BLOO

Tim Winton was born i
Swimmer (1982), *Shallou* ~~(1985), That Eye,~~
The Sky (1986), *Minimum of Two* (1987), *In The Winter Dark*
(1988), and *Cloudstreet* (1991), and two books for children. His
work has been awarded the *Australian*/Vogel Award and the
Miles Franklin Award. He has been granted senior fellowships
by the Literature Board of the Australia Council four times.
He lives in Western Australia with his wife and three children.

Also by Tim Winton in Picador

SHALLOWS

CLOUDSTREET

BLOOD AND WATER

STORIES BY
TIM WINTON

PICADOR

Scission first published 1985 by McPhee Gribble Publishers Pty Ltd,
Victoria, Australia, in association with Penguin Books Australia Ltd,
with the assistance of the Literature Board of the Australia Council

Minimum of Two first published 1987 by McPhee Gribble Publishers
Pty Ltd with the assistance of the Literature Board of the Australia
Council

Scission and *Minimum of Two* first published in this combined
edition in Great Britain in 1993 in Picador by Pan Books Limited
a division of Pan Macmillan Publishers Limited
Cavaye Place London SW10 9PG
and Basingstoke

Associated companies throughout the world

ISBN 0 330 32554 X

1 3 5 7 9 8 6 4 2

A CIP catalogue record for this book is available from the British Library

Phototypeset by Intype, London
Printed by Cox & Wyman Ltd, Reading, Berks

CONTENTS

SCISSION

Then Job answered and said,
  How long will ye vex my soul, and
break me in pieces with words?

The Book of Job

The wounded surgeon plies the steel
That questions the distempered part;

T. S. Eliot, *East Coker*

ACKNOWLEDGEMENTS

Acknowledgement is made to the publication in which these stories first appeared: 'Secrets' in *Meanjin*, 1983; 'A Blow, A Kiss' in *Simply Living*, 1984; 'Getting Ahead' in *Island*, 1984; 'My Father's Axe' in *Australian Playboy*, 1983 (also winner of the 1983 State of Victoria Award); 'Wake' in *Quadrant*, 1982; 'Lantern Stalk' in the *Age Monthly Review*, 1984; 'Neighbours' in *Australian Short Stories*, 1985; 'A Measure of Eloquence' in the *Bulletin*, 1984; 'The Oppressed' in *Southern Review*, 1982; 'The Woman at the Well' in *Imprint*, 1982; and 'Scission' in *Westerly*, 1983.

The author thanks the Literature Board of the Australia Council for fellowships in 1983 and 1984.

CONTENTS

SECRETS

OUT THE back of the new house, between the picket fence and a sheet of tin, Kylie found an egg. Her mother and Philip were inside. She heard them arguing and wished she still lived with her father. The yard was long and excitingly littered with fallen grapevines, a shed, lengths of timber and wire, and twitching shadows from big trees. It wasn't a new house, but it was new to her. She had been exploring the yard. The egg was white and warm-looking in its nest of dirt and down. Reaching in, she picked it up and found that it *was* warm. She looked back at the house. No one was watching. Something rose in her chest: now she knew what it was to have a secret.

At dinner her mother and Philip spoke quietly to one another and drank from the bottle she was only allowed to look at. Her mother was a tall woman with short hair like a boy. One of her front teeth had gone brown and it made Kylie wonder. She knew that Philip was Mum's new husband, only they weren't married. He smelt of cigarettes and moustache hairs, Kylie thought his feet were the shape of pasties.

When everything on her plate was gone, Kylie left the table. Because the loungeroom was a jungle of boxes and crates inside one of which was the TV, she went straight to her new room. She thought about the egg as she lay in bed. She was thinking about it when she fell asleep.

Next day, Kylie got up on to the fence and crabbed all around it looking into the neighbours' yards. The people behind had a little tin shed and a wired-up run against the fence in which hens and a puff-chested little rooster pecked and picked and scruffled.

So, she thought, balanced on the splintery grey fence, that's where the egg comes from. She climbed down and checked behind the sheet of tin and found the egg safe but cold.

Later, she climbed one of the big trees in the yard, right up, from where she could observe the hens and the rooster next door. They were fat, white birds with big red combs and bright eyes. They clucked and preened and ruffled and Kylie grew to like them. She was angry when the piebald rooster beat them down to the ground and jumped on their backs, pecking and twisting their necks. All his colours were angry colours; he looked mean.

Inside the house Mum and Philip laughed or shouted and reminded her that Dad didn't live with them any more. It was good to have a secret from them, good to be the owner of something precious. Philip laughed at the things she said. Her mother only listened to her with a smile that said *you don't know a single true thing*.

Sometime in the afternoon, after shopping with her mother, Kylie found a second egg in the place between the fence and the tin. She saw, too, a flash of white beneath a mound of vine cuttings in the corner of the yard. She climbed her tree and waited. A hen, thinner and more raggedy than the others, emerged. She had a bloody comb and a furtive way of pecking the ground alertly and moving in nervous bursts. For some time, she poked and scratched about, fossicking snails and slugs out of the long grass, until Kylie saw her move across to the piece of tin and disappear.

Each day Kylie saw another egg added to the nest up the back. She saw the raggedy hen pecked and chased and kicked by the others next door, saw her slip between the pickets to escape. The secret became bigger every day. The holidays stretched on. Philip and her mother left her alone. She was happy. She sat on the fence, sharing the secret with the hen.

When they had first moved into this house on the leafy, quiet street, Philip had shown Kylie and her mother the round, galvanized tin cover of the bore well in the back of the yard. The sun winked off it in the mornings. Philip said it was thirty-six feet deep and very dangerous. Kylie was forbidden to lift the lid. It was off-limits. She was fascinated by it. Some afternoons she sat out under the grapevines with her photo album, turning pages and looking across every now and then at that glinting lid. It couldn't be seen from the back veranda; it was obscured by a banana tree and a leaning brick well.

In all her photographs, there was not one of her father. He had been the photographer in the family; he took photos of Kylie and her mother, Kylie and her friends, but he was always out of the picture, behind the camera. Sometimes she found herself looking for him in the pictures. Sometimes it was a game for her; at others she didn't realize she was doing it.

Two weeks passed. It was a sunny, quiet time. Ten eggs came to be secreted behind the piece of tin against the back fence. The hen began sitting on them. Kylie suspected something new would happen. She visited the scraggy, white hen every day to see her bright eyes, to smell her musty warmth. It was an important secret now. She sneaked kitchen scraps and canary food up the back each evening and lay awake in bed wondering what would happen.

It was at this time that Kylie began to lift the lid of the well. It was not heavy and it moved easily. Carefully, those mornings, shielded by the banana tree, she peered down into the cylindrical pit which smelt sweaty and dank. Right down at the bottom was something that looked like an engine with pipes leading from it. A narrow, rusty ladder went down the wall of the well. Slugs and spiderwebs clung to it.

One afternoon when Philip and her mother were locked in the big bedroom, laughing and making the bed bark on the boards, Kylie took her photo album outside to the well, opened the lid and, with the book stuffed into the waistband of her shorts, went down the ladder with slow, deliberate movements. Flecks of rust came away under her hands, and fell whispering a long way down. The ladder quivered. The sky was a blue disc above growing smaller and paler. She climbed down past the engine to the moist sand and sat with her back to the curving wall. She looked up. It was like being a drop of water in a straw or a piece of rice in a blowpipe – the kind boys stung her with at school. She heard the neighbours' rooster crowing, and the sound of the wind. She looked through her album. Pictures of her mother showed her looking away into the distance. Her long, wheaten hair blew in the wind or hung still and beautiful. It had been so long. Her mother never looked at the camera. Kylie saw herself, ugly and short and dark beside her. She grew cold and climbed out of the well.

It seemed a bit of an ordinary thing to have done when she got out. Nevertheless, she went down every day to sit and think or to flick through the album.

The hen sat on her eggs for three weeks. Kylie sat on the fence and gloated, looking into the chook house next door at the rooster and his scrabbling hens who did not know what was happening her side of the fence. She knew now that there would be chicks. The encyclopaedia said so.

On nights when Philip and her mother had friends over, Kylie listened from the darkened hallway to their jokes that made no sense. Through the crack between door and jamb she saw them touching each other beneath the table, and she wanted to know – right then – why her father and mother did not live together with her. It was something she was not allowed to know. She went back to her room and looked at the only picture in her album where her smile told her that there was something she knew that the photographer didn't. She couldn't remember what it was; it was a whole year ago. The photo was a shot from way back in kindergarten. She was small, dark-haired, with her hands propping up her face. She held the picture close to her face. It made her confident. It made her think Philip and her mother were stupid. It stopped her from feeling lonely.

Philip caught her down the well on a Sunday afternoon. He had decided to weed the garden at last; she wasn't prepared for it. One moment she was alone with the must, the next, the well was full of Philip's shout. He came down and dragged her out. He hit her. He told her he was buying a padlock in the morning.

That evening the chicks hatched in the space between the sheet of tin and the back fence – ten of them. At dusk, Kylie put them into a cardboard box and dropped them down the well. The hen squawked insanely around the yard, throwing itself about, knocking things over, creating such a frightening noise that Kylie chased it and hit it with a piece of wood and, while it was still stunned, dropped it, too, down the dry well. She slumped down on the lid and began to cry. The back light came on. Philip came out to get her.

Before bed, Kylie took her photograph – the knowing one – from its place in the album, and with a pair of scissors, cut off her head and poked it through a hole in the flyscreen of the window.

A Blow, A Kiss

Despite their bad luck, Albie had enjoyed the night. Just the pipe smell of his father and the warmth of him in the truck's cab beside him was enough. It did not matter that they had caught ten salmon and buried them in the sand for safe keeping and not found them again. The Tilley lamp tinkled, cooling between his feet on the floor of the cab. Ahead, the unlit road rolled out.

A motorcycle whipped past, going their way. Albie saw the small red light for a moment and then it was gone.

'He's flying,' his father murmured.

'Yeah.' Albie felt his chin on his chest. He heard the lamp tinkle. His eyes closed. He looked up again, felt himself plummeting forward, heard his father pumping the brakes.

'He's down!' bellowed his father.

Albie pulled himself away from the windscreen. His father was already out of the cab and in the vortex of the headlights. On the road, the motorcycle was sprawled, intertwined with the rider, an ugly spillage. Against the blackness of machine and leather, Albie saw blood. He did not move on the seat. He held the Tilley lamp hard between his feet; he had not let it fall and break.

His father pulled the machine from the man who groaned. He took the helmet off. He held up the man's hands. They were the colour of bleeding pork. Albie had never seen so much human blood, though he had seen cut pigs and jugulars of salmon cannoning red on white sand. Groans became shouts. Without warning, the fallen man lashed out at Albie's father and pulled him down to the ground by the ears and the two men locked limbs, and rolled on the bloody bitumen in the headlights of the truck. Albie did not move. He held the Tilley lamp tight until his thighs ached. He heard the wet sound of fists connecting. Crickets and the quiet idle of the engine underlay this noise. Beyond the grovelling men, past the point of the truck's headlights, there was only darkness. In a moment there was quiet. Crickets chanted. The engine idled.

'Albee!'

Albie slid out of the cab as soon as he heard his father's voice. Every line and feature was stark in the glare. Blood ran from his father's lips. The fallen rider lay, gored jaws apart, beneath him.

'Come here, Albie.' His father motioned with a free hand. Albie smelt blood, and beer and petrol and hot metal. He saw a translucent disc on his father's cheek and for a moment he thought it was a tear but it was a fish scale. 'He's unconscious. We shouldn't move him. I'll have to call for help. Come over further. Now get on him.' Albie was astride the bleeding, still man. 'Put your feet on his hands. He won't move. He's out.' Albie wondered why it was necessary to sit on a man who was not going to move. He looked at the blood streaming from his father's lips. 'He's in shock – he didn't know what he was doing,' his father said. 'I won't be long – stay put.'

Albie felt his shoulder briefly squeezed and heard his father's boots mashing back to the truck. The lights veered from him and the truck passed and the tail-lights became tiny red points, eyes that closed and left him with the dark. He heard the man's breathing, felt the rise and fall of leather, listened to the cricket hymns, wondering what should be done, how he should behave towards this man who had struck his father. In the dark, he could not see the places where skin had been pared away. He saw no human blood, but he could smell it.

'He was only helping you,' he said to the man. The leather jacket groaned beneath him. Albie wondered what his mother would be doing. Probably ringing Sergeant Fobles, he thought; she'll be angry and blame Dad, kiss us. Albie knew she would use her kisses like blows: punishment for them.

The leather jacket was wet in parts and torn. It shocked him that leather should rip like that; it was the strongest stuff there was, and only time and sweat and constant fatigue could waste it, not those few seconds when that single tail-light disappeared and this man skittered along the road like a moist piece of moss.

'You're lucky we were here,' he said, shifting position on the mount. 'You're lucky my Dad's going for help.'

Town was only twenty minutes' drive from the coast. Farmland stretched right to the high-water mark. Albie had seen cattle on the beaches, wallowing in the surf. He hoped his father found a farm with a phone.

'Come on, Dad. Come on, Dad. Come on, Dad.' He often prayed to his father in his absence. God, he decided, was just like his Dad, only bigger. It was easier to pray to him and hope God got the message on relay.

'Dad?'

Albie flinched. The injured man had spoken.

'Dad?'

Albie's body shrank into itself. He waited for the man to move, to attack.

'Dad?'

'Yes?' Albie whispered. His throat was full of heart.

'Oh. Oh, Dad, I'm sorry. Was coming back.'

Albie listened as the man began to weep; he rode the man's sobs, high on his chest, and it hurt him to hear. Like the sound of a tractor engine turning over on a dying battery.

'It's all right,' Albie said to him, 'it's all right.' The sobbing continued, jogging him, making the leather groan and the seat of his pants hot until Albie thought he might be sick or get up and run away into the bush at the side of the road.

But he did not run. He bent down and kissed the wet, prickled face. The sobbing stopped. Even the crickets paused. Albie tasted salt, felt a jumble of things lurching in him; he felt not sick, just full.

It was that moment when Albie began to worry that the man might die.

The lights forking out over the crown of the hill took him by surprise. He watched them dip and sweep, disappear and reappear until he could hear the sound of the truck's engine.

In the piercing white light of the truck's lamps, as it stopped dead with a shriek of brakes, Albie knew what it must be to be a rabbit, powerless, snowblind, vulnerable to atrocity. The light seemed to ricochet inside his head, confounding him. He heard his father's boots.

'You all right? There's blood on your face!'

Albie felt himself swept up into his father's arms; he yielded to it. His father hugged him, touched his cheeks with his fingers and his tobacco breath. On his own feet again, Albie found his voice and asked, 'Is he going to die?'

'Dunno,' his father said, 'I don't know enough about it.'

'Oh.'

'There's no phones. I should've known in the first place. Man'd have to be an idiot. We'll take him in ourselves like we should've anyhow.'

'We didn't want to move him.'

'Yeah.' His father seemed to take comfort in this.

Albie tried to stay awake in the warm cab, seduced by the smell of his father and the crooning note of the engine. The sweat had dried on him. His arms still ached. He had never lifted anything so heavy, so awkward as that fallen motorcyclist. They had tried to get his contorted, cold machine in too, but had to leave it at the roadside. Every few minutes, Albie turned to see through the window the shape of the injured man beneath the tarpaulin on the tray beside the rods and sacks and engine parts.

He held the Tilley lamp hard between his heels. It kept him awake, a duty.

'Should've known better,' his father muttered. The featureless road wandered left and right, studded with the eyes of beer cans, mile pegs, rabbits.

Somewhere in his fog of fatigue, Albie hoped his mother would understand. She loved them; she didn't like them to be late.

Town was mostly asleep at this time of night. Only the pub and the petrol station were open. It was a fuel town at night, a farm town by day. As they pulled into the sudden brilliance of the petrol station tarmac, Albie saw Mr Stevens wave to his father, a wave without hands. His father got out. After a moment, Mr Stevens came over. Albie listened.

'That's Wilf Beacon's boy,' Mr Stevens said, peering in the back at the man on the tray beneath the tarp. 'Dead?'

'No.'

Albie wished his father would check. He was afraid. But he saw the tarp rising and falling.

'Where's Beacon, then?'

'Across the road.'

Albie knew that in this town 'across the road' meant in the pub. The pub frightened Albie. From out on the veranda, it was a roar, a sour smell, unknown.

His father poked his head in the window. 'Stay here, son.'

Not long after, Albie saw two men stumble out on to the pub veranda. One was his father. The other man had him by the throat and his father had the man's forelock in his fist. Shouting. Albie saw his father hit the man in the chest. The man fell to his knees. His father helped him up and they came across the road to Stevens' Garage.

'Just pull yourself together,' he heard his father say with a harshness that made his skin prickle.

'Where's his suitcase? He had a sleeping bag! You've done 'im over! What've you been doin' to my boy?'

'Pickin' him up off the side of the road. He's drunk like you. He's hurt, you bloody idiot!'

Albie hated that man. He couldn't remember seeing him before. He was not a farmer. Might have been a farm hand for someone he didn't know. He didn't care; he hated him. He wanted the man to see his son, and to weep like the son had wept out on the road with that hopeless starter motor sound in the dark.

His father shoved the man around to the back of the truck. Albie's insteps were cold from pressing against the lamp. He watched through the grimy little back window. The man staggered up on to the tray and knelt with a thud beside the body under the tarp.

'Little coward. Leave a man alone. Own father. Own father.' The rider's bloody face was immobile. The old man's hands touched it, lifted the head off the truck tray. 'And what've yer got to say for yerself? They bring yer back to *me*!' The sound of the rider's head being dropped on to the metal tray vibrated through the whole truck like the sound of a mallee root being tossed in. Again. Whump. The father beat his son's head against the tray. Albie's father looked helpless, did not move.

Albie got out. The flat bed of the truck resounded again. The jumble inside Albie pushed upward; he wanted to be sick. He snatched the Tilley lamp by the handle. He heard the startled voice of his father. He swung the lamp up and over, a bowling movement. Glass and sound and splintery light happened all at once and his father had hold of him as the drunk old man lay still on his son, stinking of beer and kerosene.

As they turned off the bitumen road into their own run of gravel to the yellow-lit house down in the valley, Albie ended the silence with a question. He was startled by his own toneless delivery.

'Why did that man hit his son for getting hurt?'

His father sighed. He sounded relieved that the silence was finished. 'I don't know, boy.'

'Would you do that to me?'

The truck slewed and stopped.

'Lord, no. God A'mighty, no!'

'He was going home,' Albie said.

His father's mouth moved. He reached out and put his knuckles to Albie's cheek, left them there for a long time, as though still waiting for words to come. 'Sorry about the salmon,' he said at last, 'I should've known better.'

The truck moved forward again. Albie felt those knuckles on his cheek still and knew, full to bursting, that that was how God would touch someone. He neither moved nor spoke, and the truck trundled on.

Getting Ahead

for Simon

IT WAS three years after Dad died that Mum started to get ideas, and it nearly drove the five of us mad. After dinner, when all the pots and plates were washed, dried, inspected and put away, and the smallies put to bed, Jilly and I would do our homework and Mum would get thinking. She was like a broody hen sitting there in the corner of the sofa on her clutch of ideas, keeping them warm. Dad was the one with all the ideas before that, but all of them were lousy. It took Mum a few nights to come up with hers, and without a word one evening she got up, wrote them on a Scott Towel and stuck them to the door of the fridge.

BE HEALTHY

BE ORGANIZED

BE CAREFUL

GET AHEAD

We were dumbfounded. No one in our home had done anything like that before. Soon afterwards, she went out and bought a Dymo labeller (all the rage then) with the savings in the Vegemite jar in the cupboard. And then things started to happen. Labels: warnings, reminders, instructions appeared on everything. WASH HANDS! said the cistern in the outhouse. SHUT DOOR! cried everything with hinges. On our bedheads, adhesive checklists appeared in our absence: who to pray for, duties to be done, cautionary notices. Mum began to develop powerful wrists from punching out those sticky messages. You could hear the grot-grot sound of the pistol-like gadget all over the house.

She was a big woman, my mother. In poor light she

19

resembled an untidy stack of tea-chests. She rumbled about the house at night checking us in our beds, not sleeping herself until Mahoney's rooster started to crow. We always liked the Mahoneys despite the rooster. Mrs Mahoney had what Mum called 'a generous bosom'; she was a good neighbour. Mum ironed and mended and we left her in bed when we got up for school in the mornings. She ironed and mended. And three years after the old man turned yellow and died, she got to thinking as well.

It wasn't long before the chief subject of conversation became getting ahead. Jilly and I were old enough to understand and too young to contradict. (That was another thing she said.) One night when we were working on our books, Mum ruffled herself in the corner of the sofa, putting her upper teeth in, and said, 'You've gotta get ahead.' We stopped work and looked at her gazing into the fire. 'You've got to find some way of getting ahead. You can't stand still.'

She said this once or twice a night for a whole week. Jilly and I thought she was going mental. Only mental people and teachers repeated themselves like that. But at the end of the week she looked into the fire and said: 'You know, kids, there's only two things more I'd like to try out in this life,' as if she'd done pretty well everything else; 'First, I'd like to see how long I could live off a packet of Jatz and my own wits in the desert, and second, I'd like to be a landlady.'

'I'd like to be a policeman,' I said, relieved that she hadn't gone mental after all.

'I'd like to be blonde,' Jilly said, holding out a lock of her carroty hair.

'But I'm too old for the desert,' Mum continued, as though we hadn't spoken. 'So, we're gonna get into real estate.'

Jilly and I exchanged looks of deep disturbance.

'We've got no money,' I said.

'We don't need it. We got a house. It's assets.'

Jilly wedged an elbow between my ribs. Mum took her

teeth out and held them like they were a pair of specs and she was Julius Sumner Miller gazing into the fire and not our old Mum. 'We'll rent this place out.'

'But Mum,' I said hoarsely, 'there's six of us in it already.' There was no way I could believe she was serious. It was a two-bedroom state house. Not flash, not well painted, not well furnished, and as far as I was concerned, not available. Five of us, I thought, there's Maxford (me), Jilly, Eddy, Edie and Millicent; the smallies in Mum's room, Jilly and me in the other.

'We'll move into a flat.'

'A flat!' Jilly cried. Flats were where you got yelled at from balconies as you cut across the mangy lawns on your way to school. Flats were where ladies without husbands had to live. Flats had no backyards.

'Just for a while,' Mum said.

'How long?' I asked.

'It's just until we get ahead,' she said.

The flat had a bedroom, a living room, a kitchen and a bathroom/toilet/laundry (most confusing for the smallies) and we loathed it. Mum calculated we'd be making fifteen dollars a week on top of her pension, and all the time that we lived like refugees sleeping on the floor of that flat, aching for garden space, cubby space, fences to vault, dogs and bobtails to tangle with, I kept that fifteen dollars in mind. Our tenant, the person who rented our house, was a senile old woman who smelt of cat-pee and was called Mrs Marsdale. It took her a long time to answer the ad in the paper. We chose her because she was the only one who did. We didn't like her smell. Mum didn't care for her name. Millicent cried when we moved out.

'It's only till we get ahead,' Mum would say, as if to convince herself too. 'We're saving, we're saving.' It used to be a lullaby for the smallies, long, low, sweet.

But it was lousy in the flat. We didn't open the door to

anyone except Mum in case the Health Inspector got on to us for overcrowding or the landlord saw Mum's Dymo labels all over the place, like PRESS HARD TWICE in the toilet, and MUMMY LOVES YOU policing the pantry door. The fridge had become scarfaced and confounding as Mum's old and new messages to us and herself and God (she had started praying in Dymo which, I suppose, is like doing it in tongues) accumulated day by day. We survived like this for months, clattering along balconies, passing our old place on the way to school for a look at how run-down the garden had become, at how many cats seemed to congregate on the veranda now, and coming home each afternoon to see our Mum knitting by the smelly kero heater with her teeth out trying not to look disgusted about being a landlady getting ahead.

The rent never seemed to arrive. One evening when all the others – even Jilly – were asleep on their mattresses on the floor, Mum sat beside me at the table where I was skirmishing with algebra, trying for the teacher's sake to pretend that x was the number 2 in disguise, and said:

'Will you come with me to the house tomorrow, after school?' There was a weighty tone in her voice, the kind that grown-ups reserved for other grown-ups.

'Course,' I said lumpily. 'What's up?'

'Oh,' she murmured, 'tenant problems.'

'Oh,' I replied, as if it was all too clear and much too commonplace.

Mrs Marsdale didn't seem to resent our inspection of the house. We exchanged good days and how-do-you-dos; she didn't seem to mind at all. In fact, I'm not even sure if she was really aware of our being there. She seemed to be in a kind of crooning, half-animated coma. She fell over bits of furniture as she spoke to them. She scratched herself. She scared me witless.

The house was a disappointment. The sofa looked as though someone had taken to it with a rasp. The floor was mulched with Kitty Litter, wet newspapers and wads of phlegmy cotton. Stacks of newspapers and magazines threatened to fall from every corner. Shopping trollies, bicycle wheels, steel buckets, a NO PARKING sign. And no sign of the three months' rent Mum had come to collect.

'Mrs Marsdale,' I heard my mother say as I discreetly picked a piece of blue meat from between my toes. 'Mrs Marsdale, I . . .'

I caught sight of her looking up at the ceiling where ugly brown stains had appeared in our absence. 'Mrs Marsdale, is the roof leaking?' Mrs Marsdale continued her ecstasy of falling and muttering. 'Maxford,' Mum said, 'get the ladder.'

I went out to the shed for the ladder as Mum tried to hail Mrs Marsdale. When we got up into the ceiling, we found a colony of wild-eyed cats hissing at us from the farthest corners of the darkness. I heard a glottal exclamation from my Mum. She dragged me down the ladder and out the front door.

'There's worse than that,' she said as we walked home. She looked shocked and grey. 'I have reason to believe that our outhouse hasn't been used since Mrs . . . since our tenant moved in.'

'But Mum . . .'

'A woman can tell things about a bathtub the likes of a clean boy like you would never understand. It's because the toilet is a long way up the backyard. It's a long way, I'll grant it, but there's limits to what your mother'll tolerate, Maxford.'

'It's the most exasperating thing,' she said that night as the smallies brawled from one end of the room to the other with a frisbee. 'I can't understand the ways of some people. It's not right. Oh, oh . . .' And in the midst of that tiny battleground of mattresses and rioting bodies, I thought she was going to cry. The cracking, sliding look on her face lasted a full five seconds before she said: 'Well, I'll just have to appeal to her sense of decency.' The world was a stable place again; the Laws still held. Our Mum did not cry.

In the calm after tea, by the smelly heater, Jilly and I watched her punch out an honest, forthright letter on the Dymo, a long blue strip that coiled at her feet: grot-grot, grot-grot, grot-grot. She was still at it when we flopped on our mattress and went to sleep.

'. . . just until we get ahead . . .' I heard her murmur as I dropped off.

The long blue adhesive salutation Mum stuck to the front door seemed to go unheeded. Mum went round during the day, just to watch the cats from the footpath and to think. In the flat she muttered and scowled and thumped the kitchen sink.

'Then it's persuasion,' she murmured late in the evening, polishing her teeth with cotton buds by the heater. I was hard at work with my algebra and paid no attention.

So, walking in the warm dark towards our old house the next night, I had no idea what it was we were doing.

Dogs barked all over the suburb. A few sprinklers tinkled. There was no light on at our place and none in the neighbours' either. It was very late. I followed the jumbling shape of my Mum up the side of the house and out to the back shed. She gave me a shovel.

'Dig,' she whispered.

'Where?'

'Anywhere.'

I dug, on my knees in the dewy grass. She kept watch. There was no light and no noise from the house. On the back veranda, cats watched us, starlight catching in their eyes. I dug deep, narrow holes. Four of them. Then suddenly we left. I was put to bed.

Next day after school, Mum had four potted saplings standing on the sink. She was acting most peculiar, drinking tea, humming. 'My investments,' she called them. That night she got me out of bed at midnight. We walked across to our old place again, only this time I carried two potted saplings and a bellyful of dread. Again, no lights, no signs of wakefulness from inside. Our holes were still there with their gentle mounds of sand.

'Get the big spanner from the shed,' she whispered. I did. 'Now,' she hissed, 'catch cats.' And then I knew.

I slunk across the yard. 'Puss-puss-puss.' A black cat appeared from the darkness, slowly coming to my call. It spat and scratched when I grabbed it by the scruff of the neck and delivered it to Mum. She hit it on the head with the big spanner and dropped it into the nearest hole.

'One down,' she said. Needlessly, I thought. I went back to kitty-kittying, thinking: So this is persuasion. Cats came slower and slower as time passed, but the darkness continued to yield them up all the same. Mum bedded each hole with four or five cats and planted a sapling in each, squashing down the soil around them with her boots. All except the fourth. She wanted to be sure we got every single cat. I prowled up and down, tired now, and feeling wretched about the cats. After a while it was obvious that there were no more. It was at that moment that a sound behind me caused me to go rocky with fright. I saw Mum's jaw, long and white, down in the dark. She looked shocked.

'Psst!'

I could not move. I was certain the blood had halted in my veins. I heard the clack of Mum's upper plate. With great effort, I turned to face the noise. Mum turned too. There were the big white arms of Mrs Mahoney on the fence. Our neighbour, Mrs Mahoney. She was looking at us very carefully. Her eyes seemed to glow in the dark. My head was pregnant with the consequences of being caught in the act.*Mrs Mahoney lifted a finger and motioned for us to come closer. We inched forward. I saw her eyes clearly. They were no-nonsense eyes. She pointed them at my Mum. I wanted to cry.

'Yes?' my poor Mum said.

'There's one under the woodpile.'

All the way home in the dark an hour later, Mum sang hymns and kicked stones in a clatter down the street as if nothing in the world could be a danger or a problem. It was as though she had gotten drunk on Mrs Mahoney's cup of tea. Mrs Mahoney had told us of Mrs Marsdale's disappearance. 'Two days she's bin gone. Ever since you came round for the rent. Left the cats and all.' The fact that Mrs Marsdale had gone without paying didn't worry Mum on that warm, dead-of-night walk home. The state of our old house, the brown cat-piddle ceilings, the gutless furniture, the filth didn't bother her. The fact that we were not ahead was no burden to bear. The house was empty. We were moving home. Mrs Mahoney was a sport.

'And we've got ahead, really,' she said. 'We've got four new trees.' Which was true. And still is. They're the best thing about the place. Ask my kids.

My Father's Axe

I

Just now I discover the axe gone. I look everywhere inside and outside the house, front and back, but it is gone. It has been on my front veranda since the new truckload of wood arrived and was dumped so intelligently over my front lawn. Jamie says he doesn't know where the axe is and I believe him; he won't chop wood any more. Elaine hasn't seen it; it's men's business, she says. No, it's not anywhere. But who would steal an axe in this neighbourhood, this street where I grew up and have lived much of my life? No one steals on this street. Not an axe.

It is my father's axe.

I used to watch him chop with it when we drove the old Morris and the trailer outside the town limits to gather wood. He would tie a thick, short bar of wood to the end of forty feet of rope and swing it about his head like a lasso and the sound it made was the whoop! of the headmaster's cane you heard when you walked past his office. My father sent the piece of wood high into the crown of a dead sheoak and when it snarled in the stark, grey limbs he would wrap the rope around his waist and then around his big freckled arms, and he would pass me his grey hat with bound hands and tell me to stand right back near the Morris with my mother who poured tea from a Thermos flask. And he pulled. I heard his body grunt and saw his red arms whiten, and the tree's crown quivered and rocked and he added to the motion, tugging, jerking, gasping until the whole bush cracked open and birds burst from all the trees around and the dead, grey crown of the sheoak teetered and toppled to the earth, chased by a shower of twigs and bark. My mother and I

27

cheered and my father ambled over, arms glistening, to drink the tea that tasted faintly of coffee and the rubber seal of the Thermos. Rested, he would then dismember the brittle tree with graceful swings of his axe and later I would saw with him on the bowman saw and have my knees showered with white, pulpy dust.

He could swing an axe, my father.

And that axe is gone.

He taught me how to split wood though I could never do it like him, those long, rhythmic, semicircular movements like a ballet dancer's warm-up; I'm a left-hander, a mollydooker he called me, and I chop in short, jabby strokes which do the job but are somehow less graceful.

When my father began to leave us for long periods for his work – he sold things – he left me with the responsibility of fuelling the home. It gave me pride to know that our hot water, my mother's cooking, the living-room fire depended upon me, and my mother called me the man of the house, which frightened me a little. Short, winter afternoons I spent up the back splitting pine for kindling, long, fragrant spines with neat grain, and I opened up the heads of mill-ends and sawn blocks of sheoak my father brought home. Sometimes in the trance of movement and exertion I imagined the blocks of wood as teachers' heads. It was pleasurable work when the wood was dry and the grain good and when I kept the old Kelly axe sharp. I learnt to swing single-handed, to fit wedges into stubborn grain, to negotiate knots with resolve, and the chopping warmed me as I stripped to my singlet and worked until I was ankle-deep in split, open wood and my breath steamed out in front of me with each righteous grunt.

Once, a mouse half caught itself in a trap in the laundry beneath the big stone trough and my mother asked me to kill it, to put it out of its misery, she said. Obediently, I carried the threshing mouse in the trap at arm's length right up to the back of the yard. How to kill a mouse? Wring its neck? Too small. Drown it? In what? I put it on the burred block and hit it with the flat of the axe. It made no noise but it left a speck of red on my knee.

Another time my father, leaving again for a long trip, began softly to weep on our front step. My mother did not see because she was inside finding him some fruit. I saw my father ball his handkerchief up and bite on it to muffle his sobs and I left him there and ran through the house and up to the woodpile where I shattered great blocks of sheoak until it was dark and my arms gave out. In the dark I stacked wood into the buckled shed and listened to my mother calling.

I broke the handle of that axe once, on a camping trip; it was good hickory and I was afraid to tell him. I always broke my father's tools, blunted his chisels, bent his nails. I have never been a handyman like my father. He made things and repaired things and I watched but did not see the need to learn because I knew my father would always be. If I needed something built, something done, there was my father and he protected me.

When I was eight or nine he took my mother and me to a beach shack at a rivermouth up north. The shack was infested with rats and I lay awake nights listening to them until dawn when my father came and roused me and we went down to haul the craypots. The onshore reefs at low tide were bare, clicking and bubbling in the early sun, and octopuses gangled across exposed rocks, lolloping from hole to hole. We caught them for bait; my father caught them and I carried them in the bucket with the tight lid and looked at my face in the still tidal pools that bristled with kelp. But it was not so peaceful at high tide when the swells burst on the upper lip of the reef and cascaded walls of foam that rushed in upon us and rocked us with their force. The water reached my waist though it was only knee-deep for my father. He taught me to brace myself side-on to the waves and find footholds in the reef and I hugged his leg and felt his immovable stance and moulded myself to him. At the edge of the reef I coiled the rope that he hauled up and held the hessian bag as he opened the heavy, timber-slatted pots; he dropped the crays in and I heard their tweaking cries and felt them grovelling against my legs.

During the day my mother read *They're a Weird Mob* and ate raisins and cold crayfish dipped in red vinegar. We played Scrabble and it did not bother me that my father lost.

Lost his axe. Who could have stolen such a worthless thing? The handle is split and taped and the head bears the scars of years; why even look at it?

One night on that holiday a rat set off a trap on the rafter above my bed. My father used to tie the traps to the rafters to prevent the rats from carrying them off. It went off in the middle of the night with a snap like a small fire cracker and in the dark I sensed something moving above me and something warm touched my forehead. I lay still and did not scream because I knew my father would come. Perhaps I did scream in the end, I don't know. But he came, and he lit the Tilley lamp and chuckled and, yes, that was when I screamed. The rat, suspended by six feet of cord, swung in an arc across my bed with the long, hairy whip of tail trailing a foot above my nose. The body still flexed and struggled. My father took it down and went outside with its silhouette in the lamplight in front of him. My mother screamed; there was a drop of blood on my forehead. It was just like *The Pit and the Pendulum*, I said. We had recently seen the film and she had found the book in the library and read it to me for a week at bedtime. Yes, she said with a grim smile, wiping my forehead, and I had nightmares about that long, hairy blade above my throat and saw it snatched away by my father's red arms. In the morning I saw outside that the axe head was dull with blood. After that I often had dreams in which my father rescued me. One was a dream about a burning house – our house, the one I still live in with Elaine and Jamie –

and I was trapped inside, hair and bedclothes afire and my father splintered the door with an axe blow and fought his way in and carried me out in those red arms.

My father. He said little. He never won at Scrabble, so it seems he never even stored words up for himself. We never spoke much. It was my mother and I who carried on the long conversations; she knew odd facts, quiz shows on television were her texts. I told her my problems. But with my father I just stood, and we watched each other. Sometimes he looked at me with disappointment, and other times I looked at him the same way. He hammered big nails in straight and kissed me good-night and goodbye and hello until I was fourteen and learnt to be ashamed of it and evade it.

When his back stiffened with age he chopped wood less and I wielded the axe more. He sat by the woodpile and sometimes stacked, though mostly he just sat with a thoughtful look on his face. As I grew older my time contracted around me like a shrinking shirt and I chopped wood hurriedly, often finishing before the old man had a chance to come out and sit down.

Then I met Elaine and we married and I left home. For years I went back once a week to chop wood for the old man while Elaine and my mother sat at the Laminex table in the kitchen listening to the tick of the stove. I tried to get my parents interested in electric heating and cooking like most people in the city, but my father did not care for it. He was stubborn and so I continued to split wood for him once a week while he became a frail, old man and his arms lost their ruddiness and went pasty and the flesh lost its grip upon the bones of his forearms. He looked at me in disappointment every week like an old man will, but I came over on Sundays, even when we had Jamie to look after, so he didn't have cause to be that way.

Jamie got old enough to use an axe and I taught him how. He was keen at first, though careless, and he blunted the edge quite often which angered me. I got him to chop wood for his grandfather and dropped him there on Sunday afternoons. I had a telephone installed in their house, though they complained about the colour, and I spoke to my mother sometimes on the phone, just to please her. My father never spoke on the phone. Still doesn't.

Then my mother had her stroke and Jamie began demanding to be paid for woodchopping and Elaine went twice a week to cook and clean for them and I decided on the Home. My mother and father moved out and we moved in and sold our own house. I thought about getting the place converted to electricity but the Home was expensive and Elaine came to enjoy cooking on the old combustion stove and it was worth paying Jamie a little to chop wood. Until recently. Now he won't even do it for money. He is lazier than me.

Still, it was only an old axe.

2

Elaine sleeps softly beside me, her big wide buttocks warm against my legs. The house is quiet; it was always quiet, even when my parents and I lived there. No one ever raised their voice at me in this house, except now my wife and son.

It is hard to sleep, hard, so difficult. Black moves about me and in me and is on me, so black. Fresh, bittersweet, the smell of split wood: hard, splintery jarrah, clean, moist sheoak, hard, fibrous white gum, the shick! of sundering pine. All my muscles sing, a chorus of effort, as I chop quickly, throwing chunks aside, wiping flecks and chips from my chin. Sweat sheets across my eyes and I chop harder, opening big round sawn blocks of sheoak like pies in neat wedged sections. Harder. And my feet begin to lift as I swing the axe high over my shoulder. I strike it home and regain equilibrium. As I swing again my feet lift further and I feel as though I might float up, borne away by the axe above my head, as though it is a helium balloon. No, I don't want to lift up! I drag on the hickory handle, downwards, and I win and drag harder and it gains momentum and begins a slow-motion arc of descent towards the porous surface of the wood and then, half-way down, the axe-head shears off the end of the handle so slowly, so painfully slow that I could take a hold of it four or five times to stop it. In a slow, tumbling trajectory it sails across the woodheap and unseats my father's head from his shoulders and travels on out of sight as my father's head rolls on to the heap, eyes towards me, transfixed at the moment of scission in a squint of disappointment.

I feel a warm dob on my forehead; I do not scream, have never needed to.

The sheets are wet and the light is on and Elaine has me by the shoulder and her left breast points down at my glistening chest.

'What's that matter?' she says, wiping my brow with the back of her hand. 'You were yelling.'

'A dream,' I croak.

3

Morning sun slants across the pickets at me as I fossick about in the long grass beside the shed finding the skeleton of a wren but nothing else. I shuffle around the shed, picking through the chips and splinters and slivers of wood around the chopping block, see the deep welts in the block where the axe has been, but no axe. In the front yard, as neighbours pass, I scrabble in the pile of new wood, digging into its heart, tossing pieces aside until there is nothing but yellowing grass and a few impassive slaters. Out in the backyard again I amble about shaking my head and putting my hands in my pockets and taking them out again. Elaine is at work. Jamie at school. I have rung the office and told them I won't be in. All morning I mope in the yard, waiting for something to happen, absurdly, expecting the axe to show like a prodigal son. Nothing.

Going inside at noon I notice a deep trench in the veranda post by the back door; it is deep and wide as a heavy axe-blow and I feel the inside of it with my fingers – only for a moment – before I hurry inside trying to recall its being there before. Surely.

I sit by the cold stove in the kitchen in the afternoon, quaking. Is someone trying to kill me? My God.

4

Again Elaine has turned her sumptuous buttocks against me and gone to sleep dissatisfied and I lie awake with my shame and the dark around me.

Some nights as a child I crept into my parents' room and wormed my way into the bed between them and slept soundly, protected from the dark by their warm contact.

Now, I press myself against Elaine's sleeping form and cannot sleep with the knowledge that my back is exposed.

After an hour I get up and prowl about the house, investigating each room with quick flicks of light switches and satisfied grunts when everything seems to be in order. Here, the room where my mother read, here, Jamie's room where I slept as a boy, here, where my father drank his hot, milkless tea in the mornings.

I can think of nothing I've done to offend the neighbours – I'm not a dog baiter or anything – though some of them grumbled about my putting my parents into the Home, as though it was any of their business.

I keep thinking of axe murders, things I've read in the papers, horrible things.

In the living room I take out the old Scrabble box and sit with it on my knee for a while. Perhaps I'll play a game with myself . . .

5

This morning when I woke in the big chair in the living room I saw the floor littered with Scrabble tiles like broken, yellowing teeth. Straightening my stiff back I recalled the dream. I dreamt that I saw my body dissected, raggedly sectioned up and battered and crusted black with blood. The axe, the old axe with the taped hickory handle, was embedded in the trunk where once my legs had joined, right through the pelvis. My severed limbs lay about, pink, black, distorted, like stockings full of sand. My head, to one side, faced the black ceiling, teeth bared, eyes firmly shut. Horrible, but even so, peaceful enough, like a photograph. And then a boy came out of the black – it was Jamie – and picked up my head and held it like a bowling ball. Then there was light and my son opened the door and went outside into the searing suddenness of light. He walked out into the backyard and up to the chopping block in which an axe – *the* axe – was poised. I felt nothing when he split my head in two. It was a poor stroke, but effective enough. Then with half in either hand – by the hair – he slowly walked around the front of the house and then out to the road verge and began skidding the half-orbs into the paths of oncoming cars. I used to do that as a boy; skidding half pig-melons under car wheels until nothing was left but a greenish, wet pulp. Pieces of my head ricocheted from chasis to bitumen, tyre to tyre, until there was only pulp and an angry sounding of car horns.

That does it; I'm going down to the local hardware store to buy another axe. It's high time. I have thought of going to the police but it's too ludicrous; I have nothing to tell: someone has stolen my axe that used to be my father's. A new axe is what I need.

It takes a long time in the Saturday morning rush at the hardware and the axes are so expensive and many are shoddy and the sales boy who pretends to be a professional axeman tires me with his patter. Eventually I buy a Kelly; it costs me forty dollars and it bears a resemblance to my father's. Carrying it home I have the feeling that I'm holding a stage property, not a tool; there are no signs of work on it and the head is so clean and smooth and shiny it doesn't seem intended for chopping.

As I open the front gate, axe over my shoulder, my wife is waiting on the veranda with tears on her face.

'The Home called,' she says. 'It's your father . . .'

6

The day after the funeral I am sitting out on the front veranda in the faint yellow sun. My mother will die soon; her life's work is over and she has no reason to continue in her sluggish, crippled frame. It will not be long before her funeral, I think to myself, not long. A tall sunflower sheds its hard, black seeds near me, shaken by the weight of a bird I can't see but sense. The gate squeals on its hinges and at the end of the path stand a man and a boy.

'Yes?' I ask.

The man prompts the boy forward and I see the lad has something in a hessian bag in his arms that he is offering me. Stepping off the veranda I take it, not heeding the man's apologies and the stuttering of his son. I open the bag and see the hickory handle with its gummy black tape and nicks and burrs and I groan aloud.

'He's sorry he took it,' the man says, 'aren't you, Alan? He—'

'Wait,' I said, turning, bounding back up the veranda, through the house, out on to the back veranda where Elaine and Jamie sit talking. They look startled but I have no time to explain. I grab the shiny, new axe which is yet to be used, and race back through the house with it. Elaine calls out to me, fright in her voice.

In the front yard, the father and son still wait uneasily and they look at me with apprehension as I run towards them with the axe.

'What—' The man tries to shield his son whose mouth begins to open as I come closer.

I hold the axe out before me, my body tingling, and I hold it horizontal with the handle against the boy's heaving chest.

'Here,' I say. 'This is yours.'

WAKE

SUNDAY   He wakes and finds her gone. He has slept heavily and dully during the night. The sky is pink through the curtains. He stands with his back to the window and looks at the twisted sheets. There is a hollowness in him which he ignores. Down the street, the first-gear roar of the ute is echoing in the teeth of front fences. He goes out to meet it, watches the bellowing fishermen jump fences and spring back on to the truck. They come to his house, yelling greetings, all six of them. He waves. A thick, tanned fisherman, Tuglio, jumps the small fence and slaps a snapper on to the veranda beside him.

'Good night?'

'Not bad,' Tuglio says. 'Where you lady?'

'Bed, still,' he says.

Tuglio rattles the cast-iron railing as if to wake her, hurdles the fence and runs, laughing, back to the ute.

The snapper is pink and pinker in the morning light. He takes it by the tail and brings it inside.

Near noon, he telephones his father. He smells the tannery down the road as the sea-breeze arrives.

'Hello, Dad. She there?' His father sounds surprised and perplexed. 'No, it's OK. No, nothing. You what? OK, yes.' He hangs up.

He fillets the fish slowly, carefully, the way his father taught him, and cooks two pieces for lunch.

MONDAY   He wakes late. There is a small snapper on his veranda with the newspaper and the milk. There is too much milk; he shuffles things in the refrigerator to make room. He fillets the

38

fish before he begins anything else, leaves the white flaps on the sink to firm, and sits down to his books, smelling his fingers each time he turns a page. He saturates himself with his work; he refuses to be distracted.

Mid-morning, he rings her extension number at the office; there is no answer.

In the evening, he eats dinner with his mother and father at their home. He gives his mother some snapper fillets to cook. His parents are grateful for the fish; it is expensive in the shops and his father no longer goes out in the boat. When dinner is over they sit out on the veranda in the warm night and talk. He avoids any conversation concerning her.

At about ten o'clock his father asks: 'Do you want to go for a run?'

'Where?' he asks.

'Down to the beach and back.'

'He does it every night,' says his mother with some pride.

'OK.'

For the first block, he manages to keep pace with his father, but gradually begins to drop back. His father's footsteps smack on the bitumen. He sees his father's bare back, glinting with light sweat, pull away from him, until his father slows down for him.

'You're too good for me.'

'You're damned unfit for your age. You'll be dead by the time you're forty.'

'It's not a bad age to go.'

'What would you know,' his father says.

They flash past parked cars, long, dry tresses of wild oats.

'Do you think she'll come back?' his father asks, easing.

'Yeah. Yes. I suppose.' His legs ache; his breath burns.

His father grunts and speeds up. He follows, smelling the salt of sweat and sea.

★

39

TUESDAY   There is no fish. In the afternoon he goes to the markets and loses himself in the fragrances of food and wood and incense and the crowd. As he leaves the markets, the sun is setting and the sky is purplish-pink, about to collapse into a tumult of thunder and warm rain. The colour suggests pain; he sprints home with a bag full of vegetables. He leaves his house and runs down to the fisherman's harbour to see the sunset. He watches the sun melt into the livid ocean and walks back in the warm rain, conscious that he has not come here just for the sunset. He disallows himself the memories.

He lags behind his father in the dark. He is tired of eating snapper. His father does not speak.

WEDNESDAY   This morning there is a big, mottled squid on the veranda. He is cheered for a moment, but when he is cleaning it in the sink he realizes that there is something wrong. He turns the squid over several times in his hands; there are three eyes. It angers him. He throws it in the garbage and goes to his books and works fitfully.

Running with his father, managing to keep pace with him most of the way, he mentions the squid.

'Seen it before,' says his father. 'Once. Cuvier, I think. Funny, eh? A mutation, I s'pose.'

He keeps abreast of his father's pumping arms.

'What did you do with it?' his father asks as they turn for home.

'Threw it out.'

'You're a wasteful bastard,' his father says sharply, pulling away until he is twenty or thirty yards ahead. They remain so spaced all the way back.

★

THURSDAY   Before dawn he waits for Tuglio and the others. He intends to speak to them about the squid. He has no idea what he will say, but he is still angry. When the fishermen do not arrive, he goes inside. He eats breakfast, throws the snapper fillets out to make room for the extra milk, and begins work.

After lunch, he gets up to find a pullover; it has turned cold and it is raining. Looking in his cupboards, he realizes that her clothes are gone. She has been back while he was gone. He goes, surreptitiously, to look for her. He walks downtown, the newsagent's, the bookshop, Papa Luigi's café; nothing. Then he goes to the fishermen's harbour, between the stained vessels flexing at their moorings. He sits on the end of the jetty in the rain for a few minutes, then leaves for home, chilled.

His father is quiet in the darkness. Neither lets the other ahead. The sky thunders. They run in the gentle rain. As they turn for the return lap, his father asks him suddenly: 'Have you ever wept? Cried, I mean.'

He does not reply. Nothing more is said. Rain hisses about their feet.

FRIDAY   No fish. The neighbours are asking him about her. Is she sick? He says she is not, certain that they know and have seen her, and only ask to see his response. He rings her work extension. Another woman answers. No, she is not available at the moment, she is busy. He does not leave a message; he does not identify himself. I won't give her the pleasure, he thinks.

In the evening, he rings his parents. His mother's voice is somehow hostile.

'Your father isn't up to a run tonight. You needn't come.'

'Is he sick?'

'No.'

There are long pauses in the conversation. His mother seems uncomfortable.

'How is your work?' she asks.
'Oh, all right.'
'Yes.'
'Mum.'
'Yes?'
'She's staying there, isn't she?'
'Your father's waiting for his tea.'
He hangs up.
It rains all night. The bed, suddenly vast, does not warm.

SATURDAY Before dawn he hears the fishermen's truck pass, grinding up the street. He has slept poorly, on one side of the big bed. He lies awake late into the morning, sensing the unusual heat of the day. At 10.30 he goes outside on to the veranda. It is hot in the sun; it startles him. There is a big pink snapper on the step. It is stiff and dry from the long exposure. He takes it by the unbending tail, scales rasping his palms. He leaves the milk; it has curdled in the sun.

He goes into the empty house.

LANTERN STALK

IT WAS like playing soldiers. Egg began to see it was a game they could play without shame, out here in the bush. The sergeant major called 'Parade!' from back in the clearing, and the shadows of other school cadets crumped past as he tried to secure his ground-sheet tent in the twilight. His mother had insisted he come. He was bewildered. So many pieces of equipment. Everything proceeded too fast. The sergeant major's call became a scream. Egg lifted his block-of-wood boots and fell in with the others.

Officers appeared with searing torchbeams. They were teachers in fancy dress. The sergeant major brayed: 'Atten-haargh!' Forty boys came raggedly to attention. It was the sound of a stampede. The sergeant major berated them. He was a school prefect and he played full back in the school team. Egg could smell dyed cotton and nugget and webbing and trees and earth. Stars were beginning to prick open the sky.

Captain Temby spoke. Even in the twilight Egg could see his beergut. He had felt Temby's sawn-off hockey stick on the back of his legs at PE more than once.

'Tonight, men, we're sending you on a lantern stalk.' A cheer; they liked to be called men. The sergeant major growled, 'For those of you too stupid to know what a lantern stalk is, I'll explain the aims and objectives of the exercise. You will be trucked out into the hills by the sea, and on the highest hill will be a lantern. Your task is to make it to the lantern, or inside the white circle of tape around the light, without being detected and tagged. Two men will be guarding the light. They have a fif-teen-yard circle to cover. Ten officers and NCOs will be patrol-ling the area between you and the light. The aim is not to get seen, heard, smelt, felt or tasted. In short: not to get *caught*. At nine we will sound the trucks' horns to signal the end of the exercise. Be careful, for Chrissake.'

The darkness in the back of the truck was full of elbows and knees and the vegetable smell of sweat. Someone smoked. Next to Egg, Mukas and Roper told jokes.

Egg had found make-believe soldiering fun at first. Earlier in the year when he'd signed up there was the brand-new bag of kit: boots, uniforms, webbing, beret, and the trips to the rifle range at the edge of town where he tried to shoot cardboard men off the face of the embankment. He learned to pull apart an SLR rifle and an old Bren gun, to read maps and to use compasses. His mother said it would make a man of him, but his father looked at him sadly when he came home from parade, and didn't say a word. From his room at night he heard his parents arguing. His mother's voice was strong and rich. She spoke well. Egg's parents never got along. These days he saw little of his father who worked so hard in his office, seeing other husbands and wives. Each Saturday evening, Egg heard the chatter of his father's typewriter. The phone rang night and day. Egg's mother and her friends drank sherry and spoke well in the living room. When she was angry, his mother called his father 'Reverend Eggleston' and he left the room looking whipped and pale. She kept Egg away from 'that church'. She broiled Egg with tears. 'I should have married a man,' she said. He hardly ever saw his mother and father together.

Egg was conscientious about homework. He stayed in his room a lot where it was peaceful. In the early evenings he jogged and bits of songs came to him in the rhythm of his breath. He wasn't exactly unhappy. He often thought about Stephanie Dew whom he'd caught looking at him twice in Maths. He smelt apricots in her hair when she passed him in the corridors. The proximity of her made him sad.

Some nights Egg had a dream. It was always the same: he was running up a staircase. Something terrible chased him. He could not see it or hear it but his bursting heart told him it was terrible. All along the staircase were doors padlocked against him. He hit them and sheered off them and staggered on, too scared to scream, upwards, up, twisting into the sky. Upon reaching the last step he woke. There was nothing beyond that last step, he was certain of it. Only cold space, some void to fall through forever.

'Hey, Egg, what's your plan?' Mukas asked. 'Hey, hey, Eggface!' Mukas pulled Egg's beret down over his eyes.

'Get out of it, slag-bag,' Egg said, shrugging away.

'What's your strategy? How you gonna get up to that lantern?'

'I dunno. Crawl like they said.'

'I reckon walk. Just get up and walk like you couldn't give a stiff. Reckon that's the trick.'

'Crawl, I reckon.'

'You'll never make it by nine o'clock.'

Egg shrugged in the dark. He didn't care; he was thinking about his parents. Probably, they would get divorced. He wished they could be normal. His mother was stronger than everyone else's mother. People said she wore the pants. And no one else's father was a minister.

With a whang, the tailgate of the truck swung down and someone bawled at them to get out. In the still darkness Egg heard other trucks in the distance. He got down and waited with the others by a wire fence. He smelt cow dung and wet oats. The ground oozed up wet chill. A long way off, the sea.

A light appeared small and fierce in the distance.

'All right, spread out,' the sergeant major said. 'It's a lot further than it looks. Don't let it out of your sight.'

A horn sounded, as though miles away.

'Go on, get going!'

Egg set out with Mukas and Roper, slouching along, boot-heavy. For a while there was nothing else in the night but the suggestion of crickets and the shuffle of bodies. No one spoke. They walked, hands in pockets, until a bark stopped them dead and a torch beam lanced across from the right.

'Middleton and Smythe – you're dead! Back to the truck.'

Egg fell to the ground. All around him, others did the same. He pressed into the sweet, wet earth, and he lay there listening to the others moving on. A stalk of grass poked his lip and he drew it into his mouth. For a while, he had the inclination to just go to sleep there and then, give the whole thing a miss. The whole exercise was stupid. Why the hell did his mother want him squirming up and down hills? He could be alone in his room now, or out in the streets jogging by uncurtained windows with the whole world baring itself to him.

He didn't know how long he lay there, but it was long after he stopped hearing others move past, long after he heard any movement at all. He would stick to crawling. With infinite care he began to belly-crawl to the left, clearing the way ahead before edging forward. Flank 'em, he thought vaguely. He crawled for a long time. The ground changed. In time he heard trees and began to make out their shapes against the sky. He picked his way through twigs and leaves until he rested behind a log with its smell of charcoal and ants. He was sore.

A cow bassooned softly. Egg lay on his back. The sky pressed down and it made him think that if someone knocked the chocks from the right corners, the whole lot would crash down and the world would be as it must once have been, with no margin between earth and space, no room for light or dark, plant or animal, no people. He had tried to write a class paper on the subject, but the teacher returned his opening paragraph with a suspicious glance.

Dew and cold reminded him that he had a lantern to stalk.

He struck out again with a strange restlessness, sliding quickly over the even ground so that when he keeled out into nothing he wondered insanely whether he hadn't crawled off the edge of the world. He fell, filled himself with air, and had it driven from him a moment later when he hit the bottom of the washout hard enough to make white light behind his eyes.

He got up quickly and fell down again. With his head on cold sand, he lay still and waited for the sky to settle. He was calm: it wasn't the first time he'd been badly winded. As before, he told himself he would not die, that breath would return. His heart felt engorged as it did when he dreamt his dream of the spiral staircase. He was afraid.

When he had his wind back, he rose and slewed about in the washout for a moment before aiming himself at the silhouette of the bank and scrabbling up. He came upon a fence which sang as he climbed through. He was tired of playing soldiers, so he walked brazenly through the shadows of a paddock, looking for the light on the hill and someone to blunder into for the sake of getting it over with. Only, he could not find the light. Crawling, as he had been, with his head to the ground, he hadn't seen the light for some time. He couldn't even remember when or where.

Egg marched on. He whistled. Quite suddenly, a light appeared. Below him, to the left. He galloped. Where had he been? He was above the lantern. Had he gone round behind? His boots thocked through wet, dung-thick, downsloping pasture. A dog barked. He stopped. It was a farmhouse. He was stalking the wrong light. Feeling reckless, he pressed ahead anyway. A dog spattered out of the dark to greet him, to blunt itself on his shins and whimper. Egg scuffed its cold slick coat and walked with it towards the light of the house. Lamplight streamed from a paned window, illuminating the shapes of parked vehicles. Egg moved carefully between flat-tops and utilities. In the house, people were singing, and to him it sounded like an old movie. He felt his heart fill again. He crept to the window and saw faces in the burnished light of a Tilley lamp.

Big rough-faced men and women with blunt chins and black eyes stood in a semicircle by the fireplace. A bearded man in a bib and brace held a white parcel in his arms. Egg saw the chequered smiles of the people. He saw their hands. A man near the end of the semicircle warmed the back of his legs by the fire. Tears glistened on his face. Egg was dumbfounded.

The big man with the white parcel looked around at those present and then to the window. Egg ducked. The dog pasted his face with its tongue. A door opened. Egg flattened himself on the ground.

'It's cold out.' The voice of a man. 'Come in by the fire.'

Egg rolled over and looked up at the shadow.

'Come on, soldier.'

Inside there was quiet. Roots sputtered in the fireplace. Egg felt the faces coming to bear upon him. The man with the white bundle ushered him to a spot by the fire. Egg's uniform steam-ed. The bundle in the man's arms gave a tiny cough. A baby!

'Now,' said the man with the baby, 'we'll get on.'

Egg stole a look at the people in the room. They looked like farmers, people who knew what they thought. An old woman in a pink dressing-gown had two fluffy balls peering from between buttons. They were ducklings, he saw, and she was keeping them warm.

'What I was gunna say is that this kid is a bloody miracle. That little heart just suddenly starting to beat – that's a miracle. Tonight we claim God's promises for this baby . . . er . . . Bill, what's the name again?'

'It's,' the man with the tears cleared his throat, 'it's Sidney Robert James Maitland.'

'Like Bill said. And tonight we swear ourselves to the sacred duty of raising this kid up to hear God. That's what this is about. We love each other, we try. We look after each other in our way, and that's miracle enough in this world. And now there's one more of us. Let's just hope the poor little bleeder can remember all his name.'

Everyone laughed and the man started to pray with the baby in his arms. Egg studied the still faces in the room, wondering who they all were. It was like a secret society, a Resistance meeting. The furniture in the room was pushed back against the walls: an old sofa, a card table, treadle sewing machine. The floorboards were polished. Egg felt warm and comfortable, but his heart remained engorged.

A loaf of bread came around the semicircle, and Egg, following the others' lead, broke a piece from it and ate it. The man holding the baby took the loaf from him and put it on the mantelpiece above the fire. A ceramic mug came around in the same manner and Egg drank from it. The liquid was warm as blood and it made his mouth shrivel, his belly glow. When Egg had drunk like the others, the mug went on the mantelpiece beside the loaf.

Then Egg saw that white bundle coming around, hand to hand, and his heart thickened and he felt it rising in his chest. Each person receiving the baby touched his face, looked into his eyes, and kissed him on the forehead. As it came to him, Egg felt panic. He was certain his arms would never bear the weight. The vanilla-smelling pupa slid into his arms, heavier even than he had expected. His knees creaked. He wanted to run away. How could such a thing be borne? It was insupportable. Someone coughed good-humouredly and Egg looked up.

'Serious business, soldier,' said the man in the bib and brace.

Egg glanced around at all the expectant faces. Some of them were rutted with tears. He freed one arm, reckless, and touched the infant's cheek, noticing his own blackened hands and clogged fingernails. He looked into the child's eyes. They were the colour of the night sky. Egg kissed the cool, sweet brow, then passed the baby to the man with a weak, faint sensation fluttering in him as though it had been an ammunition box he'd been holding and not a newborn.

'Amen,' said the man.

'Amen,' said the others.

'Beer and cake, then?' asked the man, holding the child for them all to see.

'Beer and cake!' they replied with a cheer and the room was suddenly full of movement. Egg stayed by the fire, almost dry. A thin woman in a mohair jumper put a glass of beer in his hand and a wedge of rainbow cake in the other, saying: 'You're a godfather, soldier.' Her smile surprised him. He was drinking beer. No one had asked him questions. A small man with no hair on the back of his head showed him how to play the spoons. The dog whined outside. Someone fiddled with an accordion. The night seemed so real. He could do nothing but stand and watch and listen and feel the panic of wonder. The beer was sour and cold as brass. His mouth rioted when he filled it with cake. He was dizzy; it was the light-headedness of the jogger. He was more than himself. He felt deeper and wider. He felt as though he was more.

Then the room went quiet. People cocked their heads to listen. Egg put his glass down. He heard the horn far out in the night.

'That's for me,' he said, going to the door. The man with the spoons saluted him. As Egg stepped out into the dark, the fat man who had presided over the ceremony put a hand on his shoulder and pushed a lump of rainbow cake into his hands.

'See you again, soldier.'

'Where?' The man shrugged.

Egg nodded.

Moving out across the paddock, Egg looked up to see the lantern away to his left, high up, miles away, it seemed, and to him it looked like a star descended from the night sky, from that darkness in his dream at the end of the staircase where he had never yet ventured. The locked fingers of his ribcage relaxed. He was not afraid. He stuffed rainbow cake into his pockets and began to run.

THOMAS AWKNER FLOATS

I

ALTHOUGH he had never been in an aeroplane before, Thomas Awkner was not a complete stranger to flight. His earliest memory was of the day the swing on the back veranda propelled him across the yard and into the fence. The ground rushed beneath him. Borer holes in the wooden paling became mineshafts. Impact was devastating. A loose picket pinched his earlobe and held him captive and screaming until his father could be hounded away from his incinerator behind the shed. Now, as the big jet staggered through the turbulence out over the desert, he twisted that earlobe between his fingers and sweated. He did not like to fly. His own height gave him vertigo.

Flight attendants lurched up the aisles. Drinks spilled. The FASTEN SEATBELTS sign chimed on and off. The thirty seats ahead of him were occupied by what seemed to be a delegation from the Deaf Society. These men and women wore blazers and little berets, and for most of the flight they had been engaged in an informal celebration, creating a disconcertingly visual babble. Words ruffled up by the handful and faces stretched with laughter, impatience, urgency. All Thomas Awkner could hear was the chink of glasses, but for the Deaf Society, he decided, it must have been a rowdy affair. Watching them gave him a thirst. He pushed the button for a flight attendant.

While he waited, he swabbed the sweat from his palms and smiled at the men on either side of him. It was a desperate grin, starched with fear, but it went unnoticed. From up ahead came a sharp, solitary belch. None of the partyers in the aisle seemed embarrassed for a moment.

A flight attendant came, but fear had knotted Awkner's throat so that he found it difficult to speak. The woman raised her sculptured eyebrows at him. Awkner's lips moved, but his voice seemed to be parked somewhere back down in his throat.

'Are you well?' the fat man next to him asked.

'The poor man is deaf, sir,' the flight attendant said. She began to mime eating and drinking. Thomas Awkner flinched.

The fat man scowled. 'I don't think he is. He's not wearing a blazer, or even a beret.'

'For God's sake, man,' the triangular man on Awkner's right protested, 'a man doesn't need a blazer and a beret to be deaf and dumb. He's probably freelance.'

'Rubbish,' the fat man said, 'he's listening to us now.'

'They lip-read, sir,' said the flight attendant.

'Could I have a beer, please?' Thomas Awkner managed to say at last.

'See? He talks.'

'So what?'

'Sir, honestly, it doesn't mean a thing!'

'Emu Bitter, if I could.'

The flight attendant beamed at him and went to get the drink. Neither man spoke to him. He felt as though he had upset them terribly. He wedged himself between their anger and their outsized bodies, and thought about his two hours in Melbourne. Right across the continent, he mused, long enough to deliver a manila envelope and board another plane home.

Since he was five years old, Thomas Awkner had been running family errands, taking small boxes to strange doors, relaying single words through holes in fibro walls, passing notes to men in grey hats in windy harbourside streets. The Awkners took for granted his apparent idiocy and he did nothing, as he grew older, to unsettle their assumption for fear of losing his only measure of importance in the Awkner web. An idiot, they thought, was the best courier possible. Understanding could be a risk. So the young Thomas Awkner cultivated complete incuriosity; he ignored message or parcel and concentrated on the trip, feasting on the world outside the asbestos house with its smoke and secret talk. But the trip always ended with a return home where nothing more was expected of him. At home, therefore, he did nothing.

He was flying. His father had never flown: that fact made him feel sophisticated. His father was a memory associated with the endlessly smouldering incinerator behind the back shed. Boxes of shredded paper were often brought through the house at every hour of the night. He recalled that long, grey face with its seedy moustache and perennial white stubble. His father died ten years before. An aerosol can had exploded as he peered into the incinerator. Uncle Dubbo appeared out of nowhere to attend the cremation service.

His beer arrived. He drank it quickly and immediately his bladder demanded relief. Lurching down the aisle toward the rear of the plane, he felt as though he was swinging across a ravine on a rope bridge. The turbulence was frightening. He fought against it in the chrome cubicle but he emerged with one hot, wet trouser leg, regardless. Grabbing at coatsleeves and the occasional head of hair for support, he found his way back to his seat and wedged himself between his large fellow-travellers. The two men wrinkled their noses and glanced knowingly at one another, and Thomas Awkner was spared no shame.

All across the continent he sweated. It took time for him to realize that it wasn't only flying that had put fear into him: it was his own curiosity that frightened him. Never before had Thomas Awkner, the courier, experienced the slightest interest in the messages, the mysteries, he bore. What was in the envelope? What did it mean? Why fly across Australia to deliver it in a public place? He longed to take it out of his pocket, hold it to a window, sniff it, rattle it, but these things would draw attention. Whose attention? His new-found curiosity brought fresh fears. Could this mission be *dangerous*? He sweated.

All he could do was deliver something and come back as always, as though a rubber cord anchored him firmly to that asbestos house in the coastal suburbs. But suddenly it seemed difficult. His filtering process was breaking down. When he went back would he still be able to absent himself from the workings of the family? He had learnt that skill early on, from the year Aunt Dilly and Aunt Celia had dossed in his room with him. Their snoring, their belches and mutterings, their stockings hanging like jungle snakes and their stares across the curtain as he dressed – these things he taught himself to ignore, and fairly soon all the machinations of the Awkner family happened on the grey, outer limits of his awareness. He did not question the prolonged absences of his brothers and his Uncle Dubbo. He never wondered about the huge unmarked containers their milk arrived in, or the boxes of unstamped eggs, the sudden appearance of a television set. Conspiratorial laughter broke through the asbestos walls like cricket balls, and all those years Thomas Awkner studied the discipline of inertia: he watched little, listened little, said little, did little. His schooling was not superb. He had no friends. And when, quite suddenly, the Awkners left town for Melbourne, he found himself alone with his mother.

2

The airport terminal was confusing: so many escalators and shops and purposeful people, and it was difficult to make headway, always casting looks over one's shoulder. He walked into the women's toilets, had to pay for a box of doughnuts he knocked to the floor, and was dragged from a Singapore Airlines queue and interrogated by customs officers. All he wanted was a taxi, and when he did find the taxi rank, the city of Melbourne seemed short of taxis.

After a wait in the sun, a cab eased up to the kerb beside him. He got in.

Pulling away from the rank, the driver asked him where he wanted to go.

'The gallery,' Thomas Awkner said.

'What gallery?'

'The art gallery.'

'Which one?' asked the driver, getting a good look at him in the mirror. Thomas Awkner was not a settling sight. His fine blonde hair stood up like wheat to the sun; he had not shaved; the flight had left his clothes rumpled. He stank of urine. 'Which art gallery, mate?'

'The proper one.' He was confused; he hadn't expected this.

The driver shrugged and took a punt and a left turn. 'How long you in town for?'

'Two hours.'

The driver settled lower in his seat. After all, what kind of man stays in a town for two hours? Not the kind of man you told knock-knock jokes to. He drove faster. Thomas Awkner skated about on the seat of his pants, smitten by the strangeness of the place. The buildings were half buried in trees, their lines were soft and their textures aged. It reminded him of Fremantle where he was born: houses standing shoulder to shoulder, old men walking in narrow streets. It charmed him. It flooded him with memories of walking to the wharf with his father. They lived in Fremantle to make it more convenient to visit relatives in prison. The air was full of gulls and the stench of sheep ships and harbour scum. Some days, Thomas walked with his father to the wharf where they would meet strange men and his father would whisper with them in the shadows of hawsers and derricks. The shimmer of the water's surface tantalized him. He always wanted to dive in. He begged his father to let him paddle at the little beach behind the mole, but there was never time and his father mentioned sunburn and rips and sharks.

'You'll sink like a stone,' his father said. They were the only words he remembered from his father.

The taxi stopped with such suddenness that Thomas cracked his chin on the ashtray of the seat in front. It cleared his head for a moment. He paid and got out into the disarming sunshine. He had an hour and a half left. He was to meet Uncle Dubbo here beside the dormant fountain in fifty minutes. It was hot in the sun. The sight of water running down glass attracted him to the building. He went in.

An atmosphere of sanctity was in the place. Tiny lights from heights. A brooding quiet. He decided to wait in there out of the heat until it was time to deliver. He saw his startled face in glass cabinets full of obscure artifacts; he recognized his hooked nose on a Roman bust and his doe-eyes in a Dutch oil painting. He saw pieces of himself everywhere. Normally he could not even bear to see his own reflection in the mirror.

It was thirty minutes before he saw the ceiling and when he did, the oddest sensation touched him. Stained glass – acres of it, it seemed. Fremantle. The old church. He remembered. On the way home from the wharf sometimes, he had followed his father into the old church where the sailors went, and he would be left to stand at the back near the door while his father went down towards the sanctuary to speak to men dressed in grey suits with hats in their hands. Often they would come away with little parcels which his father took out to the incinerator later in the day, but while they were speaking, Thomas was mesmerized by the scenes in stained glass at either side of the church. Every candle seemed to point towards the strange characters and their animals. On the way home, Thomas would dawdle behind his father, heavy with wonder.

In the middle of the gallery, Thomas Awkner took off his coat and lay on the carpet, looking up at the canopy of colours. Time passed beyond him as the panels of coloured light transported him back. He had forgotten wonder long ago and had replaced it with a dejected kind of bewilderment with which he armed himself to fight off the world from the slit-trench of his unmade bed. In those days of wonder, he had not been repulsed by his own image, he had not been afraid of his own height.

A man stooped and touched him on the shoulder.

'Uncle Dubbo?' If it is Uncle Dubbo, he thought, taking in the man's neatly pressed trousers and blazer and the well-organized face above them, then the plastic surgeons have done a first-class job.

'Sir, you can't lie here all day. There are vagrancy laws in the state of Victoria.'

'Oh.'

When he got up he saw that he'd left a wet patch of sweat on the carpet in the shape of a man, and by the time he had reached the door of the men's toilet people were noticing it. In the glittering hall of the toilet, Thomas Awkner splashed his face with water and looked at himself brazenly in the vast mirror. He was tall. His thin blonde hair was matted but not entirely disgraceful. His face was lean and his features thin and (perhaps, he thought, it's the heat) even vaguely elegant. The sight drilled him with that odd sensation again.

He heard a shifting sound in the cubicle behind and was suddenly afraid. He touched the manila envelope inside his shirt. He was a courier. A curious courier. Whatever it was he was carrying, he knew, it was important enough to be wanted by someone else. Perhaps everyone else. Thomas Awkner fled the toilet and walked quickly back to the entrance of the gallery, telling himself with fervour: 'I've got a mission.'

Out under the blinding sun, gelato vans had parked beneath the roadside trees. People sat around the perimeter of the fountain pool. A hot wind stirred deciduous leaves along the pavements and traffic passed, fuming. No sign of Uncle Dubbo. Twenty minutes left, yet. He wondered what he would say to him. A year had passed since he'd seen his Uncle Dubbo, and yet, in all the years through which his uncle had come and gone, in and out of his life, he had never really looked hard at him.

Uncle Dubbo never engaged him in conversation. Maybe he'd put the old man through a few conversational hoops before delivery. How bad did he want this envelope? What would he do to get it? What *was* Uncle Dubbo really like? What did he *do* all these years? What about those grey ghosts, his own brothers? He could barely remember them. Maybe, he thought, a few questions might be the price of delivery, this time. Was it really an aerosol can that blew the old man's head off? What does it all mean? What's my life honestly been about, for God's sake?

Thomas took out his return ticket and turned it over. Stuffing it back in his pocket, he bought an ice cream and sat at the edge of the pool. Two small boys tugged their shirts off and made shallow dives into the water, stirring up a sediment of leaves and potato-chip bags as they skimmed along the bottom and came up gasping beneath the NO WADING sign. People clucked in disapproval. Thomas watched the boys, envious. He had put his jacket on again to cover the bulge of the envelope, and the heat was unpleasant. He watched as the boys duck-dived and came up with coins. A woman next to him, long breasted, long faced, crinkled her shopping bags and rattled her tongue.

'Decent people throw their money in there. To make wishes.'

He looked at her. Reflected light from the water was unkind to her face. He opened his mouth to speak, then closed it again. A moment later he came out with it anyway, grinning like a clergyman.

'Well, so will they when they grow old and stupid.'

She cut him with a stare and turned away. With their hands full of coin, the two boys ran across the pavement to the ice-cream vans, footsteps evaporating behind them. When they came back with dripping cones and smeared faces, Thomas Awkner was untying his shoelaces. The woman turned to stare at him. He returned her stare and without taking his eyes from hers slipped sideways into the water. She screamed, brushing drops from her dress, while Thomas Awkner struck out across the mucky pool, ice-cream cone in hand, to the cheers of the boys. Cool water rushed through his clothing and he felt like singing. His head cleared and he remembered his father's words. Resting at the end of the pool, he watched the boys finish their ice creams and churn across to where he floated in the shade of the gallery. Behind them he saw the sports jacket and feather-duster moustache of Uncle Dubbo. Thomas lay on his back. He spouted like a whale. He had not been seen. Uncle Dubbo had black eyes. His fists opened and closed as though he might lash out with them at any moment. Thomas recalled suffocating clouds of cigarette smoke, toneless instructions, a plate thrown.

He patted the soggy lump in his shirt. The boys dived around him and he felt the rumour of a laugh in him. The strange city rang in his ears: sound and sight limitless. Uncle Dubbo paced, fists in his pockets. Thomas Awkner floated.

WILDERNESS

FOR FIVE days and five nights the man and woman had been in the wilderness. The last good stand of karri was hours behind on the bluish hills against the sky. In the mist of early morning the scrub and rock of the coastal hills were the same steel-grey, and each footfall resounded, steady and unambiguous. They could not see the ocean but they knew it was less than an hour away. They had not come to see it. Marsupial droppings flattened moistened underfoot. Their packs had not yet begun to weigh heavily upon them; it was early.

He waited for her to catch up. It was unnecessary but it gave him an illusion of leadership. She read her bird identification book as she walked. Even as he watched she stumbled on a stump and fell to one knee, driven to the ground by the weight of her pack. He waited. She turned the page. Clouds skated in from the south. They were at the end of the continent. After the ocean there was only the half world of the Antarctic.

'You shouldn't read while you walk,' he said.

'It's a skill worth having,' she murmured.

'Well don't break a leg acquiring it. I couldn't carry you out.'

'It's just that we should be able to name all the birds we see. It makes seeing them worthwhile,' she said. 'Common sense.'

'I wouldn't have thought so. While you've got your beak in that book you're not even seeing the birds.'

They walked another twenty minutes. The bush, as the light grew, turned blue and was unbroken on every side, unmarked until the paler blue of the sky capped it at the uneven horizon. On the spine of a long, granite-studded ridge they took compass readings and, looking eastwards down the valley, saw – for only a moment – a metallic glint. When they moved their heads it flashed. The man took a reading from it. She thought: Metal? This is wilderness. God, don't let it be a car. The idea itself was a desecration to her. Neither spoke: As they cut down the valley through the thick strew of boulders on the slope, the bush rang in their ears. They lost sight of the flash immediately. For five days there had been wilderness, no person, no sign of a person, not even a footprint. They moved down in the direction of the flash.

The valley was thick with head-high trees and dense, scrubby undergrowth around lozenges of granite in the cracks of which grew nests of pigface. The walking became difficult.

Bush-bashing, he thought; just what we need.

They stopped before a thick wall of growth that appeared impenetrable. Resting, packs cast aside, they were beset with a strange feeling: they had left their planned route, broken the timetable. In all their walks this was the first time. They had digressed.

'Maybe it was something in the rock that glittered,' the woman said, fingering her book.

'Like fool's gold.' He sighed and opened his canteen. He saw seams of dirt in the earliest lines of her face. 'We said we'd walk six hours. We've exhausted ourselves.'

'This isn't as good as the Bibulman walk,' she murmured. 'Or others.'

'There's a gazetted stream a kilometre east.'

'Funny, isn't it,' she said, 'how we always walk to water.'

'Common sense, I'd have thought.'

She looked at him and sucked her furry teeth. It was the same answer she'd have given to such an uncharacteristically whimsical statement. After all, she thought, chastising herself, who but a mad person would walk out away from water?

Hoisting themselves into motion again, they skirted the dense growth for several minutes until they came to a space, a tunnel in the tangled and matted foliage, that looked as though it had been made by animals. The man bent down to it. On his belly, there was enough room for him to move forward with his pack. The woman stood behind, watching his rump disappear, thinking: We've gone off course for a flash in the bush. It amazed her. A ludicrous thing to do, quite out of character. She got on to her belly and followed the scent of his sweaty buttocks.

The undercut in the bush widened until the man and the woman could crawl abreast of one another across the tortured roots and between the stems and wizened trunks of the vegetation. Marsupial droppings and the shadows of birds coloured the detritus. The woman and the man came out into the light together and helped each other to their feet. What they saw caused them to cry out simultaneously. Fifty yards further downhill in the clearing stood the aluminium frame of a dwelling.

'My God,' she said.

He shook his head. Within the frame hung a wooden door. A petrol-powered cement mixer stood to one side and with it, a shovel, a trowel and a screed. An aluminium window as big as a man leant against the near side of the frame.

'This is *wilderness*,' he said.

'Impossible,' she whispered. All around the cleared site, the scrub was the same: knotted, olive-drab and seven feet high. The lower side was confused and thickened by boulders and some taller trees. The woman pointed out the stumps and dead brush trodden flat on the ground all about. The clearing was man-made, someone had slashed the vegetation flat.

The man went to the door and opened it. It was eerie to step over the threshold and into the square of ground enclosed by that cage of metal. He walked through the space where the exterior wall would be.

'Yes,' he muttered, 'impossible.'

'And illegal,' she added in disgust.

'How could people carry all this gear in here? The nearest vehicle track is eight kilometres away.'

In all the bushwalking they had done over the years they had never come upon anything as inexplicable as this. They had done a lot of bushwalking. In their five years of marriage they had become connoisseurs of national parks and wilderness trails. The passion had not visited them by chance. After their first married year when it became evident that beyond their shared enthusiasm for courting, they had almost nothing in common (they read little and disliked team sports, and though minor, their musical interests were irreconcilable), they drafted a list of hobbies a husband and wife could share, drank a bottle of wine over which they had bickered bitterly, and arrived at two final possibilities: the Gestalt Club and bushwalking. Being afraid of religion and expense, they chose bushwalking. They bought their equipment, did their reading, and after the first year found they had a taste for it. Being teachers, they had a good number of lengthy holidays and their walks became more adventurous. Between walks they bored their schoolteacher friends with their hobby. In time, they were not invited to dinners and parties. They stayed at home and planned new walks. To the fresh crackle of survey maps, they filled their evenings with sensible conjecture and reminiscence. They upgraded their equipment. They became connoisseurs.

The husband lowered his pack to the ground and sat. 'I want to find out about this,' he said, wiping his brow with the sleeve of his shirt.

'Me too,' the wife murmured. 'It doesn't make sense.'

Later they retreated to the hedge-like vegetation and crawled just inside its shade and its tintinnabulation of cicadas. He took water from his pack and she the Hexamine stove from hers, and they made a billy of tea. They rested in the shelter drinking tea until the late afternoon, each secretly annoyed that they were allowing this strange discovery to distort their itinerary.

'It makes no sense,' she kept saying. 'You don't build houses in a gazetted wilderness.'

'And if you do, you don't build a kilometre away from the nearest water, and you don't build a house with those materials. And hack your own clearing. Only a lunatic would.'

They settled in to wait.

Night fell. They unrolled their duck-down sleeping bags, and after a meal of reconstituted rice and vegetables, slept lightly, listening to the rustlings of tiny animals in the invaded space beneath the scrub. The husband woke in the darkness before dawn with an aching bladder. He slid from his sleeping bag and crawled out into the clearing and was only beginning to relieve himself when he heard a metallic rattle somewhere out of his vision. He cut himself short, cursing inwardly, and slipped back under cover. The sound repeated itself. He woke his wife. They listened, peering out into the dark. A jarring thud; it was closer, but the bush, they knew, was deceptive. The thud again, and the rattle. Excitement prickled in the man and the woman. They strained until they thought they could hear each other's pulse. Then the bush down across the clearing began to vibrate and they heard scrapings which continued for several minutes. She was the first to see the outline of the figure that emerged and the shape that so slowly followed it. She touched her husband's arm and whispered: 'There.'

'A bloody wheelbarrow,' he whispered.

The figure was hunched and moved with the hesitancy and weakness of an old man. His coarse breathing was quite audible. With the convergence of dawn upon them the man and the woman began to see with less difficulty. For some time the man stood over the barrow, grunting and cursing. Then he straightened, puffing, each breath a bellow, and kicked the barrow over. A bag of cement thudded to the ground. A few tools chattered down beside it. Then the man himself fell. He did not move. For some time the wife and husband remained silent and motionless, watching, but there was no movement. They stared. The woman shifted her gaze to see her husband in the corner of her eye and she felt something turn in her belly. She thought: He looks sort of handsome when something gets his whole attention. Like a child, all intent. She had never experienced this distracted, disturbing sensation before; she was admiring him. At her side, he was thinking: This is a madman we're watching. We're losing walk time.

From beneath their shady hollow the wife and husband felt the day's heat creeping overhead, taking hold of the wilderness, claiming back the glittering jewels of dew, and as the morning came on and on, the man in the clearing by the houseframe and the spilled barrow did not move. They assumed he was sleeping; there was no sign even of his being alive.

But the man lying beside his battered barrow was breathing, albeit in narrow snatches. He had walked eight kilometres in the night, pushing his barrowful of cement, and he intended to repeat the trip as soon as it was dark. Inside his exhausted body he was dreaming. In his dream there was only the ultramarine sound of the wilderness sky and the sound of his heart labouring and he felt a profound satisfaction as he was raised up into Heaven. Flies dozed on the domes of his eyelids. Not even they sensed the intruders on the perimeter of the clearing he had hewn in the wilderness.

By noon the husband and wife had become quite uncomfortable in their nook, changing prone positions carefully, front, side, back. They hardly dared crawl back whence they had come for fear of alerting the man in the clearing. They did not consider revealing themselves and greeting him as if by accident. He looked unpredictable. Besides, their curiosity had grown and their resolve had hardened with every uncomfortable hour. They communicated by facial expressions and occasionally a whisper. As they waited and endured, an exciting sense of complicity took hold of them. In that cramped lair there was a novel intimacy. It was unnerving. He fed her tiny bits of chocolate, taking infinite care with the foil so as not to make a sound. She took it on her tongue silently as a communicant, tasting the salt on his fingers, holding one fingertip captive between her lips until his thumb buttoned her nose back and he smiled.

There was none of this at home. Their home was a place of business. No time, no gestures, no thoughts wasted. There were careers to attend to, unlikeable children to teach, Remedials to suffer, Exceptionals in whose glory to bask. Evenings were begun with sociable complaints about the staff and equipment of their respective schools. Then papers were marked, lessons prepared, and before bed a little mild gossip was exchanged. It was not a frivolous life. Even in their walking they were not frivolous. They mapped out their journey, they walked from A to B to C without unnecessary deviation or lingering at any point, and they gained their satisfaction from telling themselves, and the few who would listen, that they had *done* this walk and *done* that wilderness trail. Walking was a means to an end. They did not believe in things that were ends in themselves.

Somewhere inside her, the woman, taking chocolate from her husband, felt the impulse to explain their behaviour as a means of passing time. But the feeling was hollow. Instead, another sensation, a springing of nerves in her pelvis, in her chest, her feet, had come upon her, and though part of her demanded to stifle it, she drew it upon herself deliciously, licking her husband's fingers, pinching the tips in her teeth, holding her tongue out to him before he had another piece of chocolate to hand. And she noticed his quickened breathing, the reckless way he opened a second bar, the way he thrust his finger into her mouth and moved it across her teeth and around her gums.

Without pausing from this intensifying ritual, the woman unbuttoned her heavy cotton shirt and saw her husband's teeth meet and his lips move as she revealed her small, damp breasts, and from that moment, as she pushed him back on to the uneven ground and felt his breath in her mouth and his belt buckle hard against her belly and her waistband stretch and the vegetation against her shoulders and in her hair like frenzied fingers, the man prostrate in the clearing was forgotten. She heard her husband's breathing in her ear. She tasted chocolate and sweat and felt him reaching inside her without fear, without reserve, without precision. He bore her down on him. It was passion. It made no sense.

In his dream, the man in the clearing rose out and away from the curve of the earth, the compromising sounds of nature, the expressionless and unseeing eyes of those ugly little boys he lived with five days of the human week, the spiritless books that crowded his bedroom and his reference lists, the bloodless words and meaningless syllables he taught – all of them fell behind as his exhausted body and his burning soul lifted free and rose and rose. He felt himself yodelling and hooting, tumbling upwards to that clean, well-lit, sensible and airy room in which he would be received.

When he woke to find himself earthbound, he let out a groan and watched the dusk sky passing overhead. His legs, his feet, his back, his head ached. He thought: dark . . . time to go again . . . time to work. In one ragged movement he got to his feet, righted the empty barrow and began his agonized shuffle back across the clearing to the scrub. Down on his hands and knees, he dragged the barrow through and under the clot of vegetation. Twigs and trunks tore at his hands and his hair, snagging on the awkward shape of the barrow, until he was through and into the thinner open scrub outside where he could wheel the barrow ahead of him, jolting it over rocks and stumps downhill. It was eight kilometres to the Land Rover.

Lying in a stupor, feeling the sweat dry on their skin and the guilt creep into them, the wife and husband heard the man go. His groan of disappointment had made them flinch because they had forgotten him. They followed the progress of his shuffle and the creak of the barrow wheel across the clearing, and then listened to him bashing through the scrub until nothing more was audible.

'That's bloody odd,' the husband said, startled by the sound of his own voice after so long a silence. It was the longest period without speaking he could remember.

'Is it safe?' she asked, noting the lack of intimacy in his voice.

'I suppose so.'

She scrambled out to stretch and to urinate and brush herself clean and button herself up. Stars had appeared in the sky and a chip of moon was illumined just above the uneven horizon.

'We need water,' he said, tasting the residue of chocolate on his tongue.

'Why is he doing this, do you think?'

'He's either a criminal or a lunatic.'

'And he's coming back, I'll bet.'

They had wandered cautiously down the clearing to where the bag of cement lay near the door of the skeleton house. In the moonlight they could plainly see the weals his boot heels had left in the ground.

'He's no econut, that's for sure. Look at the materials, the way he's hacked the bush.'

'Still curious?'

He nodded. 'What about water, then?'

'We'll get some and bring it back. He's got hours to cover. We could find water pretty quickly, if we're lucky. Enough for tonight and some of tomorrow.'

He shrugged, agreeing. But he was still uneasy about the broken itinerary.

They took the waterbottles and the billy and with a map and a compass, made their way east, the same way the man had gone. It was difficult and dangerous work in the dark. There was no time for small talk.

★

It was late in the night when the man came willing his body up the incline towards the clot of scrub. Two bags shifted and shook in the barrow before him, one of builders' sand, the other of bluemetal, and he held them in his gaze as though they were sacks of precious stones. Sweat slicked him, and his lungs felt blistered and broken. He didn't even bother to confuse his movements or to stop and start again at odd times or to swap trails or lie and listen any more because he knew deep in his rawness of exhaustion that any deviation, any pause, any confusion would be final, that if he lost sight of that tangible bar that connected him, pointed him to the scrub clot on the slope – he couldn't tell if the white bar was light or pain – then it would be over. All his life, it seemed, he had been working towards this. Energy burned white in him even now, but his body was failing him; it did not understand that all things were possible. God help, God help me, he thought. Fifty weekends, a hundred trips, had not been enough. He had taken sick leave, holidays, even a day-trip after which he fell asleep in front of a class of thirty-eight teenagers. But still the structure went up slowly, awkwardly, fell down and was put up again as he read from how-to manuals and held screws in his teeth and felt the righteous anointing of sweat on his body. At first the work had been frenzied and the results quick to be seen by the eye. He cleared the circle in the scrub in four days: his machete flew, blinded him with its sunflashes, moved of its own accord. But the structure, the carting under secrecy and peril of darkness, the logistical odds . . . Men, he knew, had dragged riverboats through jungles and over mountain ranges, built pyramids, towers, walls that were impossible but for the will. It would go up because he had will, and because it was the most logical thing in the world.

From their position under the nest of scrub at the perimeter of the clearing, the man and woman heard him coming. They had washed and drunk at the tiny creek at the bottom of the valley, finding it by ear in the end. They had returned several hours before, and were roused from their light sleep by the noises. The woman, washed of this afternoon's stickiness, felt a renewed excitement at the sound of his approach. It was as if a great secret was about to be revealed.

The husband moved back slightly further into the foliage. There was no wind, no bird sounds, only the wispy, close movements of nocturnal animals and the distant creak and rattle of the wheelbarrow. The man was already wondering how he was going to make this story credible to the others in the staff-room. He never listened to a story that was not credible, and he would certainly not tell one. He was proud to be a teacher, a man of reason, disseminator of rational learning. This afternoon's incident in the bush had unnerved him. He tried to organize the past twenty-four hours in his mind, but the creak of the barrow wheel, ever louder, distracted and confounded him. He gave up and listened to the madman's pained respiration.

Down at the lower end of the clearing, the undergrowth rattled and snapped and screeched against the metal of the barrow. Each expiration was a distinct groan: 'Ugh, ugh, ugh.' It was like the sound of a labouring locomotive. The moonlight caught first the slick of sweat on his back, and then the metal sides of the barrow, and the man and woman, close to the ground in their hiding place, saw at once how fiercely his limbs trembled. His shoulders jerked, his legs danced beneath him. His mechanical breathing underwent a change as the laden barrow tipped suddenly on its side and then he was down on the ground, beating feebly at the earth, weeping. The sound became more and more animal, more shocking in the quiet of the wilderness. His body sent out a vibrato distress call like that of a wounded ram. They listened for a few minutes until it became obvious that he would not get up and the bleating would not stop.

Everything in him hurt. Everything. His soul ached like a tourniqueted limb. His body jangled him, smothered him, refused to move, refused to stop, refused. Stars closed in upon him, shining drops of sweat. He tasted salt. Remember, he thought, you are salt. He wedged his tongue between his teeth to stop them battering. He felt himself looking outside his body to the night above, as though he had scratched two holes in the lid of his own coffin. And that strange mewling sound in his head that disgusted him slightly would not cease. Beneath the sound, something in him said: 'I am trying, I am trying,' in a mellow, patient tone. Shivers rolled over him, end to end, faster, until there was no calm between swells. The black bowl of sky glittered benevolently.

I have to mix cement, he thought. I have to build, to measure, to carry, to make. I have to establish here to wait. I have to be here. I have to be here. Then his body stopped for a moment and he heard in the calm the sound of his heart punching, working, building, carrying, and his body relaxed as his soul's voice said, 'Then I'm here?' and there was only the bleating sound far away and the mild heat in his throat.

He was not surprised to see the two angels hovering above him, pinned against the velvet bowl of black sky. Their faces were clean and well fed. They were decent-looking angels; he was not disappointed. There was concern and innocence in their decent-looking faces and he was touched. Warm hands on his chest. A woman angel with black hair that fell over him, a warm ear to his swampy breast. Then they were looking at one another with worried angel faces. Although their lips moved, he could not hear their words for the mewling in his ear. This is it, he thought, this is truly it.

Their decision was reluctant but inevitable. There was only one reasonable path of action: the man had to be carried out of the wilderness. He was gravely ill. The husband and wife were grateful in a way that the situation and common sense itself left them with so few options. There was no argument; it took only a few moments. She stayed with the trembling, wailing, sick man while her husband went up to get their packs. His eyes were open, following her in an odd, unalert way, and sweat continued to appear on his bare chest and on his blackened, unshaven cheeks. She prised open one of his fists and saw nests of white blisters in his palm. Crazy, she thought; this is absolutely crazy. His jeans were tight and heavy with sweat. From one of his pockets she extracted a leather wallet, fat with money and an identity photo she could not see clearly in the moonlight. The money was a surprise to her. She wondered if perhaps he had stolen it.

At her side again, her husband, panting slightly, began sorting the contents of the packs.

'We'll have to go absolutely light,' he said. 'Anything superfluous has to go. Anything that'll weigh us down that we don't need in order to get him out.'

The spare changes of clothing spilled on to the ground. A pair of carnival-coloured underpants made him wince momentarily before they were obscured by the roll of the tent, the billy, the birdwatching manual, spare maps, excess food, and tiny items that looked anonymous and useless in the moonlight.

'Can we do it?' she asked. She watched him stuff the essentials into one pack.

'We'll have to. Besides, can a man do all this?' he said, with a gesture taking in the clearing and the partially built dwelling.

The woman pursed her lips and looked at the sick madman whose cries had begun to subside. 'Who knows?' she murmured. 'Does he look successful to you?'

The man zipped and sealed the pack and turned to the prostrate body. 'Let's get him into the bag.'

After they dragged his heavy boots off and shunted him feet-first into the sleeping bag and had him zipped up and hooded, they began the arduous task of lifting him into the barrow. It took ten minutes. His body bent and sagged awkwardly. The nylon exterior of the bag slipped between their fingers. His body was like a bag half full of stones. And all the time, as they heaved and dropped and cursed and staggered, his eyes passed from one to the other of them, infuriating them with a lack of expression. When he was in, feet out between the handles, buttocks in the hollow of the tray, head out over the front lip of the barrow, they wedged him tight with the spare clothing and rested for a moment.

He saw their earnest faces moving above, and the sky still benevolent over their shoulders as he felt himself levitating and moving away, the earth turbulent under his back. He wondered if his mother would miss him. She, even this past year, had never suspected, never known where he had been coming every weekend, never even understood or detected his sudden and vast dissatisfaction with his life, with her, with his useless job. Never, as they sat at dinner with the ABC news gently whispering to them across the room, had she suspected that he raged inside. But he ate his chops or his meatloaf and the cabbage that tasted like wet newsprint without letting go his secrets. Yes, he thought, she'll miss the company at the table. But she'll get in a boarder. And I forgive her. I forgive it all. These thoughts saddened him. His mother had, after all, given him a home, a room of his own, the chair at the end of the table after his father left them. But he had never known much feeling for her. The day he saw her in X-ray vision he knew why: she was an empty vessel. The white light of her soul, that radioactive ball, was deep in her large intestine, lodged firm, unable to be shunted through her bowels. He understood then.

Now he felt himself floating downhill, saw the pale biscuit moon running along the tops of the faraway trees, and felt himself at a so-long-awaited peace. But it puzzled him that things proceeded so slowly. He had imagined death and ascent into Heaven as more or less instantaneous.

The night seemed determined to last for ever. There was nothing to marks its passage but the endless punctuation of jolts, curses, near-spills and the occasional soft bleats from the invalid in the wheelbarrow. The husband and wife did not speak; there was no room in their lungs. The husband felt the gradual lengthening of his arms and sagging of his burning shoulders as he held fast to the handles, forbidding himself to let go. The woman at the front expected at any moment to have her heels fall away. Walking by turns backwards and sideways, she struck rocks and stumps on the tenderest parts of her feet. She sensed the track. She guessed. She could rarely see where the barrow bade her walk.

This is not impossible, she thought, catching a glimpse of the long cocoon in the barrow and the wild-eyed face of her husband and the featureless shadow of the bush all about. Her husband's beard glittered with sweat each time the moonlight touched it. His breathing was mechanical, hurtful to hear. She found herself avoiding the sight of him. In his fatigue he looked as mad as the man they were carrying.

Every few minutes, after each passage of near-spills and slips, the husband found himself thinking: This can't happen, people can't do this, people don't even imagine this. But not for one moment did he hesitate. Even when they stopped to rest a moment and taste the PVC-tainted water from the canteen, there was no doubt in any part of him that he would continue.

The invalid settled back inside the coffin of himself, feeling nothing but slight puzzlement. In an effort to orient himself, he went back to the start, that lunch hour twelve months ago in the staff room when he saw the ragged noticeboard on the wall opposite become a window. It frightened him. His coffee went cold as he watched. There was bush, just bush and sky through that window, the kind of bush he had never entered before. It was lonely, untouched, risky-looking bush and it gave him an inflated feeling in his chest. When the siren sounded the end of the lunch hour, the bush and the window were gone and there was only the scabby pin-up board and the everpresent haze of cigarette smoke. Then in the first class after, while chalking up the current facts on the Russian revolution, he saw his thirty-six students lose their heads. He stopped chalking. Their hands continued to copy down his scrawl, their torsos squirmed, shins were still kicked; he saw a note being passed, but for a full minute there was not one child with a head. He turned, shaken, back to the blackboard. He sneaked a glance. They had their heads on and they were giggling at him.

It was that evening when he saw his mother's skeleton inside her. His chops actually became live coals. The ABC newsreader's jaw swung like a garden gate. He went to bed early. Every evening that week he went to bed early. That weekend, he decided to drive out of the city to the hills to think. I'm having a nervous breakdown, he thought driving up. I'm off the edge. But the moment he got out of the car a few miles off the main road overlooking a valley and a series of uncleared ridges, his body ticked like a geiger counter. Bush. He experienced the same sensation as that first day in the staff room. His blood went mad. He began to walk. He half galloped down a ravine to where pools of water and reeds and shady trees were all about, huddling in secretively. And it was there that he heard the voice coming up out of the ground.

'Go into the wilderness and wait,' it said, and the logic of it made his nauseous with excitement and apprehension. He had no doubts as to whom had spoken.

All in a rush he bought Forestry maps, tourist maps, bush-walking glossies, visited the state library, drove hundreds of kilometres on weekends to find a wilderness. I'll have to build a house, he thought, I'll need a house to wait in. He began to hike and search, feeling his whole being jangle like an alarm bell as he stood on isolated crags where nothing human was visible, where the sky seemed close enough to whisper to, until he found a place that sent his blood ricocheting about in him enough to tell him *here, begin*. A white cord of light or heat rolled out before him and he stumbled in and along it until an impenetrable clump of shrivelled trees came into his vision and he saw that nothing was impossible, that all things could be done and had been done.

Here, he thought, I'll wait here. But first I have to build a house. Not even God would make a man wait out here without a roof over his head.

Every night for a year he dreamed foreign dreams in strange languages. The last few weeks, a phrase coiled through him like a loop-tape in the darkness. *Ich kann nicht anders . . .*

And now, as he saw the moon rise like an aura above the angel's head, he understood, was content, and he glided, weightless.

For a moment, the husband had the gut-sinking feeling that they were lost. The moon, behind them all along, now seemed diffuse on the horizon ahead. He called a halt. The woman, afraid to lie down for fear of never getting up again, slumped across the cocoon in the barrow, her sweat running down past her ears and into her eyes. From his pocket the husband took the flat, tiny compass and was surprised to see that he could read it without the light of the torch. East. They were still heading east. They were not off course at all. He peered at the pale light in the distance. East, he thought. East. Light. He glanced back over his shoulder to see the faded moon. East. It was the sun. He pulled a sleeve back and saw that it was five-twenty.

'Dawn,' he said. His voice sounded close and alien in the bush.

'Far?' she whispered, not looking up. She could see the barrow wheel with its tread full of little stones and burrs.

'No,' he wheezed.

But it was no comfort to them. They were appalled at the thought of willing themselves to move again. They knew such a thing could not be done. Ahead of them the earth curved upwards to a point, a ridge against which the eastern sky had begun to blanch.

A minute later, stone by stone, bush by bush, they were climbing it, the woman backwards, pulling, digging in with her raw heels, her husband hard behind with the ends of the handles almost piercing his palms as he pushed and steadied and made ground barely off his knees. Birds had begun to blur by. Their hesitant songs were lost on the man and woman who heard only the blood in their ears and the infinitely slow creak-creak of the wheel's revolution. They had forgotten the man in the barrow. Since his bleating had ceased hours before, there was only his impossible weight to remind them of his presence, and even that, after a time, became an anonymous, abstract thing that only their bodies sensed.

Once or twice during the night, the woman had thought of the warm, sensible staff room at her school: the lively, decorous chatter, the tobacco smoke, the yarns, the certainty of it all, but now such things did not exist for her. There was only the stone-by-stone impossible certainty that she was making ground. Her husband saw the mask of her face. It had begun to remind him of the mummified monster he saw in a film as a child. The image had terrified him and his father had laughed coming out of the cinema. His laugh had sounded so confident, so matter-of-fact, and as he grew he came to remember his unreasonable fear with disdain. But he felt it again now when his wife's tortured face came into his vision, stronger with each step as the light grew on the crest of the ridge and the crest itself became close enough to seem attainable. He heard his breaths become sobs. He bent and pushed and heard the wheel creak and turn.

Through the holes in his body, the man in the barrow saw the light coming and heard the sounds of birds stirring in the scrub all about. The steady labour of his heart was still with him, racing a little as mind and soul reacted to the intensified sensations of ascent. Excitement coursed through his tiny, warm core.

The moment they reached the razor spine of the ridge and

took the fresh yellow sun in their surprised faces, the man and the woman lost their grip on the barrow. It tipped their passenger into a nest of pigface. They gazed like animals at the Land Rover.

'It's impossible,' the woman said.

'No,' murmured the man in the sleeping bag, hearing the final blow of his heart and the comforting silence that succeeded it. He felt himself slipping, curving, lifting away, rising up through the orifices of his body with a silent hiss that sent his warm core out and away into the impossible, colourless light. He did not look back to the figures embracing on the ridge with his body shrouded beside them; there was no time and no need.

Neighbours

When they first moved in, the young couple were wary of the neighbourhood. The street was full of European migrants. It made the newly-weds feel like sojourners in a foreign land. Next door on the left lived a Macedonian family. On the right, a widower from Poland.

The newly-weds' house was small, but its high ceilings and paned windows gave it the feel of an elegant cottage. From his study window, the young man could see out over the rooftops and used-car yards the Moreton Bay figs in the park where they walked their dog. The neighbours seemed cautious about the dog, a docile, moulting collie.

The young man and woman had lived all their lives in the expansive outer suburbs where good neighbours were seldom seen and never heard. The sounds of spitting and washing and daybreak watering came as a shock. The Macedonian family shouted, ranted, screamed. It took six months for the newcomers to comprehend the fact that their neighbours were not murdering each other, merely talking. The old Polish man spent most of his day hammering nails into wood only to pull them out again. His yard was stacked with salvaged lumber. He added to it, but he did not build with it.

Relations were uncomfortable for many months. The Macedonians raised eyebrows at the late hour at which the newcomers rose in the mornings. The young man sensed their disapproval at his staying home to write his thesis while his wife worked. He watched in disgust as the little boy next door urinated in the street. He once saw him spraying the cat from the back step. The child's head was shaved regularly, he assumed, in order to make his hair grow thick. The little boy stood at the fence with only his cobalt eyes showing; it made the young man nervous.

In the autumn, the young couple cleared rubbish from their backyard and turned and manured the soil under the open and measured gaze of the neighbours. They planted leeks, onions, cabbage, Brussels sprouts and broad beans and this caused the neighbours to come to the fence and offer advice about spacing, hilling, mulching. The young man resented the interference, but he took careful note of what was said. His wife was bold enough to run a hand over the child's stubble and the big woman with black eyes and butcher's arms gave her a bagful of garlic cloves to plant.

Not long after, the young man and woman built a hen-house. The neighbours watched it fall down. The Polish widower slid through the fence uninvited and rebuilt it for them. They could not understand a word he said.

As autumn merged into winter and the vermilion sunsets were followed by sudden, dark dusks touched with the smell of woodsmoke and the sound of roosters crowing day's end, the young couple found themselves smiling back at the neighbours. They offered heads of cabbage and took gifts of grappa and firewood. The young man worked steadily at his thesis on the development of the twentieth-century novel. He cooked dinners for his wife and listened to her stories of eccentric patients and hospital incompetence. In the street they no longer walked with their eyes lowered. They felt superior and proud when their parents came to visit and to cast shocked glances across the fence.

In the winter they kept ducks, big, silent muscovies that stood about in the rain growing fat. In the spring the Macedonian family showed them how to slaughter and pluck and to dress. They all sat around on blocks and upturned buckets and told barely understood stories – the men butchering, the women plucking, as was demanded. In the haze of down and steam and fractured dialogue, the young man and woman felt intoxicated. The cat toyed with severed heads. The child pulled the cat's tail. The newcomers found themselves shouting.

But they had not planned on a pregnancy. It stunned them to be made parents so early. Their friends did not have children until several years after being married – if at all. The young woman arranged for maternity leave. The young man ploughed on with his thesis on the twentieth-century novel.

The Polish widower began to build. In the late spring dawns, he sank posts and poured cement and began to use his wood. The young couple turned in their bed, cursed him behind his back. The young husband, at times, suspected that the widower was deliberately antagonizing them. The young wife threw up in the mornings. Hay fever began to wear him down.

Before too long the young couple realized that the whole neighbourhood knew of the pregnancy. People smiled tirelessly at them. The man in the deli gave her small presents of chocolates and him packets of cigarettes that he stored at home, not being a smoker. In the summer, Italian women began to offer names. Greek women stopped the young woman in the street, pulled her skirt up and felt her belly, telling her it was bound to be a boy. By late summer the woman next door had knitted the baby a suit, complete with booties and beanie. The young woman felt flattered, claustrophobic, grateful, peeved.

By late summer, the Polish widower next door had almost finished his two-car garage. The young man could not believe that a man without a car would do such a thing, and one evening as he was considering making a complaint about the noise, the Polish man came over with barrowfuls of woodscraps for their fire.

Labour came abruptly. The young man abandoned the twentieth-century novel for the telephone. His wife began to black the stove. The midwife came and helped her finish the job while he ran about making statements that sounded like queries.

His wife hoisted her belly about the house, supervising his movements. Going outside for more wood, he saw, in the last light of the day, the faces at each fence. He counted twelve faces. The Macedonian family waved and called out what sounded like their best wishes.

As the night deepened, the young man dozed between contractions, sometimes walking, sometimes shouting. She had a hot bath and began to eat ice and demand liverwurst. Her belly rose, uterus flexing downward. Her sweat sparkled, the gossamer highlit by movement and firelight. The night grew older. The midwife crooned. The young man rubbed his wife's back, fed her ice and rubbed her lips with oil.

And then came the pushing. He caressed and stared and tried not to shout. The floor trembled as the young woman bore down in a squat. He felt the power of her, the sophistication of her. She strained. Her face mottled. She kept at it, push after push, assaulting some unseen barrier, until suddenly it was smashed and she was through. It took his wind away to see the look on the baby's face as it was suddenly passed up to the breast. It had one eye on him. It found the nipple. It trailed cord and vernix smears and its mother's own sweat. She gasped and covered the tiny buttocks with a hand. A boy, she said. For a second, the child lost the nipple and began to cry. The young man heard shouting outside. He went to the back door. On the Macedonian side of the fence, a small queue of bleary faces looked up, cheering, and the young man began to weep. The twentieth-century novel had not prepared him for this.

A Measure of Eloquence

ALONG THE clay cliff-edge the sagging old radio wires cut the wind with a yawl. The young man and woman saw that down on the point in the grove of trees were two tents and a caravan.

'Jerra told us this place was deserted,' said Ann, looking down at the campfires.

Philip paused, hand on the door of the hut, and looked down to the beach and the trails of footprints that looked so tiny from up there. He said nothing, there was nothing he could say. The exultancy had receded and disquiet had come upon them, the kind of restless anxiety which visits people in the wake of momentous actions. They had been married for two days.

Before last night in the motel room, they had never slept together in a bed. Now, in this rough hut on the cliff, they found themselves straightening blankets too hastily, tucking the corners with awkward, terribly casual movements. The big iron bed consumed most of the space in the single room. Ann slotted a cassette into the tape recorder and the music helped diffuse some tension. The interior of the hut, with its patchwork of tin and asbestos and pine packing-cases, seemed more benign in the light of the Tilley lamp. There was a deal table, two chairs, a bench with a bucket set into it, a few shelves fastened to each wall, and an oblong strip of linoleum on the floor. The hut belonged to the father of a friend. Their friend had lived here for a year after a nervous breakdown. There was no sign of his occupancy except for a few books on the shelf by the bed: *The Coral Island*, *Under the Volcano*, *Reach For the Sky*, *The Sun Also Rises*. Philip pulled down *The Coral Island*. The dust made him sneeze. Ann turned from the window and smiled.

'Did you read it as a boy?'

'No,' he said.

'I did.'

'You were never a boy, though,' he said, trying to shrug the heaviness from him.

'Sometimes I was.'

'This marriage could be embarrassing, then.'

'Don't worry,' she said with a grin, 'I won't tell.'

He put the book back on the rough shelf and sat on the bed. It sagged in the middle like a hammock. Rain started to fall and the tin roof chattered.

'You want some tea, something to eat before bed?' he asked.

'No,' she said. She drew the salt-stiff curtain.

Ann woke to the sound of the camera shutter. Pink light made the blankets and the linoleum floor and the bedstead blush. Philip, elbows on the windowsill, focused the zoom lens. She saw the dawn in his hair, on his bare shoulders, on his right cheek.

'The sea,' he said.

'The what?'

'The sea. The sea.' The camera plunked. He wound on.

'What about it?' She bunched the pillow beneath her neck.

'Nothing. Just . . . the sea.'

'Now you sound like Jerra. You don't even like the sea. You hate fishing. You even hate people telling stories about shipwrecks. You don't even go to the beach in summer.'

'Yes I do,' he said. He was conscious of his untanned nakedness.

The day came out of the sea at them. Birds hovered on the updraughts before the cliffs. The gas stove hissed. The smell of eggs overpowered the dust and the mildew and the last scent of sex on their bodies.

★

Neither mentioned last night as they wandered along the beach with the cliffs and the hut and the old radio wires high above. Ann held her folio hard against her hip to keep the wind from having it. Philip's camera swung from his neck like a grotesque charm. Rain had pummelled the roof in the dark last night, drowning their cries. In those first moments after waking, Ann had a feeling of having flown. Philip recalled her boyish shoulders against his teeth, and the taste of talcum. Both, even now as they kicked up sand and saw the distorted shadows of gulls on the beach ahead, had the sensation of having come somewhere, the night traveller's disorientation upon arriving, at dawn, at a town which bears no recognizable features, no signs, no immediate relation to the last stop.

A mile up that endless beach they stopped and Ann sat to sketch. She sketched poorly and they both knew it, though it remained a tacit secret. Philip watched her work from a distance, close to the shore where the sea ate at the sand.

'How does it feel to be married?' he called.

She did not answer; it seemed as though she had not heard. How does it feel? she was thinking. It feels like waking up on your twenty-first birthday and realizing that there's no change, that you don't feel an ounce older. That's how it feels. So why ask me? You know how it feels, it's written all over you.

Through the zoom lens Philip saw that she was not drawing at all; she was thinking. He snapped that sad expression on her lips and the thread of hair in the corner of her mouth, and wound the film on with a sigh. We shouldn't have come here, he thought.

On the cliffs at dusk, just at the soft edge where run-off wore steep veins in the clay, they found a pair of brogues, toes pointed out towards the sea. In each shoe was a sock. They were still warm. Footprints embossed the clay surface near the brink.

Behind them, the sun was far gone in the hills. It took Ann a moment to realize that she was alone. She saw Philip running along the brow of the cliff towards the safe path to the beach. She did not call him; her throat was swollen with dread. She stood at the edge peering over. She could see nothing; even the beach and the vegetation at the bottom was dissolving rapidly into night.

When finally he joined her again, wheezing and wet with exertion, his embrace told her that he had found nothing.

'I don't understand,' she said.

'No.'

'It might be a joke.'

'Yes,' he murmured, 'a joke.'

They could not find the shoes again in the darkness. They went back to the hut where they had left the lantern burning.

That night, a storm bore down and the little hut quivered in the wind. They picked at their food and drank too much wine and lay in the big hammocky bed, listening, unable to shed the sensation that enclosed them. The wine had fuelled their sadness and apprehension. They touched each other; their nakedness seemed frivolous; their bodies felt ludicrous.

'I can't,' he said. 'I'm sorry . . . I can't.'

She turned her head into his chest in the dark.

'No, neither can I.'

'We shouldn't have come here,' Philip said. 'It was a mistake, it was my fault.'

'We were both there when he offered it to us.'

'It just doesn't feel right. Like sleeping in a morgue, or on a deathbed.'

'You're exaggerating,' she murmured. 'Anyway, it should be the opposite. It's where he came to get well. It's a haven, a refuge.' But all the time she was thinking of Jerra's tears, his tossing and twisting, his great sadness in this single room. And the shoes, the shoes would not leave her mind.

'You know, if we were fishermen, fisherpersons,' he said with a shallow cheerfulness, as pieces of dust were forced from the cracks in the wall by the force of the wind, 'we'd be up planning for the morning's fishing, making lines and putting hooks and things on them, telling tall tales, not getting depressed. We'd be—'

'But we're not,' Ann said without expression, and immediately he regretted having sounded so desperately light-hearted. The wind in the falling old radio wires that had once linked boats and crews to their families ashore gave out a cry that made him think of boats lost at sea, families grieving – even the out-of-work shearers over on the point with their campfires and their taffy-haired children and the piles of beer bottles by their tents. And he thought of those shoes and the warm socks inside and wondered whether it was a sick joke or whether he would find a broken body on the beach in the light of dawn.

An hour before dawn Ann woke, weeping. She saw only darkness and felt Philip close beside her.

'What's the matter?' he asked, half-conscious.

'I had a dream,' she said. All her limbs restrained a sob.

Philip sat up. The air was sharp. It was beginning to rain again.

'I dreamt that this hut fell off the cliff and we were killed. Someone found us with our feet cut off. We were dead, all bloody, without clothes, and there were people all around.'

He put his hand to her cheek, felt her wet face in the dark. 'Well, we're not dead.'

After a long silence she said: 'Have you ever seen a dead person?'

'No.'

'I have. When I was thirteen my aunt died and before the funeral started my parents made me go in and look at her. She was . . . like something out of a sideshow. They made me.'

'One of my friends',' Philip said quickly, 'father was killed when we were in high school. He was a road worker. A carload of kids ran him down. My old man was the local copper. He had to take my friend to identify the body. His mother was in hospital having her appendix out or something. Dad brought him home to our place after the morgue and he was weeping like a baby. Dad left us in my room. I put my arm around him and then we were both really embarrassed so I took it away. I think I was expected to say something, but I'm not like my old man. I don't have those kinds of things to say. Fine bloke, my Dad. I always wanted to be him. I still want to be like him, I suppose.'

'What? Dead?'

He smiled after a moment, thinking her comment a desperate joke, but in the half-light he saw her face in her hands and he was wounded. 'What's wrong?'

'I don't want to die. I don't want you to die.'

'People die,' he said hopelessly.

She gave him a traitorous look. Now they could see the rain on the window, long cords of it torn out of plumb by the wind. They slept and woke spasmodically, watched the weather through the window, heard the linoleum flap and the wires wail until late in the morning. They spoke little.

When they rose, they ate thick squares of bread daubed with honey and drank the Irish Breakfast tea they had brought specially. The other treats and specialities they had brought for this week were still on the shelves: Spanish olives, ambrosia cheese, chocolate, pecans, kiwi fruit, things they had gloated over on their way south that seemed so unappealing now.

'Let's see if we can walk to the end of the beach,' he said. He had honey on his chin.

'Which way? Towards the point?'

'The other way.'

'It's miles.'

'Why not?'

She shrugged. 'I had thought of reading.' She pointed to the book at the foot of the bed.

'Don't bother. I've read it. About that legless pilot—'

'Douglas Bader.'

'Well I thought you'd rather walk than read about artificial limbs.' Then he laughed. 'Has this got anything to do with your dream?'

She scraped the honey from his chin with her index finger. 'Let's go then.'

It took them ninety minutes to come to the end of the seemingly infinite white curve of the beach. There was a headland, some rocks, and a half-exposed reef. They climbed along the rocks to the reef and saw nests of cockles along the waterline. Philip lowered himself feet first to where the water surged in, and filled with cockles the bag they had brought for shells.

'I suppose you can eat them,' he said as they walked back in the afternoon sun.

'Jerra says they're like mussels or oysters.'

'Poor ol' Jerra.'

Half-way back they noticed two figures moving towards them on the beach. It annoyed them and made them walk faster to reach the path up the cliff and regain their seclusion. But it was further than they thought and they soon tired. Before long, they saw the figures were the old couple they had seen arriving with their caravan on the first day.

'Oh God,' Ann muttered when she realized they were going to meet.

The two couples met. They exchanged pleasantries and the old man asked them what they had in the cloth bag. Philip told him.

'Cockles,' the old man said. 'Lovely things. Where'd you

get 'em?' They told him. He seemed disappointed. 'Give my right arm for a feed of cockles.'

His wife agreed. She was a small woman with her white hair braided and pinned to the side of her head.

'You want some?' Philip offered, annoyed.

'Oh, no.'

'It's a long walk,' Ann said, 'and it's pretty precarious down on the rocks.'

'Oh, Jim couldn't do anything like—'

The old man seemed to cut her off with his grimace.

'Here, take half of these,' Philip said, pouring cockles into the old man's doffed hat. Ann looked as surprised as the old man. Philip felt a secret pleasure.

'Jim has a marvellous recipe for them,' the small woman said. 'We'll trade you.'

'Yes, yes,' said the old man. 'We'll trade you. And I'll give you a cup of Sauterne to marinate them in.'

Twenty minutes later the four of them were sitting in the caravan. The old man poured Philip a beer and the women lemonade.

'Lovely set-up you have,' Ann said. She felt trapped in this over-furnished mobile home.

'Oh, you'll have one like it, someday,' the small old woman said. 'Always nice to start small.' She then went on to talk about her five daughters and their weddings. Philip observed her husband across the table. The old man had a tremulous air about him, little hair, gold rimmed spectacles, a good suntan, and moist eyes. Philip wondered whether he was an alcoholic.

'Of course,' the woman continued, 'Jim would have liked a son. Fathers like to have sons. But he had his work.' She told Philip and Ann how her husband had taught at the technical school for thirty-five years, and of his recent retirement and the sale of their house, her husband all the time moved his spectacles about on his tanned nose as if graciously allowing himself to be spoken about. 'He got tired of those boys. They had no home discipline.'

'But some of them could really work with wood,' he said. He was assuming control of his story. 'And I liked them, tried to get them on side for thirty-five years. I just didn't have the tongue for it. Not a good enough tradesman to be a carpenter, and not good enough talker to be a teacher. Wanted most of all to be a teacher.'

'But you *were* a teacher, dear,' his wife said with a worried glance.

'But not a teacher with his class in the palm of his hand. All I needed was that little measure of . . . eloquence.'

'His last class put in together to buy him a gold-plated drill-bit.'

'Their little joke.' He smiled thinly.

Philip looked at his watch. It was late. The cockles in his bag had begun to smell.

'Married long, dears?' the old woman asked as they made to leave.

'Two days,' Ann said, drinking the last of her lemonade with some effort.

'Well, if you could have some of *our* forty years, you'd be a happy couple, I'm sure.'

'Yes.'

Half-way along the cliffs where the radio wires drooped like laden clotheslines, Philip laughed suddenly and swung the bag of cockles up high.

'The old bastard didn't even give us the Sauterne.'

★

There was a coldness in the hut that night. The delicacies remained untouched, the cockles went rank on the bench, the wind blew and the lamp hissed. They ate bread and honey and put their elbows up on the deal table, unable to say much. They found it difficult to even allow their eyes to meet. In bed, Philip thought of his friend, the one whose illness had shocked him so. As she tried to read the opening of *Under the Volcano*, Ann thought of the old woman's words: 'You'll have one like it, someday,' with a turning in her belly.

Ann whimpered in her sleep. Philip was awake. Surf cracked down on the beach. The wires kept up their mournful sound.

Towards noon the next day Ann and Philip sat in the sun on the broad beach, and sketched and took photographs.

'What are you drawing?' he asked.

'The cliffs. What are you taking pictures of?'

'You drawing the cliffs.'

'Here come our mates,' she said.

Philip turned the zoom down along the beach, focused and groaned. 'And they're bringing a bag. He's gonna get some cockles, I'll bet. Not to be outdone.'

'You shouldn't have put them in his hat.'

'He wanted them. Hang on . . .'

'What?'

'Hang on . . .' Philip got to his feet. 'Something's wrong. The old man's down.'

'But what's wrong?'

Philip saw the woman moving frantically about the prostrate figure. 'Oh, God, we better help.'

They ran, folio flapping, camera chest-beating, and the sand broke their gait and made them stumble. The old woman was now flailing the air with her hands, hat fallen to the sand beside the head of her husband. She began to shout, then scream.

As he leant over the old man, the swinging lens of the camera caught Philip on the nose and he was blinded. Ann put her head to the man's chest and heard respiration. The woman cried: 'His heart, his old heart!'

They hoisted him on to Philip's back and tied his wrists together with his belt and threw his arms over Philip's head. For a few moments Philip felt the old man's breath in his ear. He could barely see. His nose bled. Fifty yards away, the path up the cliff began. Words, talking noise, plans, advice, regrets, they were all mashed in his ear with the sound of his own exertion. Near the top, where the footing was firmer and the noise of the wind in the wires could be heard, Philip felt a hot wet flush down the small of his back, in the waistband of his jeans and down the back of his legs.

Ann did not drive as fast as she could have. No one had conceded the old man's death yet, even though his body, sprawled across the back seat, head in the old woman's lap, was quite lifeless. She saw Philip's white face with its congealed blood smears. He looked out at the road. It was an hour before a word was spoken. The town limits were visible. Then the old woman spoke.

'Jim loved his cockles,' she said composedly. 'Loved them.'

Ann, watching in the rear-view mirror, asked: 'Did you know his heart was bad?'

'Oh yes, dear, only I didn't know *how* bad. He didn't enjoy teaching those boys, I'm sure. No, his heart was bad. I should have guessed it was giving him funny turns the other night when he went for a walk before dark and came back without his shoes. He was all confused, said he didn't know where they were. He went straight to bed. I heard him crying in the night – it must have been the pain, poor love. Well, we had a good life, dears.' She began to weep.

Philip's mouth was open slightly. Ann had noticed it was the way he slept. She seemed to be driving faster, the curves seemed more centrifugal. Ann cleared her throat. The sound made Philip flinch. Their eyes met. It was only a moment. Then they were inside the town.

THE OPPRESSED

for Loi Hong Quan

They are like children sitting in the market-place and calling
to one another,
'We piped to you and you did not dance; we wailed and
you did not weep.'

Luke vii, 32

I

WE ARE hugging. Our arms and faces and palms touch. Skins
brush contrasts across one another. Their eyes glitter in their
tall, pale bodies. They are Australian. I am still Chinese. We
laugh exultantly. It has been months since we met. They used to
visit me at the migrant hostel. But I have not come alone: by my
side, Hoa is silent, half afraid of the strange boisterousness of
Mary and Simon. They tug me and punch me on the back,
though they become subdued when they notice Hoa and her
stillness.

'You're back, mate,' says Simon who is a shaggy-haired
youth. He is younger than me, friendly, and impatient, it seems,
to be friendlier. 'Quoi, you're back!'

Mary slips an arm around his waist as she often does, with
her weight on one foot. She is sensitive, I feel; she wants to
know things, to feel things. These are young people, and I, so
little their senior, feel like an old man with them. And yet, what
do I know that I would have them experience? Her narrow,
pleasant face beaming, Mary asks many questions at once,

almost in a single breath. There is a smell of roses in this park
with its crusty statues of horses and men poised, rising and
rushing forwards, clamouring silent. And browning roses.

'Yes, I am back.'

Their faces smile until they seem they may split like
mangoes.

'It's great,' Mary says. I call them 'mate' and they laugh as
we stroll in the sweet space between rosebeds. We are quiet for a
moment; even the traffic is subdued. Mary smiles at Hoa, uncertain, but friendly. Hoa is unused to their ways and remains
silent. She feels like an intruder, I am sure, but my relationship
with these people is difficult to explain. They invited me into
their home. They helped me. How can I explain such a thing?
She folds her hands neatly over her cheap cotton dress. Her
figure is minutely fine compared with the motherly thighs and
hips of Mary. Their bodies seem to have thickened during these
months, whilst mine has strengthened and hardened. They tell
me so, and seem ashamed of their softness.

'Who's your friend, Quoi?' Mary asks.

I introduce Hoa, embarrassed at my neglect. They say hello
in unison and Hoa nods politely. They are noticing her silence
and I can feel them wondering. Silence worries them.

Those long reeking, wallowing nights we learned silence, huddling
on the aft deck of the stolen boat watching lights pass us spectrally on the
water, that water which yields more than fish and weed, throwing
bloating things upon the beaches, that water which knocked fists of
wavelets against the boat's hull, beckoning, taunting us with the men
and women it still withheld . . .

As we walk down William Street towards the art gallery, I tell
them of Broome and the other towns they have yet to see. It is

very like home, I say, explaining the climate and the palms and the tides, and describing the humid, sultry nights drinking beer with the noisy Aboriginals who frighten us, but smile often and whitely in the dark. Some Europeans drink with us, call us Charlie, speak rudely to the Aboriginals. Beautiful, lonely nights sipping draughts of prickly-cold beer with froth boiling over the lip of the glass. Saigon beer, I say, has not been so good for years. Simon says he thought we drank rice wine. He is joking, I am sure. Both he and Mary seem disturbed when I say Russian beer is no match for American beer. I feel sure Simon wishes to reply, but he refrains from comment.

'Where did you meet Hoa?' Mary asks, avoiding more talk on beer.

Dismissed from my job as deckhand without warning, I sat by the post office watching the waves bracing the rugged piles of the jetty as a new boat berthed, off-loading tired men who came up to collect their mail. In my hands I clutched two letters, one from my company who regretted this and that, and the other from Simon and Mary who joked about a string of illegal pearls I should bring back to use as checkers to renovate the battered set we idylled over by the river on summer evenings when we ate freshly netted prawns. It was hot and I clenched the paper between my fingers, for the first time without a reservoir of resolve, only apprehension. People speaking in the post office . . .

I begin to tell Simon and Mary the parts that are not so tedious to tell.

The people at the post office were asking me did I want a job. I walked down to the jetty with them, four Eastern European men with difficult accents. A deckhand died at sea, they said, and they seemed dazed. Perhaps they too knew death, but not at sea as I did. It was something new to me. I noticed these men were speaking to me as though I was stupid. This would be a hard job, I was sure. A girl's face appeared for a moment near a hatch. She was also Chinese. My spirits rose. She did not smile . . .

'Many Vietnamese working up there?' Simon asks. He forgets what I have told them of our origin. Does he do this on purpose? I tell him of the Chinese, Filipinos, Malaysians and others. No one else could allow themselves to be treated so poorly, except the Aboriginals who no longer seem to bother. Few need money as badly as us. Fewer know what Australian money is worth in our country.

I speak of the advantages of the black market and how I send money home through its revaluing channels to my parents and family in Saigon. Simon and Mary speak in gently disapproving tones. I cannot explain. There is too much for them to know.

As I mounted the gangplank, the girl's head appeared once more and I stared and lost my footing. My belongings bobbing sulkily about, I swam to the jetty, with the crew laughing down at me . . .

Hoa's shoulder brushes against me. Is she glad that these people are my friends? More than once have I thought they would make formidable enemies, so irrepressible is their idealism and goodwill. Hoa is frightened. She does not know how they will react. Her mouth is tight.

'Rough seas?' asks Simon, perhaps he is testing me.

'Nothing is too rough when there is somewhere to go,' I say with a smile. Simon nods soberly. They react this way when I mention the refugee boat. I feel they mention it to remind themselves. Sometimes they are angry and tearful about it, but more often sober and quiet.

We go into a dirty café which smells of bacon and coarse antiseptic, the sort of place Americans eat in. I am confused. Simon and Mary cannot afford to buy food. This is why we are going to the gallery which costs nothing. We sit at a slippery Laminex table with a chromed napkin-dispenser and a cracked glass sugar bowl. Simon puts the dispenser against the wall to make it like Australian toilet paper. We laugh, not really embarrassed. My brother, who designs American bathrooms, would laugh loud if he were with us.

Four egg and bacon burgers come, the sort we ate in the American places in Saigon. It was fashionable for students then. Hoa is gripping my hand. This will be hard for her. Mary and Simon seem not to notice as she spills lettuce and tomato into her lap, eyes down, humiliated. She has not yet learned to eat without her front teeth. I am embarrassed for them. People are staring, some nudging and making unquiet fun. I am embarrassed for Hoa. And perhaps myself. And my people.

She only ever told me once, late at night when most of the crew were resting and in Chinese in case they weren't. How the Thais dragged her across the deck by her legs and tied them apart with all the other people sobbing and looking away. How she had heard them beating the young men, tearing the instruments from the boat, smashing, urinating, threatening, leering as she waited mutely, too frightened to speak until she saw things which made her cry out, and she tasted the brass end of the rifle butt in her mouth, the oily, bloody taste, and the fragments and singing nerves she could not spit out. I could not know it as she did, but I had things of my own.

Some I have told to these, my innocent friends. I say nothing of Hoa's boat. They have guessed and Mary is crying.

The night I spoke of the Gulf of Thailand, Simon, too, cried; ashamed, he said. Even the Thais will not fish there, now. Their nets are invariably snagged by sunken vessels and often break under the strain of the bodies dredged up. Was Simon ashamed of mankind, or ashamed of crying?

2

Massive as walls, the paintings lean down upon us, clotted oils glistening as if still wet. I watch the 'cybernetic structure' whose photocells react to my presence, my shadow, my height. It beeps and blurts sounds, audibly reacting to me. Can it tell what I am thinking? It is a marvellous thing.

Mary and Simon steer us down long rows of pictures to a small collection of watercolours. There, says Simon. The water-colours are of men and women – peasants – working in rice paddies. They form a progression. Dread plummeting through me, I realize that these are of the war. Helicopters, candy-bars, the rickety skeleton of a live child, huts aflame. Old miseries. Hoa and I walk away, leaving Simon and Mary peering carefully at each frame, murmuring to each other in serious, indignant tones.

Puzzled, they join us at the display model of the new Congress Hall the government is building. 'Parliament House'. The model is beautiful, so pure, precise in its engineering. I feel the formulae in my mind, the slide rule hingeing against the heel of my palm, and for a moment I am resentful of such things as dirty pearling boats. The symmetry and wholeness of the structure are not apparent to Simon and Mary who pass sarcastic comments.

'Such technology,' I say. 'Marvellous.'

'Bloody marvellous,' says Simon, straining to be polite.

'You have made great advances. Like the Americans.'

They nod, and I am uncertain about the cause of their sudden ill-feeling.

'Bloody America,' Mary whispers.

On the boat with the crew sleeping around me, my hands sore from the shells and the salty cuts, I thought, not about the starless nights huddled on the deck of the other boat, but felt the old formulae in my head reeling outwards, ready to unfold themselves on paper, to do my work for me. I longed to write them into the stiff, brief postcards to Mary and Simon, but they would not understand. In any case, the formulae are different here, they told me at the Institute of Technology. Not even Hoa would understand the formulae. She has had little education. It is easier, sometimes, without.

3

Christmas Eve. On the way to a party in Mary's old car, we speak of small things, avoiding the subject of the watercolours we saw yesterday. The exhibition was called 'The Oppressed'. Mary and Simon want to discuss it with me.

'Hoa is at the dentist,' I say. I miss her tonight.

'On Christmas Eve?'

'He is Chinese. A favour.'

We become quiet.

'Those pictures,' Simon says. 'Yesterday, those pictures – I thought you'd like them, Quoi.'

I shake my head.

'But it's about cruelty, destruction, oppression.'

'Yes.'

'But you've been there,' says Mary.

'And do not wish to return. Such things are for those who have not been there.'

These people are concerned about politics, but only of a sort. They think in fiery, innocent terms – in principles. But politics – it is how much food and who will die. We have grown up without time to wield these principles, only a numbness.

I had never lived in a bamboo hut and worn no shoes until the Area Camp. My father, a taxi driver, saved for our education over many years, before the Americans, even. Saigon had no rice paddies where we lived . . .

Simon is trying to distract my attention from a slogan on a bus shelter which almost glows in the dark. I wish they would not worry.

'Bastards,' said Mary, driving faster.

On the back lawn we sit drinking good beer, eating the grapes, watermelon, cheese, apricots and biscuits that Mary's friends bring around. I have read nothing on Christmas, and it has not been explained to me. No one mentions it. The beer is good and for a while we talk quietly between ourselves, joking about the seeds Simon is spitting into the garden. They are trying to protect me.

'Have you ever had food like this before?' a wriggling curly-haired girl asks, holding a stick of English cheese under my nose. I answer politely, telling her I have. She calls to a friend. Simon and Mary are ill at ease.

'Hey, come and meet this Vietnamese bloke!'

'He's Chinese,' Simon says with a measure of authority. I cannot help but smile.

The drinking is heavy, many people are dancing to music I cannot understand. American music. Some serious young people are talking around me.

'Who were the worst?' asks one. 'The Yanks or the French?'

Before I can answer another speaks over me.

'Was the corruption in Saigon—'

'Ho Chi Minh City,' interrupts the other.

'Bullshit!'

'What do you do?'

I tell them my qualifications and those of my eldest brother. I tell them my father drives a taxi and how he bribed an official to ignore my absence temporarily.

'Poor bastard's a victim.'

'American product.'

They speak about me as if I am not present.

'Shut up!' Simon is shouting. 'Go bite your watermelons or something.'

'Geez, Sime,' someone calls, 'the proletariat cries out.'

They all laugh. Simon and Mary gather their things and we leave, climbing over the bodies in the garden and the asbestos fence. They are apologizing for their friends as we get into the car.

'Bloody idiots,' hisses Mary, looking helplessly at Simon.

'We're sorry, Quoi,' he says.

Both are confused and embarrassed.

'It was good tucker,' I say, a word from the lugger. It catches them by surprise and they smile, and Mary leans over and kisses me on the forehead.

'They wish me to be a peasant,' I say.

'Yes,' says Simon. 'I suppose it would be easier for us, too.'

4

Tonight I must tell them.

The lights move on the river, rippling like long tapering silk worms that dance in the night. Prawns are soft and still warm from the boiling pot we have cooked them in. Vinegar runs down our chins. Mary has her feet in the water where the little bodies of gobbleguts and smelt lie discarded from our net. I run my fingers over the mesh. The piles of the jetty across from us smell of barnacles and slime. Odours I remember well.

'She's a nice girl, Quoi,' says Mary. 'I hope you're very happy.'

'Yeah,' Simon smiles. 'Good luck.'

From my pocket I take the tiny medicine bottle which has been hidden in so many places, and shake out the pearls. These are what I have collected from the bad shells, imperfect greyish-white pearls, small enough to be hidden in an ear or under a fingernail. The skipper would have beaten me, had he found out.

I show them the big one I have chosen for the ring for Hoa and they marvel at its beauty. It is not perfect, but it is surely beautiful.

'And this is for you,' I say shyly, uncertain of how they will react. The two pearls are faulty, oblong specimens with lines in their skins like scars. Simon and Mary hug me and say thank you. I am grateful, because I know they do not agree with pearls.

'Why, Quoi?' they both ask.

'Because I am going to Brisbane. Hoa's brother has been found there. She must see him before we marry, and there . . . is no money for a return fare.'

'Going? Again?' Mary looks hurt.

'We could get some money together for you,' says Simon.

'No, you cannot,' I say, truthfully.

'What about your Uni course?'

'It cannot be helped.'

We sit awhile, the light flickering in our faces, and I observe the limestone monument behind us set with a metal plaque. The limestone thing is indecipherable. I wonder if they notice it? Mary, crying, hugs me. Simon is turning the pearls over meditatively in his palm.

'They're probably not worth anything, commercially,' he says.

'No,' I admit. I am ashamed.

'A peasant's gift?' Mary asks.

I smile. I will miss these strange people.

THE WOMAN AT THE WELL

THE TIRED horses shuffled in the dust, burying their heads in the buckets the soldier had drawn. The creak of the rope made them prick their ears, half alert. The well was old, the stones worn from animals and women.

Heavy blowflies knocked against his brow as he grunted, carrying the heavy buckets. The horses also grunted, half submerged, almost satisfied but for the wet rope that bound them. The well jutted out of the smooth, packed dirt of the deserted market-place, and the buildings around the square were full of soldiers as young and old as he. Shouts drifted from the shade. A two-up game was spilling on to the street, a nodding mass of curses and thudding coins.

It was a strange place, but the men, like all soldiers, brought their country with them. They fought and swore and slept and waited. The liberating forces called this resting. Women in the area were as scarce as in any other pock-marked town on the peninsula. They stayed indoors; too many things had happened.

Returning to the edge of the well with an empty bucket in each hand, the soldier noticed a shawled woman walking, bucket on her head, towards him. He lowered the rope again, feeling under his palm the smooth stone.

Although he did not hear her footfalls, he knew when she was behind him. Turning, he saw that she was quite young – scarcely out of adolescence – but there were lines in her face.

The woman stood, hands limp by her sides, and stared at him. He busied himself with his buckets in the dirt around the well. His arms were hairy and streaked with sweat, his shirt prickling with moisture. She watched him.

'Will you draw me some water?'

He swallowed, his mouth dry, and croaked.

'Ah-er, sure, miss.' He wound slowly, searching for something to say. 'It's a bonzer day, eh?'

She didn't seem to hear. He didn't feel like saying anything else. The bucket came to the surface, brimming with clean desert water which forced the sun into his face. The two-up game was rowdier, with the laughter of winners and the grunts of those on the lose.

'Do you have money?' Her English was perfect. The question startled him; she seemed to be speaking to someone else. Perhaps she was mistaking him for another man.

'Er, why do you ask, miss?'

Covered in a sprinkling of fine dust, the black shawl over her head was holed, and there were callouses on her feet.

'Do you have anything?'

'Pardon?' Sunlight danced in the creases of his face. He squinted at her. 'Listen, I haven't got anything you'd want.'

'Have you money?'

'. . . Yeah.'

'Will you trade?'

'In what exactly?' He grew cautious.

She put a hand on his arm. His body contracted. He was quiet for a moment. The horses drank and shuffled. There was peace here. But her hand was on his arm and his breath came out with a sigh.

'What the hell; here today, gone tommorrer. Where?'

Turning from him, she walked slowly across the square towards one of the crusted, flat buildings. With the sun on the back of his neck, the soldier loped along behind.

She stopped in the shade of what looked to him like a shop or an office, then disappeared into the entrance. Coming to the step, he peered inside, hesitant. He saw nothing in the musty darkness, heard nothing. Her face appeared; she took his hand, her palm cool against the damp heat of his.

For a few seconds the contrast in light left him blind. Led through the front room, he could see the forms of a desk and an empty bookcase. The desk was bare, edges burnt. Papers crackled under his feet. The woman padded and he clumped across the floorboards, following her into an equally dingy room that smelt of ash and sweat and urine. There was a small window high on the wall; the ceiling was black from smoke and flies. On the floor lay a large pallet, stolen from the barracks, he supposed. There were a few boxes in one corner, and a wooden chair covered in cigarette burns and graffiti.

Hands in his pockets, he stood as the woman began to undress by the pallet.

'How much, love?' he croaked, throat tighter.

'Two pounds.'

Still standing, he watched her as she lay on the gritty mattress, naked, resigned, absent. Her breasts were small, her ribs like an ugly corset beneath her skin, her belly scarred and limp. He unbuttoned his shirt, and as he peeled it from his back he heard a shuffling sound. Standing still, with his head cocked to one side, he waited and heard it again. Then a baby wailed.

'Where's it coming from?'

The woman stayed stretched feebly on the floor. Her eyes were expressionless. The cry continued as he went over to the boxes in the corner.

'Gawd, who's this, then?'

A small head poked from a rag in the smallest of the boxes. Its eyes oozed yellow. Shaking his head, the soldier turned to the woman.

'Forget it, blossom. Here, take a quid. Buy Mohommed here something to eat.' He gave her a pound note, moist with sweat. He showed her his open wallet.

'See these? That's my kids and my wife.'

She nodded again.

'The littlun'll be two soon.'

She stared.

'I'd better get back to the nags. I'll probably be in for it already.'

The sun burst into his eyes as he strode out across the square to the well. No one had noticed his absence. The two-up game was nearing a climax of anger and laughter as he drew a bucketful of water and splashed his face and arms. Refreshed, he turned to the stomping horses and noticed the woman's bucket at his feet. He filled it then stretched his back. He saw the black robe at the doorway across the square. Chuckling, he returned to the horses. She was coming to thank him, he thought.

An insect hum crept into the air, but his mind was on other things as he checked hoofs and mouths. The woman, now halfway across the square, looked up and then fell flat as a shadow. The blur of the plane hurtled overhead, the Turkish pilot beetlelike in his goggles and yellow scarf. The two-up game continued, a few of the less engrossed gamblers scuttling to safety, and the horses stirred.

The soldier turned. A bullet pierced his left arm, throwing him sideways to his knees. It was then that he heard the cicada sound of the machine-gun, and felt another blow in the side, just above his pelvis, and the third seemed to open his chest inwards. The horses thrashed against the ropes, falling over each other with wounds in their legs and bellies. One lay broken backed, crimson ribbons gouting down its belly. In their fear, the others trampled the beast, staggering and snorting.

On the earth near the well, the soldier lay spreadeagled, bleeding into the dust. The sound of the aircraft faded and the horses calmed a little, still disturbed by the presence of their dead.

At his side, the woman. Her eyes were empty, her mouth tight. Pinned to the dust, he breathed loud and spoke.

'There's ten quid in my wallet . . . top pocket. Keep it.'

The woman moved closer, to hear him better, he thought.

She was reaching into the bloodied pocket above his heart.

'But . . . keep the pictures, the wife and kiddies . . . promise.'

She paused as he spoke, and when his words faded and his eyes were as empty as her own, she pulled out the wallet, red with blood and blue with the ink of his burst fountain-pen. Opening the leather, she took out the ten pounds, wet and torn. The bullet had passed through money, photos, papers. She noted the name embossed on the inner flap: Pte. W. Williams. Stuffing the money into her robe, she closed the warm wallet and dropped it into the depths of the well.

Turning again to Bill Williams whose blood had disappeared into the dust, she stepped over his splayed figure and picked up her bucket. It was holed and empty, so she left it by the well and walked back to the dark entrance across the square.

SCISSION

I

IT IS four o'clock. He paces through ribbons of glass, stepping hard on his heels to feel the shift and snap. As he stares at the walls with their dainty pictures of women, he inserts a magazine, secures it in the weapon with his palm. He feels the rifle's dark weight and observes the plaited sinews locking in his forearms.

He sits on the piano stool and surveys her room. In one corner there is a vase of peacock feathers on a small table. He notes carefully the fine spray of colours. The feathers ease up out of the mouth of the vase like soft words. Everywhere, inflated armchairs, animal rugs, knotted, baked pieces of clay. He is a stranger in this flat.

Light through the shattered window is soft. A breeze brings in the dry grass smell of late afternoon.

There is another smell, though he is puzzled because it is also a quality of light. Hers.

He lifts the lid of the piano gently because he is afraid of its dark smoothness. With his thumb he depresses the last key but one, and then, the last. It is like pushing white teeth. To him it makes the word:

A-MEN

and the last, lowest, darkest note trembles in the wood until his breath is gone. He sees his face, distorted in the polished wood. And smiles.

2

'McCulloch.' He says his name aloud. His voice is close in this room. He takes pride in his name; it is the brand name of a chainsaw. He looks at his hands curled about the tube of gunmetal. There is no paint on these hands. They are soft. He once loved to roughen her flesh with his spirit-hardened callouses. He stirs at the thought.

McCulloch is a big man. His muscles have grown soft with the years and he must constantly will them into firming. It makes him squint as though in pain.

In the bedroom the vast bed is unfamiliar. Posts, big pillows, eiderdown. He faces the mirror. The T-shirt is tight; the outline of his nipples shows through. He holds the long barrel before him.

He keeps a careful eye on the space around his image in the glass. Nothing moves in the dimness.

3

Rosemary McCulloch lounges perfectly in the fortified sunlight by the pool. Her thoughts are far from the chunk-chunk of heavy camera shutters and the talk of the photographer. She is possessed by whiteness.

Behind her eyelids there is quivering white. It reminds her of the past; clean, fresh brick pulsating in a street of salmon-pink and terracotta, bright, pale faces of the family just out from England (she remembers the woman's accent as she called for her child – 'Murr-rraaay!'), and the modest chiffon of the bride arriving next door. At dusk the sound of other people's children. Everywhere yards barren with pale coastal sand and harassed-looking runners of buffalo grass.

Sweaty summer nights in white sheets, under his biceps, listening to the sprinklers.

4

A small woman moves among the empty cardboard boxes, and, after a moment's indecision, crosses the glass-strewn floor to the bookcase. She notes, despite herself, that it has not been dusted. She pulls books out, Herbert Kastle, Helen MacInnes – scruffy paperbacks that she drops into the nearest box. *Anna Karenina* she remembers and pulls the cardigan tighter about her as if to secure the memory of debate through the pickets of the fence. *Pure Metaphysical Knowledge* and *New Idea* join the thrillers in the box. Then she scoops out an armful of Simenons and reads the back covers once more and turns and says: 'Remem . . .' and puts a hand to her mouth. Yes, always Maigret, she thinks.

For a few moments she is happy and strong, moving along the shelves, boxing books and discarding more issues of Bilbert Kann's *Pure Metaphysical Knowledge* with resolve. She breathes shallowly, scuffs aside the broken glass.

5

The weapon rears in his hands.

A red geyser issues from an eye socket. The woman staggers.

There is a roar like the heavens opening.

6

Soon after the Housing Commission opened up Playne Street there was an influx of young married couples and English migrants who found deposits for the sandy, treeless blocks, and waited and saw State houses built on them. There were only four styles but designs were often reversed, as if copied in a mirror. Instead of the door of the terracotta double-front opening on the left of the little cement porch, it opened on the right. Tile colours varied.

The McCulloch house, however, was none of the four, and this set it apart. McCulloch, a signwriter, worked at home much of the time and this also held a certain prestige. His wife stayed at home; it was expected of her, but she, like most of the young wives on Playne Street, was happy with her new life in which she had a home that would one day have a garden and a greenhouse and a concrete driveway.

Next door, on the left, lived another young couple. The husband, Phillips, was a clerk with the government; his wife, Ruth Phillips, spent her housecleaning hours planning her new home, nuggeting and polishing the jarrah floorboards each week. Rosemary McCulloch could be sometimes seen standing outside her white house brushing the spiderwebs from the asbestos eaves with a broom, whistling. Her neighbour watched through the pickets.

One afternoon, after the Phillipses had their driveway bituminized, Ruth Phillips, who was lashing the sandy verge with water to coax the buffalo grass, saw the McCullochs pull in on McCulloch's motorcycle. Flinging dark hair from her eyes, Rosemary McCulloch met her neighbour on the kerb. They spoke shyly, asking girlish questions, laughing in little ragged shreds, often turning to point out things about the two houses, salmon-pink and white.

Thereafter, the two spoke daily – often by the hour –

through the fence. They shared cups of Robur tea in each other's kitchen and shopped together in the Phillips' Morris Minor. The two husbands spoke little. Sid Phillips thought conversation with McCulloch was like talking to a small boy; he found himself being patronizing and he tired quickly of talking cars and women. McCulloch spent hours after dark working on his motorcycle with his friends. He thought that Phillips was a bore. Phillips tended to share this view, though his wife did not.

When the Beatles came to Australia, all of them went together; it was Rosemary's idea. For the Phillipses it was deafening and terrifying. For the McCullochs it was like being near the Queen or seeing the Pope. There was a poster of Paul McCartney in their hallway.

The rest of the people living on Playne Street noticed that numbers seven and nine had become close. People told stories of wife-swapping and other titillating atrocities, but there was no truth in them.

Ruth Phillips had a baby, Rosemary McCulloch had a miscarriage and a long depression.

Soon after, McCulloch almost got the contract for a concert tour of Billy Thorpe and the Aztecs, but the promoters decided that they did not like the funny slant he gave to all his letters. Other clients did not like the long shadows he painted into his signs, although most never complained. Many were afraid to offend him.

A woman, a year later, gave birth to a baby with no arms. She and her husband moved from the street. A Yugoslav woman moved in; she was no more popular.

On Sundays 'the kids' came to see McCulloch. They were his old friends from school; he still called them 'the kids'. Rosemary and Ruth, for a year or two, went on picnics on Sundays. Sid Phillips took up golf, despite his loathing it. McCulloch and 'the kids' lifted weights with a transistor bellowing, threw empties over the fence and tuned cars all day.

The Phillipses had another son. Rosemary McCulloch gave

birth to a son, and the next year, another. The Phillips children grew to be noisy, happy children. The McCulloch boys were quiet. Sullen, some said.

It sometimes occurred to Ruth Phillips that Rosemary was like a young sister. She thought of herself now as a woman, and could not help but feel as though Rosemary was still a girl. Rosemary had a worldly air about her – she knew more about sex than Ruth – but her speech betrayed a schoolgirl's naïvety. Because Rosemary was beautiful and Ruth plain (though her husband did not agree), Ruth Phillips thought of herself as a much older woman. In fact she was five years older.

The children did not play with each other. The Phillips children were wary of the McCullochs and thought the boys were 'a bit slow' because they did not speak much. The McCulloch boys did not seem to have an opinion of the Phillipses, they paid attention to no one.

For her twenty-second birthday, Ruth gave Rosemary a hardcovered edition of *Anna Karenina* which cost a great deal and so seemed to her to be a good book. Rosemary read it slowly at first, then quickly towards the end, and when she had finished, lent it back to Ruth who struggled through the first half, left it for nine weeks, and finished it quickly on a holiday at Dunsborough. Neither of them understood everything in the big, unwieldy book, but the scenes and some of the dialogue became a secret between them. Phillips read *Time* and *National Geographic*, McCulloch read *Phantom* and *Man*.

Rosemary's mother died of cancer and to Rosemary it seemed to happen very quickly. She was quiet and introverted, brooding for several months afterwards. The next year, McCulloch's father suicided, but nothing was ever said about it. The Phillipses, and the others in Playne Street, were not told.

Soon after, a smartly dressed man and woman went to all the doors in the street speaking to people about 'Spiritual Existence' and 'The Sin in What You Eat', selling subscriptions to or stuffing into letterboxes copies of a glossy magazine called *Pure*

Metaphysical Knowledge, which some people browsed through as if it was a sales catalogue, and others read carefully for a few pages, then tossed into the rubbish as soon as Sin and Death and Eternal Life appeared in the columns.

Ruth and Rosemary never discussed the magazine, though both read it through independently. Things had already been uneasy between them for months since Phillips had sprayed a hose into McCulloch's carport at two o'clock in the morning a few months before. McCulloch had been tuning his motorcycle. The McCullochs began to behave 'differently'. They were never seen outdoors from Friday night until Sunday morning. No lights were seen in the house. The children became more sullen.

The Phillipses did not know that each Friday morning a new issue of *Pure Metaphysical Knowledge* appeared in the McCullochs' letterbox. The Phillipses puzzled about the strange weekend behaviour of their neighbours and were even more surprised when Rosemary McCulloch asked them to water their lawns and feed their cat for a week.

Rosemary McCulloch did not tell them that they were going to Sydney. Ruth did not ask, and Phillips would rather not have known.

While they were gone, the cat had kittens in the baby's cot. It rained in an unseasonal manner all week. The Phillips children went next door to feed the cats and look at the *Man* magazines in the loungeroom. It was an adventurous week for them.

7

At the window, he sees a woman come off the street past the banks of letterboxes. She pauses at the foot of the stairs and looks up. Her face is lit in the afternoon sun. It is unfamiliar to him. Her face contracts as if in fear, her lips move, and she turns and walks briskly away.

McCulloch waits two minutes. He hears noises through the

walls, other people cooking. As he leaves, he slowly tears a poster from the wall. Fragments of cheesecloth and flesh stare at him.

She is working late, he thinks.

He shifts the weight of the weapon from one arm to the other as he moves to the door.

8

He is thinking about her. It bubbles hot within. Crooked notes from her guitar; those first awkward tunes. 'I am learning,' her mouth says. 'No, no,' he is firm. His fingers knot . . . he sings along, stumbling. She smiles. Is it encouragement? Or ridicule? She is laughing!

His brother is a state cricketer!

Her fingers learn to caress the strings. They furrow delicately through dark-backed books that he hates and fears.

He hears the notes as they begin to link with each other, then a gentle strumming, a purring of strings and she is singing.

> *Please release me, let go,*
> *For I don't love you any more . . .*

The voice is cracked and horrible to him.

But his brother is a state cricketer! It warms him for a moment.

9

When the taxi stops outside the agency she bounces across the pavement on her heels and decides that tonight she will ring her sons. Rosemary has not spoken with them for two weeks. She remembers her last conversation with Robbie. How can I explain it? she thinks. She has nothing to tell them, only a twinge of fear, like pain. And sometimes a nauseous guilt she does not understand. Like steamy nights lying awake in the damp sheets, aching, afraid of the blackness that loomed above.

Her son's voice:

Why don't you live here any more?

What's wrong with Dad?

I hate you.

Dad bought me a surfboard today. A six-foot-six Cordingley.

No, Simmy doesn't wanna talk.

Yer lying. He never hurt *us*.

Yes, the toothpaste thing was good. It didn't look like you.

No, I don't wanna talk to you any more; you're tricking me.

10

The carved chest in Ruth Phillips' unsteady hands is made of fragrant wood. She sits on a cardboard carton and opens the lid. Inside, there is a tangle of pearls, beads, balls, bangles.

The pearls untangle themselves first. They are strange to her, their faces like the skin of the moon, mapped with minuscule marks that might be the landmarks of another world. She lays them aside.

She turns a bangle over in her hands. Its tarnished surface gleams dully; there is a smell of incense.

An ugly pair of clip-on earrings with jade settings. Why would someone keep these? she thinks. Oh, Lord, Rosie, she chuckles.

Amid the twisted, blackening chains crouches a red, shapeless stone like a clot of blood. She rolls it in her palms. Yes, had all the best, our Rosie, she thinks.

'The best, Rosie,' she says aloud with a hardness in her voice.

11

The gushing roar as she spins, a perforated hand flung against the wall. Plaster falls like confetti.

12

McCulloch weaves through the suburban streets, past his house and joins the afternoon traffic on the artery that leads to the city.

The engine of the Fairlane vibrates slowly. He owes a large amount on this car that he will never pay.

He switches the radio on. The news is over; it is ten minutes after four.

He catches his eye in the mirror and acknowledges it with a wink. He senses his brown arm on the sill of the door.

> *Tie a yellow ribbon 'round the old oak tree,*
> *If you still want me,*
> *If you still want me . . .*

He switches the radio off.

'. . . 'round the old oak tree,' he sings brokenly.

13

So what's an E-type Jag? Stuff the bloody Jag! Had enough! Enough filth and greed and stupid talk. Feel this thing corner! Maybe Bilbert (you bastard!) was right . . . Oh, those days of doin' all the right things . . . the way it was supposed to happen . . . Yeah, that was better. But the kids, they still wanted to come over. Still gotta live, you know. And her bloody whingeing.

Stupid, rotten car. Knew it would bust the family up. So, what's it matter? She should know better. Oh, a hard, hard, hard heart. Rotten bitch.

It was that miserable little tit next door what did it in the beginning, asking all them stinking questions — ALL THAT TALK AND BOOKS! — looking through the fence, doin' filth in the baby's cot. Turned her black inside, she did. Ah, but she went to piss just lookin' at me. Never had it properly in her whole life. And Sidney-kidney-blidney. Agh!

Suddenly the Fairlane feels cumbersome in his hands. He grinds his palm into the centre of the wheel and the horn squeals.

14

There are more photographs to be taken. Rosemary McCulloch smiles the 'oh, you big man you!' smile and leans on the dummy in the three-piece suit. Later in the afternoon her face will ache from the forced tightening of her lips. She will slick her teeth with Vaseline to keep her mouth from drying out. Her veins will ache from standing.

Cameras chew film.

'C'mon, Rose,' the photographer says smoothly, 'this isn't the old "I did it for Smirnoff" girl I used to know.'

'No?' she says. 'Where did you know her from?'

'C'mon, let's have some life, eh? You know what *life* is, don't you? *Life!* Show them you have life, they want to buy you! They want to eat you!'

'Shit, Charlie, that's sick.'

'Yeah,' says the photographer, sheepishly.

'Anyhow, I don't taste good.'

'No?'

Rosemary tilts her head and catches the mannequin by the pink chin.

'C'mon people, buy me, eat me.'

'Yes, yes,' mutters Charlie.

15

The phone rings. It has not yet been disconnected. It is the executor. Ruth speaks to him for a while. No, he cannot come yet. She needs more time. No, nothing of value, really. Later in the afternoon, yes. She hangs up.

The boxes of cosmetics are open before her, swirling up a foul, sweet odour. She does not touch anything.

The first time Ruth noticed Rosemary wearing cosmetics was when she needed it to cover lovebites and bruises. Why was it such a show of prowess, she thinks, to show me her big, battered breasts in the privacy of her room? 'This is what he does to me,' she would say with her tongue on her lip.

Then, later, powder and make-up base to cover the welts.

Ruth Phillips remembers the times she ran into her own room, sobbing at the horrible things.

The last year, the plush tones and textures of cosmetics were all that kept her on the billboards.

. . . Much later, no attempt at make-up. No viewing, only a screwed-down lid.

16

Corner from her mouth. Choir of thunder singing.

17

Monoxide fumes ascend in the slanting light. McCulloch fixes his stare on a long, high billboard towering over the intersection. Pedestrians flood across the road. He sees the slit fabric of the dress and the dark recesses of cleavage, bare, smooth skin of the small of the back – and satin, folds and folds of lascivious satin.

I DID IT FOR SMIRNOFF . . .

'And how many others,' he says quietly to his speedometer.

18

During those bare, safe years, McCulloch was torn between the security that Bilbert Kann gave them in delivering to them the Truth, and hatred of the man (he had filed a law-suit against him which was later withdrawn) for inflicting upon them the poverty and despair of his Knowledge.

To keep the Sabbath, the house was locked at dusk on Friday nights. They sat and slept and thought, and the children brooded and fought, and the McCullochs read from *Pure Metaphysical Knowledge*:

> . . . *For whatsoever man he be that hath a blemish, he shall not approach: a blind man or a lame, or he that hath a flat nose or anything superfluous* . . .

and spoke words at the ceiling and the slick covers of the source of Truth, and cried and hated and hated and hated.

Meanwhile, the Phillips children called through the pickets to come and play, safe from answers, safe from playing with 'the horrible McCullochs' who were both 'twice as slow as their old man'.

McCulloch painted signs for the Knowledge Fellowship for a pittance and they gave him specifications, forbade him some images, compelled him to others. Some nights McCulloch sat in the semi-darkness of his workshop and slashed with the brushes at things for himself that he kept under padlock. He threw foreign substances on to the tin flats that he daubed – honey, chocolate, gelatine crystals, chunks of lipstick, petroleum jelly – things that sent the paints into chaos, running out of control, or coagulating stubbornly, or merely losing their colour. The paintings had a dark, uneven terrain, livid – even in twilight – whilst wet, but as dull as dried blood when left to stand a while.

After painting, he would clean off, then go to the blackboard and check off the sins at random. The sins were gleaned from a multiplicity of sources, half-sentences, snippets from the *Koran*, the *Book of Mormon*, *The Himalayas of the Soul*, Leviticus and Deuteronomy, and many personal inspired insertions from Bilbert Kann himself. McCulloch comprehended the literal meanings of few of them, and did not for a second imagine the textual significance or origins of any.

Be thou to me as thy mother's back . . .

19

Rosemary McCulloch's children were a great disappointment to her; her sons were rough replicas of her husband, and, looking into their wooden faces, she wondered whether or not, in giving birth to them, she had done something wrong. They bit and whined and had the animal instincts of their father, and she pretended to be proud of them as she pretended to be proud of him. But she saw them under his spell, as if the very odours he gave off stunned them into a trance. As they did her.

And she was aware of a vacancy inside her.

She read to them from a *Pure Metaphysical Knowledge*, 'Recite thou in the name of thy Lord who created; created man from clots of blood: Recite thou!' It arrived each Friday from the other side of the continent, from across the desert. Monday they would put the cheque in the mail (THOU SHALT NOT STEAL!). She read from the Truth and was sometimes ashamed. 'Or are ye sure that He who is in Heaven will not send against you a stone-charged whirlwind?' For herself? For not believing? For believing? 'Woe on that day to those charged with imposture!'

20

The wallhangings are mostly photographs by David Hamilton; furtive, voyeuristic, but tranquil. Their apparent innocence puzzles Ruth Phillips. She cannot tell if they are pornographic or beautiful. In one place on the wall there is only a corner, a triangle of paper held to the plaster by a dob of putty. She tried to peel it away, but it sticks to her hands; she cannot rid herself of it and she dirties her dress and leaves smudges on the wall. A feeling of nausea comes upon her.

On a table is a smaller photograph in a light frame. It is Rosemary; she is wearing the cheesecloth blouse and the sensuous pout, brightened by waxy sunlight, like the children in the Hamilton pieces. But this woman is thirty-four years old.

Ruth Phillips puts a hand to her face in confusion.

21

A furrow appears diagonal to the serrated edge of her spine as she slides down, facing, and defacing the discoloured wall.

Thunder has become numbness.

People pass in the street below. No one moves in the corridors. Each shot has no time to cannon off into the distance of silence before it is overtaken by the next.

22

At four twenty McCulloch parks the Fairlane carefully in the midst of the city. His heart moves at a set pace.

He has counted again the sins of the Smirnoff advertisement. He has found seven, though more will come to mind later.

This city has grown with the years since the Beatles came. He is unsure if this is a good thing or a bad thing; no one has yet told him.

23

School has been out for an hour. Bag-swinging children dawdle along footpaths.

McCulloch is proud of his children; if they are in pain he feels it himself. Since babyhood they have played in his paint-tins, fingering the dried, gummy edges; they sprayed their pedal-cars before they could speak properly.

Now they are schoolboys. Robbie truants from school – all classes except Art where he buries himself in a mute world of colours and viscous materials. Simmy, the younger boy, wants to be a weight-lifter. He is thin and asthmatic. McCulloch has encouraged him in his ambition, despite, or perhaps because of, the opposition from his wife.

Teachers worry about Robbie McCulloch's paintings. The distorted figures are unsettling; they are framed – all of them – by arch-like shadows, or the images are visible through foliage or lace curtains. The Art teachers say they are passionate and surrealistic; other teachers say 'Yes, but . . .' Notes home are ignored. The headmaster, a weak little man, has 'gathered some information'. Yes, the boys are disturbed, he has been told by a teacher of Social Studies; their mother has left them only recently. The headmaster has some paintings in his office. He covers them with his academic gown in the corner.

24

Twice today Rosemary has thought of Ruth Phillips. She has not seen her for nine months. It is a year since she left her home. For a few months she dropped in to see Ruth when she knew there would be no one at home next door, and they talked over cups of well-brewed tea. It was difficult to speak in the end; they were so different, and Rosemary was part of a new world.

'Not bad, eh?' she had said, pointing through the little kitchen window to the pink Jaguar poised in the driveway. 'Not bad for a mother of two, my age,' she said, half-congratulating herself, wanting, at least, confirmation from Ruth.

'Yes,' said Ruth, uncertain, intimidated. 'Yes, you've reached the top, all right.' She said it into the collar of her dowdy gown.

The second time Rosemary went back they tried to talk about the past, but Rosemary was embracing what Ruth feared the most; the future.

The last visit, Rosemary was drunk. She slewed the Jaguar into the drive, crushing the heads of the roses growing along the edge.

'You've gotta help me, Ruthie,' she said. 'He's after me. I think he's gonna kill me.'

'Calm down, Rosemary,' Ruth said.

'He's got a gun.' This was true; he had an American service weapon. A number of people living on Playne Street knew that he had it. He told people about it; it brought him a great deal of respect.

But Ruth Phillips was irritated.

'Go back to your flat,' she almost spat the last word, 'and get yourself a good sleep.' She deplored drunkenness; it made people say/things they didn't mean.

Rosemary decides that she will ring Ruth. She yearns for her soft, reassuring voice from the other world. She wishes she could tell Ruth some things. She's a good stick, she thinks.

Sometimes it occurs to her that she is older than Ruth. Despite herself, she longs for the days when they were both new brides and new friends. She wonders if those times were so good because she did not know certain things.

Rosemary's attention is distracted from her work. She is hearing her voice and Ruth's voice: '. . . *you've got a lovely shoulder to cry on, Ruth love,' pulling down her mini. 'You too, love,' Ruth says, dripping tears that smudge the polish of her floorboards.*

25

Ruth Phillips lingers over the furniture in the flat. Rosemary's chairs are delicate, with soft curves and cushions and dark, rich wood, not the strong vinyl and wipe-clean surfaces of the stuff in her own house. In her place things are cheap and useful, and nothing has changed since 1964. Tasteless old Ruth, she thinks, flopping into an armchair. She sits a while, becoming dispirited, before getting up to stack it all by the door.

26

An arm lifts as it is struck, the wall vibrates. And the endless thunder.

People are screaming, but their voices are smothered in the roar.

27

Office workers streaming out of shadowy buildings do not notice the automatic rifle that McCulloch is carrying by his side in the rush, even though it enters and leaves the vision of scores of them. It is twenty-five minutes past four and they are going home. McCulloch pushes against the surge and enters the sleek glass doors. Inside, carpet muffles all movement, and seems to exude a narcotic breath which tempts him to lie down and go to sleep in its burgundy pile.

Young women, some of whom he recognizes from places he cannot recall, walk past him from the lift. One woman, a tall, black, lithe creature, turns her head in surprise.

Weep ye that lie down with other tribes and with animals . . .

McCulloch walks towards the potted palms near the lift.

28

Billboards, plaques, all signs attract McCulloch's attention. He has been a signwriter since the age of sixteen. He was a sign-writer when he was married. He is a signwriter now: it says so in the telephone directory below his name, though he has not had a client for almost eight months. No one recommends him; he is lazy, they say, late, they say, and he does not always paint what he is asked.

The most recent thing he has painted is on the wall at home in Playne Street. It is a long piece of masonite with a white background and big, red, Gothic letters. It says:

GOD IS LOVE

The staccato words puzzle him. He put them there to remind his children and himself. Beneath the bold letters, niggled pencil lines show through. Even though he had not thought of God or Love for some time, he had suddenly been seized by the idea after his wife left him. She left a note:

> *I do not love Bilbert Kann's God. I do not know him. I never knew him. I don't love you, either, though I know you only too well. I don't think I've ever loved you, really. I have spent my whole life pretending. No more pretending. I have finished pretending. I have. You can't even pretend. That's what you are like.*

He crushed it in his fist and brought his hand down on to the Laminex with some force. He went to work quickly, in fright, splashing on the primer.

29

The session is finished. Rosemary sits with some other girls in the studio drinking coffee, listening to their talk of cruises to Noumea and jobs on television quiz shows. Some even talk about getting married, though they are wary around Rosemary. They treat her with a respect for her position, the most enviable in the business at the moment, and resentment for her age and her sudden ascent.

Rosemary is in great demand. People want to see a woman who has had children, who has married and experienced life, who is both homely and glamorous, voluptuous in her ripeness.

As a new wife Rosemary was an object of interest, to herself, her husband, and her husband's friends. She lived an endless procession of Sunday afternoons when her husband 'had the boys over'. They drank beer and ogled her, McCulloch displaying her like a sleek new road-machine, fanning their heat, their stares and catcalls, coaxing them to stay longer, to come again. He knew they liked to come to his place. After all, they were his best mates. In later years, they began to lose interest, when McCulloch began to mutter about the Meaning of Life and the Tithing of Time, so he asked her, begged her, sometimes, to wear clothes that were more daring. He dressed her to look like Nancy Sinatra. They patted her and they were all great friends. She loved those beery afternoons because they gave her an outlet after the dreary Sabbath, and she enjoyed the attention. Afterwards she was always left with an elusive nausea, as if she might throw up something that lurked deep inside her, and she took a sleeping tablet and dreamed till morning whereupon she rose with a clear head and not even a dim memory of what she had dreamt.

She listens to the girls' self-conscious talk.

Rosemary McCulloch is a model. She is the woman-model. She gives life to clothes, libido to car bonnets, meaning to vodka. She sets the pace for mothers and daughters who want to be like her.

Her husband is haunted by her reproductions, and her sons have learnt to hate her.

30

The wardrobes are fragrant with the smell of Rosemary's perfumes and the odours of her body. Ruth Phillips recalls the smells from when they gardened and jogged together. They tried hard, then, to disguise and dispel their body odours. They tried roll-ons, spray-ons, dab-ons, and stick-ons. As she grew older, Ruth tired of trying, and she spent less time worrying about her appearance. Phillips grew accustomed to her odour, and had said, once, that he even liked it, so she saw no need to bother.

Rosemary pursued deodorants; she could not afford to have a smell of her own. But she had one, nevertheless. Ruth recognizes and remembers it.

'Funny think to think of,' she says aloud.

She feels the fabrics of pullovers and cardigans, lingering over the older, less fashionable things that smell of dowdy innocence. Chenille brushes between her fingers. Old jeans, faded and patched, are difficult to fold into the box.

Ruth Phillips feels old.

31

The bullet that enters the chest sounds like an old football being kicked two doors away.

32

McCulloch is light-headed with the feeling of ascent. Lighted numbers pop and ping above his head. If he was alone in the lift he would jump to see if the floor would overtake him.

He is soaring.

The woman beside him is more alarmed by his breathing than by the stock of the weapon brushing against her thick hip.

33

On a summer evening McCulloch came home with a trunk full of costumes. He dressed up and faked magic tricks for his boys who were thrilled at the colours, half-believing. He pulled caps from false-walled boxes and knitting needles from handkerchiefs. His wife acted along with him, despite herself. She could see it was good for the children and for him. He had been upset of late, despairing at the admonishments they had received in the mail from Sydney. They had no money and their faith had weakened. Kann was calling them to the half-completed Opera House and they refused. McCulloch had nightmares.

She played along with the games. The boys made costumes. There were others in the trunk.

34

As she sips coffee in the hubbub, Rosemary thinks also of her eldest son, Robbie. She loves him; he is her own flesh and blood, like a piece cut from her, but she has never liked him. She is honest about this. So honest that she once told Ruth Phillips whose face darkened with confusion and discomfort.

'Look, it's just the way it is,' she said. 'I can't explain it properly. You know what he's like.'

'But he's your child,' Ruth said, always grateful that Robbie McCulloch was not hers.

Robbie McCulloch has a 'speech problem'. He hardly spoke until his second year at school. He shows no affection. Sometimes he smiles at his father.

There were times when Rosemary believed that she had been cursed with such a son because of the manner in which he had been conceived. McCulloch copulated with her as if she was a carcass from an abattoir. At first she wept at the sounds he made and the things he made her do when sex was something new to her, something frightening and exciting. But she soon learned the techniques of sex he taught her: endurance, agility, and a measure of dramatic exaggeration. She loved to shock 'poor Ruthie Phillips' who understood little of sexual matters. Ruth sometimes introduced The Right Thing and God to their discussions about sex which she endured. But she knew less about God than she did about sex, and cared still less. She had a home to take care of and had little time for either. She also spoke of Love, but it was a puzzling subject.

35

Ruth Phillips, when she notices something odd about the underwear she is refolding, suddenly puts it down and sits on the floor. A cry escapes her. She sits, mute, for a few minutes until her mind clears. Then she gets up again and stuffs all the torn, soiled, alien garments into a box and runs to the bathroom to wash her hands and splash her face.

It leaves her with a light head. Her stomach tolls.

36

He aims where it gives him most pleasure and the lower half quivers again. He is alone in the room with her and the choir in his ears.

37

There is no one in the corridor down which he is stalking. He feels as though his feet are not even touching the ground, though they leave heavy prints in the pile. Photographs on the walls. Pieces of her float by. They shower him, spurring him so he glides faster.

38

In 1969 McCulloch's father committed suicide. He was a big man, like his son, who often spent hours, days even, contemplating, brooding about things that mattered to him but of which he never spoke. He was a cattleman who owned big land in the North. Regularly, he left the staff at the station homestead (his wife, an ex-barmaid from Boulder, had died some years before) and spent two or three days in the bush. On his last day he drove out into the heartlands and shot himself. Birds and animals gradually robbed him of his flesh and he was identified, months later, by his yellow teeth. He was a lapsed Methodist. He grieved constantly over his son's becoming 'a half-Jehov-wit-Latter-Day-Saturday-Cultist', and he thought that worse even than the 'useless, ignorant nothing' his son had been before the cultists had knocked on his door. He had never ceased to grieve for his wife who had died suddenly of a stroke. Also, he was bored and scared. He felt bad things about his son, though he did not believe too strongly in omens because, even if lapsed, he was still a Methodist.

The station staff buried his shabby remains after the inquest, on the station, and he was bought along with the place when his son quickly sold it.

39

Pieces fly at him. He is flying. Into pieces.

40

Her second son, Simmy, is as much of a disappointment to Rosemary as Robbie. He has a prominent brow that divides above his nose like the swelling from a boxing blow. He speaks without difficulty but he is totally expressionless; his words are like the monosyllables of a plastic doll. His cheeks are bright, as if rouged; his teeth are sturdy and white, like his father's. When he uses barbells he wheezes, a clicking hiss deep in his chest. He will never lift weights properly.

Rosemary remembers the first words he spoke. The da-da-da-da-da was as accentless and unremitting as a heartbeat.

Simmy is a product of the 1965 Multiplication for the End. But there had been no End, thus far.

During her second pregnancy, Rosemary often stood naked before the mirror to see the evidence of her swelling. She watched each day, minutely aware that she was becoming two people. She knew very little of either of them. Afterwards her flaccid torso revolted her. Her baby disappointed her, and the image of an unkempt, dumpy woman before her in the mirror added to her depression.

Her second son gained his name from the author of a book Rosemary and her friend had read years ago: *Red Lights*. He has never been told this. It is unlikely that he would understand or show interest.

She cannot help but see Neanderthal in him.

41

Stalks through the carpet . . .

42

Ruth opens the trunk with a gasp. Slowly, she draws out the top garment. In a few moments she understands what it is.

'*Spiderman,*' she says, remembering her children's comics. It is sparking something in her memory; a stone striking metal. Snakeskin, long strips of it, comes out. It is smooth and evil-looking. A schoolcap. A pair of grey shorts like her sons wear; she shudders. She digs into the voluminous box. Moons; a magician's outfit. A horse's head, creased and rubbery, bares its teeth. Her hand touches something coarse. She pulls gingerly and what she pulls out she cannot identify for a few seconds until she comes to the head and the hands; it is an ape suit.

'Oh,' she murmurs, half in recognition, half in fright. She is not angry yet, because she is not allowing herself the pain of understanding. Somewhere in her mind is a vivid memory she refuses to see.

She stands at the broken window watching traffic easing out of the city into the suburbs.

> *Spiderman, spiderman,*
> *does whatever a spider can . . .*

She remembers it from television, glad she is remembering that which is of limited importance. Ruth Phillips refuses to recall forty-five seconds of her life. It is this:

. . . She is looking through the pickets, idly. She sees a man dressed gaudily in red, white, and blue with knee-length boots and a cape. He has a helmet on his head. Stars cling to all his garments. On the concrete paving there is another figure sprawled, in bountiful skirts, with a hat and white wooden clogs like a china doll. Above the squirming doll is the man with his shield brandished . . . then there is nothing as the pickets recede.

'Captain America waves his mighty shield,' she says. She puts the winged helmet aside, gazes at the righteous pyramid the 'A' makes, embossed on the brow. Her mind convulses, free of her. She sobs, remembering. He's polluted her, she thinks, it's in *her* now, she's tainted even now when she's dead. Can't she be free of him?

Everywhere she smells sickness and she is hopeless, perfectly ineffectual. God, I've always been useless to her, useless to myself, she thinks through a falling curtain of tears. She remembers, irrational with guilt and hysteria, that she and her brothers pulled the limbs from dolls and inverted their puckers with a thumb inside their heads. They always reassembled them, later, though. But the thought ceases to comfort her.

'Waves his mighty bloody shield.'

43

Four twenty-nine . . .

44

A shoulder strap dematerializes as the flesh beneath it shatters into white pieces that quickly shade over.

Rosemary is in the burgundy carpet, broken face buried in its scent. Once, she might have imagined this roar to be the God of Bilbert Kann descending on the Opera House with his business associates. But it is a roar of vacancy and vacuum, and, in any case, she does not hear it.

45

. . . and fifty-eight seconds.

46

At exactly four thirty by the not-always-defective clock in the
corridor (a joke shared by the models who work here; they often
wish it was defective more often), McCulloch confronts the
glass doors and watches them open obediently without his
touching them. He feels as if he is expected and welcome. A
hero's welcome, he thinks. The glass clicks together in frigid
union behind him.

47

Bilbert Kann left the United States of America after a scandal
involving his advertising company and certain members of the
Senate. He resurfaced in Australia soon afterwards to take part in
the optimistic new growth of the early 1960s.

Many who knew him then described him as a prophetic
businessman. He understood the nature of people. With this
understanding he discovered and developed a marketable god
which he promoted in a glossy magazine, *Pure Metaphysical
Knowledge*. His god, as the market-culture demanded, was a
low-profile, uninterfering one. People observed certain codes
and legalities and Kann's god kept out of their way. No one but
Kann ever met this god. He had a blueprint for him in his safe, a
patent, an artist's impression, and a volume of inspired writings.
Kann's disciples were grateful for a mediator; it spared them a
great deal of effort and discomfort to have a go-between.

Kann aimed at the Lowest Common Denominator. He borrowed and patched until he came up with a vague but versatile image.

Since 63 AD, he maintained, no True Religion had been preached. 'God has revealed himself to me,' he said on 24 December 1959. Ten years, fifteen years later, he had begun to believe it himself. It was a logical thing to happen.

In the first national issue of his magazine he gave ten or more commandments, and mated these with clipped phrases from fashionable and forgotten religious canons. He found that Australians were naturally legalistic and therefore eager to subscribe to the Worldwide Fellowship and pay tithes.

In a very few years, the Fellowship was truly worldwide. In 1971 when he had five hundred thousand subscribers in Australia alone, he predicted the End of the World within the year, and located the Divine Appearance at the yet incomplete Opera House in Sydney. Fifteen thousand people gathered, many of them staying in hotels operated by Kann's syndicate. The crowd included many entertained spectators. The sun rose and set. At length, the scoffing crowds went home or to the airport to fly home. As the hotdog stands were dismantled, Bilbert Kann and his son Macabee-Dowell told the press and television reporters that God had seen the leaden hearts of his people and rebuked Earth by postponing his Coming.

The next year Macabee-Dowell slipped the country with one of his father's wives and a considerable fortune and was publicly denounced. After two more false second comings and a tightening of monetary rules, subscriptions waned and many ex-disciples sought legal advice. Late in 1974, Kann shifted his assets to European banks. In 1975 he moved to South Africa where his racial legalities were highly marketable. He was assassinated by black youths during a tour of an industrial township in the same year. In 1976 his son founded a syndicate of drive-in churches across the United States of America. He foresaw a great resurgence of profitable legalism in the country within years. He died of cancer in Utah during the presidency of Jimmy Carter in 1979.

48

Rosemary is thinking of soft light and the smell of incense. She is thinking of her lover, a woman who is mute. They have been in love for two months. Her lover will sit on the edge of the bed and watch Rosemary perform. Rosemary sings and dances for her, mimes, reads poetry to her, nuzzles her, and lies in bed with her all Saturday, every weekend. This is the most secret thing in her life. Her husband does not know; he will never find out.

At times, in bed with her sleeping mute lover, Rosemary is bound by a weight of melancholy she does not understand. Other times, it is a prickling violence. She gazes out through the open window of her flat at the black awning of sky and feels its inky vastness descending upon her.

Her lover does not know she is a model. This is a novelty for Rosemary; she is entertained by innocence. Her lover stays more nights now. Rosemary is fascinated by her expressive face, the softness of her body, the absence of the brutality Rosemary fears and often feels within herself. She mimes with her lover; the woman is silent as a soft doll.

With some of her heart Rosemary wishes to tell Ruth Phillips about her new friend, but she can no longer tell anyone. And the secrecy is much of the thrill.

Suddenly, jerkily, she puts down her coffee cup and decides she *will* ring Ruth Phillips, and yes, she will tell her. It would only be . . . right . . . she thinks without conviction.

And tonight, she thinks, I'll be with my lover who makes no sound.

49

GOD IS LOVE!

It shouts at him; he withholds the urge to run screaming. His biceps quake.

50

Ruth Phillips' sobbing rises to a moan as she uncovers the alien apparatus. She has never seen a dildo before, but she understands its intent; the straps with it upset her more. She finds oily jars and jellies and some pornographic photographs of women as well as dark, heavy leather garments thick with the concentrated stench of mildew and sweat. The floor is now carpeted with costumes and the odours overcome her. She is driven to her knees and she cries out.

'No! No! It's not true!' But she knows she is mocking herself. She nods, acknowledging something she does not understand. She realizes what she does not know. Have I ever met Rosie McCulloch? she asks herself. She spins inwardly. She is uncertain about who she has ever known.

She collapses in a heap with a photograph in her fist.

51

Clicks together, like a snip.

52

The last image in Rosemary's conscious existence is a rose enveloping the world with its cool, impenetrable petals. She is gone, but her twisted body is undeniably present, mutilated on the floor. Another eruption gives it a semblance of life, but the deception is momentary as the pelvis quivers. Her body is dead.

53

> *I swear by the declining day,*
> *Verily, man's lot is cast amid destruction . . .*

He shakes his head. The pink Jaguar knifes into him, long, glistening, sleek.

54

And before him is his wife Rosemary McCulloch of Smirnoff fame who passes the receptionist's desk and whose eyes recoil as their gazes meet. A sharp intake of her breath. McCulloch has the weapon before him. He brandishes it at her. She does not move. He takes careful aim and triggers its unalterable mechanism.

55

In the last seconds before entering the reception office, McCulloch has discarded all excuses. There is no thought of Sin or God or Truth in his mind. These are things he no longer needs. He can think of nothing but the pink Jaguar roaring, leaving and entering his vision with spurts of speed. He sees his wife in all poses in it. He sees the boys pawing it with sighs of wonder, looking into her face. He sees Rosemary in an aura of pink reflection. 'Well, look what I got,' she says sneering. He sees her packing. Things she has paid for. Scribbling in the jotter on the Laminex table. He sees himself. Smashing furniture against the white wall and Paul McCartney.

He could feel her behind him as he ran out with the axe. Felt her breath teeming against his bare back as she clung on to him with her nails and teeth as he smashed the headlights and struck the long, pink nose and skittered windscreen glass and pierced the pouting roughed cheek of the fender and saw steam, and the car expired audibly. The removal men looked on with amusement.

The bloody Jag! he things. Aaaaah! It makes him shudder with sickness. Her solid-framed, immovable, luxuriant reproductions beam from the walls and hound him. He flexes forward, aware again, of flight.

His sons hate him for the Jaguar.

He hears the rending of metal and he feels the unused muscles creaking within him. He flexes forward, aware again, of flight.

'God will—' he begins, but remembers he has no need of God and he surges on to do some kind of duty.

56

There are times when Rosemary McCulloch can look back on the hardest period of her life with a sort of longing. In the first years of Membership and Fellowship, she spent many hours locked away with her young children. At times they mimicked her; they listened to her stories. They acknowledged her presence when she shared her portion of food with them. They sat with her on the floor without furniture and listened, like her, to McCulloch's puzzled intonations from the Law. Perhaps they shared a stubbornness. They dozed while McCulloch called with staged enthusiasm and tried to feel his soul move. Perhaps, too, they felt his hate soaking everything, but they were young.

When Rosemary feels these things she is usually alone in her flat and she is half drunk with vodka. It is poor consolation. Even Ruth Phillips seems a spectre to her. She looks for her strong, happy face in the faces of her mute lover, but none of her lover's masks will fit.

She knows she can never look back on these things for help. She feels the still resilient firmness of her body, feels her lover responding to it, and knows that she still lives. It is my future, she says to her mute lover who caresses her.

She leaves the room. No, I will not ring Ruthie, she muses. She won't even begin to understand. Anyway, it's all over between us. Come on, Rosie, don't be a baby. She is still undecided about a phonecall to the boys. She is waiting for a call from the insurance people to see if her car is worth salvaging.

The buzzer rings. The receptionist is in the toilet. Rosemary knows this, and to help, she goes to the desk for her.

57

The executor of the will is due in an hour and a half. Ruth Phillips has been crying. Now she is in control. She is thinking clearly. She steps outside and looks into the rear courtyard near the half dozen parked cars of the other tenants. In the corner of the shaded yard is a blackened incinerator. She watches it for a few moments. A snake of smoke escapes it. Somebody is burning something already.

She walks through the boxes she has packed: books, jewellery, cosmetics, curtains, wallhangings, clothing, underwear, costumes and sexual tools. She has stuffed all the repugnant things into one box. She hefts it to her waist and begins towards the door. Before she reaches it, she stops and drops the box at her feet. It seems deceitful, somehow, to burn those things she does not like to remember. Now that she knows a great deal about her friend, Rosemary McCulloch, she is tempted to withdraw to the image she has held previously.

But in a surge of relief and honesty, and thinking of the children that she never liked, she takes the box to the door to fulfil what her mind will do in any case.

58

She sits, truly grieving, waiting for the executor to inspect with expertise and calculation. She takes up *Anna Karenina* from the box, aware of the smell of plastics burning, and realizes that she remembers nothing of it; not a thing.

Inside the cover is scrawled in pencil:

> *In a mirror*
> *you can only see your front*
> *and what's behind you.*

She does not remember the inscription. It does not surprise her, though. The book's musty odour is repulsive to her.

59

The receptionist runs blindly in from the toilet. There has been a long silence. The others are back in the studio, hiding, but she does not know this.

She screams when she sees the bloodied mess before her and she reels as McCulloch rises from his chair in fright.

The bullet hits the metal frame of a photograph and rico-
chets.

The receptionist falls as if the burgundy carpet has been
pulled from beneath her. Blood issues from a small wound in
her ankle. She screams. And screams. And screams.

McCulloch sits again; the thick barrel between his knees. He
shifts in his seat and reaches for a fashion magazine.

60

There were ten shots. Police arrived at five o'clock. They
pushed through the crowd and made an arrest and called an
ambulance.

MINIMUM
OF
TWO

These belong to Jesse and Denise: my blood, my water.

One and one make one
and one
and one and one make one . . .

      Playground chant

ACKNOWLEDGEMENTS

A number of these stories have appeared before, in *Island*, *Bulletin*, *MJ*, *Australian Literary Magazine*, *This Australia*, *Matilda*, *Sydney Morning Herald*, *Meanjin*, *Follow Me*, and *Scripsi*: the author thanks these publications.

CONTENTS

FOREST WINTER

EACH DAY the young man left his wife and child asleep and went out into the forest to saw wood. Winter had closed in. The sawing was bitter work, but it had come at the final moment, before they gave up on the country and went back north to the city and the hardship of the dole. He drove out in the boss's utility and searched for fallen timber which he would cut into blocks and cart back to the tiny valley to store for the holiday season. The bawl of the saw hurt his ears so that at the end of a day's work his head had the same stuffed feel as it had after a night's playing with the band, before everything fell apart.

At noon he sheltered in the utility and ate his lunch of bread and cheese with the rain trickling down the windows and the quiet of the forest coming upon him. It was lonely in the middle of the day with no company but the pale trunks of karri trees. During his morning break, the circumstances of the past few months rested hard on him. When the light was weak and if the wind was especially hard and cold, he would sit, chewing, motionless, almost catatonic from misery. But when it came time to take up the chainsaw again and sharpen its teeth before going back to whichever great, dead tree he was dismembering, he knew with certainty that he was still all right, and the fact that he could swill his tea dregs into the bracken and rise from his haunches with the saw was enough for him to know that he wasn't broken. He had been broken once before, years back, when he was still half a boy, and he knew that when you were beaten properly, you didn't get up; you had to wait for some obscure grace to put you together, and there was no guarantee it would come by a second time.

Most days he returned to the crooked little valley before

dusk to see the two dozen timber cabins and the shop and the old school and the ruins of the sawmill echoing with the misanthropic calls of magpies. His boss was a retired farmer who'd bought the valley years ago and turned the remains of the logging town into a holiday village for the spring and autumn. Summer and winter were extreme down here and the place deserted but for the owner and his wife and whoever he hired in the off-season.

It was here the young man and his wife and child found themselves the day their money ran out. By then they were just driving without purpose. Too many things had gone against them. The job and the cabin were a sudden mercy.

A month after they arrived, the young man came home one evening to find that the stove and the fire were still unlit. The small house was cold and in darkness and the baby was screaming.

'Rachel?'

He found his wife on the mattress on the floor with the child beside her. When he turned the light on he saw her on her back, mouth wide, struggling to breathe. Her eyes were so big in her face they frightened him. He scrabbled around in the bedclothes. The baby shrieked.

'Where's your Ventolin? Your inhaler, where's you inhaler?'

The young woman was concentrating too hard on getting air to be able to speak. The noise she made in her throat was like the sound of a bough tearing loose in a storm, back and forth, creaking.

He picked the baby up and took the full force of its squall in his ear as he flattened it to his shoulder. He found the inhaler on the floor between tissues and ointments and folded nappies. He felt panic. He brought the inhaler to her mouth with a spare hand, but she pushed it away. That tearing sound faltered for a moment and she managed a single word.

'Old.'

He looked at the cylinder. It was a pressure-pack the size of a bottle cork. He read the expiry date. Months too old; it was likely useless, perhaps dangerous – he didn't know.

'Oh. God.'

He went into the dark kitchen with the baby. Tears and saliva ran down his neck. He wrapped the pink-faced little boy tighter in his blankets and put him in the carry basket. He took the basket out to the car. The sun was well down but the tops of the karris were visible in silhouette and he could still make out the skeleton of the old water tower. For a moment he considered going to the boss for help; it was only a moment.

With the child screaming out in the car, he dressed his wife and wrapped her in blankets and hoisted her up.

The nearest town was twenty-five kilometres east. As the young man drove the old station wagon hard along the narrow road between the bodies of trees and the eyes of feral cats and foxes, he could barely hear the motor over the baby's screams and the pendulous, tearing respiration of his wife.

Everything was changed. How long had it been since they were happy? The music was gone, the money. And Rachel, what had happened to her? Having the baby had muted her. The forceful, funny girl he had married, had suddenly become placid, listless, sickly, as though she'd had the life torn from her as well as the child. He was afraid the breaking of things had let that old helpless panic get back into him.

Winding down the hill towards Bridgetown, he began to sing madly.

A frog went walking on a summer's day, a-hum, a-hum . . .

Rachel lay against the seat with her head back, eyes wide. He drove hard. He couldn't let this happen. A scream rose in him, like the night the baby was dragged hollow-chested from her.

A frog went walking on a summer's day,
He met Miss Mousie on the way, a-hum, a-hum,
A-hum-a-hum-a-hum!

The pharmacist was still inside the shop – the young man could see him moving about – but the doors were locked and the CLOSED sign was up. The young man bashed on the glass and noticed in the high beam of the idling station wagon how cut and crusted his own fingers had become. The pharmacist ignored him. He beat the glass harder. He shook the door until the burglar alarm set to ringing. Shedding his white coat, the pharmacist came down the aisle between rows of cough medicines and sweets and stuffed toys. The young man saw he was angry.

He thinks I'm a junkie, he thought; he thinks I'm a fuckin' junkie. In the city, a pharmacist might carry a gun at night. But, God, this was the country. He saw the man mouthing words at him.

'Ventolin!' the young man cried back. 'We want some Ventolin. Turn the alarm off, for God's sake! Open the bloody door.' He looked back in the headlights. Oh, Rachel.

The pharmacist stood looking. The young man pointed to the car.

'Asthma, bugger you. She's sick!' His fists rested on the glass and he was stiff.

The doors opened a crack. The alarm rang on. It rang in his head, right through him.

'My wife's got asthma. She can't breathe. She needs Ventolin.'

'Doesn't she carry it?' The pharmacist was tall. He squinted.

The young man realized the man couldn't see with the car lights in his eyes.

'It's expired. Look, she's nearly had it.'

'You need a prescription. And money.'

'We've got a nine-week-old baby boy in the back. Or how 'bout my index finger as a deposit. Will that do? For Chrissake!'

'Stay there.'

'Oh, listen to it.'

When the man came back with the tiny cylinder, the young man snatched it from him and ran to the car. Rachel had begun to sob. It was pitiful. He stuck the inhaler between her lips and sprayed it. The bitter smell seeped out. The baby whimpered hoarsely. He sprayed, catching her on the intake. And again. He sank against the seat with the lights on and the motor still running. He saw the pharmacist locking up. The alarm died.

Late in the evening the young man sat in the darkness and drank the coarse volatile claret the locals called Kirup Syrup. The stuff found a big emptiness in him. Relief had consumed something inside. Mother and child were asleep on the mattress in the bedroom. He was weary. There was a day's work ahead in the morning. He could not sleep. Kirup Syrup puckered his mouth and made his lips fatten. After midnight he reeled out into the still forest night and saw clouds rushing across the moon above the crown-shadows of the trees. It was an eerie sight; not a flurry where he stood, but up there a maelstrom. He was grateful for the sight of it. He was thankful for Rachel and the baby. They were something to check himself against. And now he was drunk and would have fallen down asleep in leaf litter if the cold hadn't driven him into bed.

★

Before dawn, he woke and crept about in an unaccountably cheerful mood. He drank steel-cold water and washed his face and looked at his hands in the half-light. They no longer looked like a guitarist's hands and the fact was suddenly of no consequence. For a while he stood at the bathroom window and watched light and mist and birds moving at the feet of karris where bracken and grasses hung sluggish with dew. Then he went to the bedroom where Rachel and the baby were stirring. He took the old kerosene tin they used as a wastepaper bin to the kitchen.

At the stove, he tipped the contents of the tin into the firebox. The papers were old bills and envelopes, Kleenex, and a few crumpled sheets that were his latest clumsy attempts at songwriting. He laid some kindling on top and lit it. He went out for more wood.

When he opened the firebox again a few minutes later, the blaze exploded in his face with the sound of a gunshot. He squealed. In that instant his vision was gone, and he fell back against the rickety deal table.

'Jerra? Jerra! What's wrong? What's happened?' He felt her propping him up.

'I can't see,' he cried. 'Nothing.' His eyes felt scorched. There was soot and charcoal grit in his mouth.

'Let me see.'

'Oh, Jesus.'

'Get up.'

'I—'

'Get the hell up, Jerra. Come to the sink.'

He felt her pinching grip on his forearms. Water splashed on him. For a moment he saw those clouds rushing across the sky; he felt delirious. Somewhere, the baby burbled. He was happy, he felt crazy.

Then there was light. Water in his eyes.

'Better?'

'I dunno.'

'Don't be wet, is it better or not?'

'Yes.' He saw the fogged outline of her arm, and for a moment, a clear vision of her brown eyes. He listened to her wheeze. In a few minutes he could see properly, though his eyes felt as though they were full of ballast.

The kitchen floor was black with soot, and as far back as the opposite wall, pieces of kindling and charcoal were strewn about.

'What was it?'

Rachel straightened from the firebox of the stove and held up the distorted remains of the old Ventolin cylinder. She showed him the metal fragments all over the linoleum.

'Must have tossed it in with the wastepaper,' he said.

'You could have lost your eyes, Jerra.'

'I'll be more careful.'

Out on the back stoop after breakfast, the young man watched the rain coming in from the south. He heard Rachel coughing as she sang to the child.

A frog went walking on a summer's day, a-hum . . .

He sharpened the teeth of the chainsaw and prepared to go out into the day.

No Memory Comes

THE BOY leaves his parents on the beach and wanders up through the dunes. Night has fallen and the lights of holiday shacks are budding on the hill. There is no wind. He hears a voice, slows down, homes in on it, and falls to his belly at the vegetated lip of a razorback dune. Down in the bowl between hills he sees two bodies. Hears them whispering. The sand on the declivity is fine and wind-smooth. As he shifts, a tiny ripple begins. He moves back. Another swell rolls down.

A shout!

The boy sees a man's body rising against the luminous sand, pulling up his pants. The boy turns and surfs back down the face of the incline with the sound of a silhouette behind him. He fights his way through the white seas, up slope, down-trough, from shadow, to light, until he comes out on the flat beach where his mother and father sit talking low and he sees no one behind.

Happy New Year, his mother says.

Happy New Year, his father says

A year has passed. He is older. He does not believe it.

That night he climbs into bed between his parents. His father muffles a weedy fart. His mother sleeps with a glick in her throat. The boy worms in and gets ready to dream that the new year will never come. Everything is fine right now. He has no need of it.

2

The boy is in love with school. He knows he is young. He knows he doesn't need to fly to Hong Kong every week or wash clothes. He only had to go to school and say things right and try hard. He only has to see his friends and not get caught playing British Bulldog.

On the way home he walks with a boy from a Catholic school. They both live on the hill behind the beach. In the summer they are in the same swimming classes – their patter kick and their duck dives are about the same. By the end of the summer they are best friends. Summers go by, but the boy knows everything stays the same. Even at twelve he doesn't feel any older.

At the end of one summer, the boy and his friend, on their way to the beach, find a man dead in his car. There is a hose from the exhaust going into the boot. It takes them a long time to decide the man is not asleep. When the ambulance comes and the men break the windows to pull the man out, the boys see the upholstery look of the dead man's face. When the ambulance leaves, the boy's friend begins to cry. He tells the boy that he wets the bed every night. And once his father tied the wet pyjamas round his neck and sent him to the Catholic school like that. This is his biggest secret. The boy sits on the kerb and watches his friend's fists. In the vacant lot behind, the wind stirs the whispering wild oats.

Later that week, the boy visits his friend's place and pisses in his father's golf buggy. He is older now, he knows, but he knows too that he and his friend will never change.

3

The boy goes to high school. He likes it after a while, though it is never as good as primary school. His friend leaves the Catholic school and they are in the same classes.

The boy still had weekends up the coast with his parents in the little asbestos house. His father drinks beer and his mother reads.

After school the boy and his friend ride down to the beachfront, and if there is no surf they play pinball and pool at the Snakepit and Minderbinders. They see bikies and rockers. The boy knows his mother came from here when she was a widgie. He has never seen a widgie, but he feels it is right that the place should still be there for him.

Sometimes the boy and his friend lie on the sand and talk about where they will hide when the world ends. They talk about God now and then, but it always brings them back to the end of the world. One afternoon, there on the sand with a dollar's worth of chips, they make a vow to look out for each other when it happens. They know it is only a matter of time. The burger joint winks and gulls hang over them and everything is solemn.

4

The boy hears his mother on the phone. When she is finished, she tells him his father is not coming back from Hong Kong because he has fallen in love with the housegirl. She lights a cigarette. He goes into the bathroom, locks the door, turns the shower on full belt, and cries. He beats the tile wall and his knuckles lift.

His mother gets a job. The boy comes home to an empty

house. He does his homework, he mucks around with his best friend. He doesn't go up the coast any more, even though his mother got the beach house in the divorce settlement.

The boy looks through old photo albums.

5

The boy bores people at parties. He tells them everything he remembers. He remembers everything. He knows the name of every song on every old record. He knows the name of every member of his first school class. He knows the name of every boy a girl had ever liked. When everyone gets their hair cut and gelled, he keeps his long. His Hawaiian shirts make people laugh. Girls get drunk and go to sleep in his lap. After every party he waits for his friend, cleans vomit off him, separates him from a clinging girl and they go home together. Everything stays the same between them.

At sixteen they buy a car together. They save by selling milk bars their own empty bottles. They sell their bikes. The boy sells his newest record. They wash cars. They get a paper round. The car is an old HR Holden. They paint it green with brushes and housepaint.

The boy's friend is the first to turn seventeen and get a licence to drive. Together they cruise along the coast and into the city. One night rockers kick the windscreen in at traffic lights. They U-turn into a one-way street. They have to turn around again on the footpath. Back on the beach where it is quiet they buy a bottle of green ginger wine and remember it.

The boy's friend gets a regular girlfriend. The boy doesn't mind. They all ride around together. She graduates from the back seat to the front. After a while the boy finds himself sitting in the back. He doesn't mind. In the back he stretches out and tells old stories. On lonely hills overlooking the river, cruising down neon streets on hot nights, parked beneath the sound of gulls and pinball machines, he tells them how it used to be.

The boy's friend and the girl are voted Head Boy and Head Girl at school. He votes for his friend because they are best mates. He votes for the girl out of loyalty. People say they make a fine couple.

At the school ball the boy gets so drunk his friend makes him go outside and sleep in the car. He wakes to the sound of rocking on the front seat. At the girl's final squeal, his jeans fill with a terrible heat. He swears things are the same.

The boy's friend keeps the car at his own place, even though they both drive now. The boy doesn't mind. His friend still picks him up and he rides in the back and drinks beer and passes out and wakes to a little squeal.

Signs go up all over the beachfront. Redevelopment. Highrise project. Luxury hotel. Observation tower. The boy doesn't believe it will happen. The beach has always been the same. Even for his mother.

Through his bedroom window in the early morning, he is woken by the sound of bulldozers. Someone will stop it; he knows they will.

6

The boy finishes his final-year exams. The year has almost ended. A year no longer feel like a year. Summers seem patchy and short. After the graduation party he rides with his friend and the girl down to the beach where they drink beer from the jagged end of a bottle they open on the door. The burger joints and pinball parlours are gone. Security fences and puce floodlights surround the cranes and the ugly bones of the hotel tower. The boy feels a hole open in him. He strains beer through his teeth.

His friend and the girl flex on the front seat but he can't absent himself. There's a faint, wet breeze, but nothing moves outside. Twisted cartons and stuck-flat wrappers park on the asphalt. The cyclone wire fences glint salty with moisture. Down on the sand, gulls make lumps of themselves in sleep.

In a week he will no longer be a schoolboy. Every morning he wakes with a hard ball of panic in his stomach.

The wet, butcher's-shop sound of lips and tongues. The girl sighs. From the back seat, the boy begins a story about how he once caught so many prawns in the river with his father that they had to take off their clothes and tie knots in the arms and legs and used them as bags to carry prawns that overflowed the tubs. The girl springs up off the seat in front, breasts afloat, and turns the radio on full belt. For a while the boy stays stuck fast in a corner of the back seat. The song makes the whole car vibrate. He feels his eyes itching. He holds his breath.

> *The beach is a place where a man can feel*
> *he's the only soul in the world that's for real . . .*

It's an old record. A mob of things rush him. He remembers. He remembers.

> *And I see a face coming through the haze*
> *I remember him from those crazy days . . .*

People should be born old and die young, he thinks. Grow back; grow back. Memories everywhere.

His friend starts the car. The boy jerks. Next year no one will know them.

They buy more beer. Under the lights of the drive-in bottle shop, the boy remembers the shack up the coast. He remembers sunburn so bad his mother bathed him with vinegar. No beginnings then, and no endings.

From the back seat he tells them about the beach shack. The girl says it's too far and why didn't he remember it before. He shrugs. Thought you were a professional rememberer, she says. They drive up the highway with her laughing. The boy sits in the back trying to catch his friend's eye in the rear-view mirror. He gulps down a can of beer. He sits back with all the windows open and feels the wind take him. Remembers the haze coming down on the beach.

Outside the city, the hot, moist night smells of grass. Backyards, summer. The girl's perfume streaks back to him, triggering. His mother? No, a squeal outside the gym and a flush of heat.

Down a narrow limestone road they wind. Here the dunes are bald and creeping. Sound of heavy surf. The air smells of peppery coastal plants. Black shapes emerge as houses. The boy points out an asbestos place. He opens his third can and pours it scalding-cold down his throat.

With the motor off there is only the sound of the sea. There is no key. The boy gets the jack out of the car and puts it through a window. He doesn't feel drunk. He is starting to feel dead. The girls calls him an idiot. His friend sheepishly turns the power on. Inside, everything is carpeted with dust. Walking on the linoleum they leave footprints. Around the walls stand big iron beds, and on shelves, fat paperbacks. A wicker craypot. In the sink drain, the skeleton of a mouse. Out of his deadness, the boy feels panic coming.

They sit on beds. The girl sighs. His friend looks away. The boy looks at his friend's girl. She is slim and brown and her breasts stand up under her singlet top. She has dark, small lips and deep eyes. He asks: Aren't you afraid of getting old? She asks: Is there any beer left? His friend goes out to the car. She sniffs and follows. The boy watches their footprints.

Nothing.

His friend comes back. No beer left. Is he all right? Doesn't he want to go home?

But the boy springs up and begins to hunt for beer. His

father kept loads of it. The boy tears cupboards open and guts them, tossing aside bloated tins of pork and ricecream while his friend stands by.

The girl comes inside and asks where is the toilet. The boy points the way and keeps rooting in the cupboards. When she returns, she holds out an old can. A rusty, unopened beer can. The boy takes it. Must be a thousand years old, his friend says. It has no rip-top. It is the kind people used to open with a knife-like opener.

The boy drags a drawer out and finds the old, black opener. It looks like a scythe. You can't drink it, his friend says. But the boy knows he can. There are no memories coming, of course he can.

He slams the flaky old can on to the Laminex table. Braces it against his thigh. Brings the point of the blade to rest on the corroded top. Hard to get a purchase. He leans down hard on the blade. The can slips aside. He feels the cold shock of steel in his groin. He takes in a jet of air. The can rolls across the table and thumps on the floor, keeps rolling.

What? His friend looks at him.

What? the girl says.

The boy looks at the blood on his hand. His friend grabs him and for a moment they hold hands like that, gore slipping between their fingers.

His friend looks down. Oh, shit! Oh!

Laugh, the boy thinks, losing his grip; laugh!

7

Wind tears at him, tearing him down. The motor beats like a heart in his ears. There is heat in his jeans. A warm, warm bath. A year starts to feel like a year again, but no memory comes.

GRAVITY

JERRA NILSAM sat with his son at a café table and the breeze was in his shirt. The day was all but gone from him now, and there was a party to attend. To host, in fact. It was a friend's birthday. He was late but he was in no hurry. A party didn't seem to matter a damn today. He felt a little punch drunk. How could a party count for anything on the anniversary of your father's death? He wanted to know: how the hell could anything matter?

This morning he'd woken full of ghostly sensations like those he'd always associated with amputees. He was afraid.

With great concentration, the little boy made a handprint with ice cream on the glass table, and looking beyond him, Nilsam saw the traffic pass. He had come to love the city. It was no capitulation on his part; merely a gradual awareness of new beauties. He was older now, he felt it.

'Go home, Daddy?'

'In a minute, mate. Let me finish my coffee.' Wait, little man, he thought. Let me linger.

Nilsam's pulse quickened, as though he were about to take a leap.

The three-year-old's eyes were intent on him. They were black, beneath his fair hair.

'Pongs?'

'No, you can leave your thongs off, if you want. But finish your ice cream.'

The child held the dripping cone out to show he had eaten enough. Nilsam took it, licked it once, and upended it in the ashtray.

'OK. Come on, me mate.' His throat felt tight and he heard his heart working hard.

Through the flat streets they rode with the wind in their faces. The boy sat strapped into his seat over the rear wheel with his rubber thongs threaded up his forearms. He shrilled a song Rachel would sing him in the bath in the mornings, the quiet time when Nilsam transcribed with an ear to the sounds of the house.

'Green for go!' cried the boy, beating him on the back.

Nilsam coasted through the lights. Heat. Sweat. Pulse.

'Ready for the party?' he yelled back over his shoulder. The boy clapped. Oh, God, the party.

'Yaaa!'

They rattled past parked cars to beat the sunset home.

Their street was always full of cars, but now there were so many there didn't seem to be enough room for houses. As they coasted into the driveway, Jerra heard the music. It was his own music they were playing, his not very famous songs. His heart contracted.

'Party!' the boy cried. 'Yaay!'

Nilsam got off and wheeled the bike up the leafy side of the house. He had to struggle to counterbalance the child's excited lurching. The sudden light and roar of the packed yard stopped him dead. People, some friends, greeted him. They tickled the boy. He smelt the thin, cutting edge of tobacco smoke and the subtlest hint of dope. Everywhere was light, in jewellery and bottles and eyes and glasses. Food passed him. He saw how trodden the lawn was. He was glad to see the door to his studio padlocked. It was an old shed his father had renovated for him. Rachel turned from where she stood speaking with friends across the courtyard and saw him. He knew there was trouble,

'Juice? Drink, Daddy?' the little boy shrilled. 'Loud.' He covered his ears. 'Loud.'

Nilsam leant the bicycle against the paling fence, unstrapped the child and led him to a table where he let him pour himself a drink. Lemonade sloshed on to the hired tablecloth. The boy smiled around the glass,

'Good?' Nilsam asked. His mouth was dry and a heaviness was in him.

'Marvellous.'

'Where'd you get a word like that?' But the child was drinking again and the bubbles made him giggle.

He felt Rachel at his side. She was tall and slim. Her dark hair was out and she wore a cotton dress. Her tan made her look as though she was made from polished jarrah. He was sad.

'Where were you, for God's sake? I thought you must have had an accident.'

'We stayed too long at the Italia. It was cool, wasn't it, Sam? Sorry.' He thought he could smell suntan oil. It was the frangipani in bloom.

'You haven't done a bloody thing for this. Poor Ann thinks you've snubbed her. Philip is drunk—'

'OK.' She was beginning to cry, it always frightened him. 'What do you want me to do?'

'Oh, Jerra.'

Rachel went inside and left him with the heavy scent of the frangipani and a strange, hurtling sensation. His music jangled out at him. He went across, under the pergola, to the tapedeck, cut the music, pulled out the tape and put something else in, something fashionable.

Philip intercepted him on his way to the back door.

'Modesty strikes him down.' Philip pointed at the cassette in Nilsam's hand.

'Hi, Phil.'

'My wife is offended.'

'And you're drunk. I've heard.'

Philip had got thin these past years. Eight years back he'd married Ann and they'd honeymooned in Nilsam's shack on the south coast, though it had not been a success. Ann had grown fat. Nilsam carried too much weight himself and it had begun to annoy him. Philip looked pasty. His soft, hairless face had the practised vulnerability of the social worker. Nilsam liked him, but not tonight.

'Tell her I'm sorry, eh?' Jerra said. He touched Philip on the arm as was expected. 'And tell her she's a silly bitch for getting offended.'

He left Philip with a cheap hurt look on his face and went inside. People fussed in the kitchen. In the laundry, someone broke ice with a hammer. He heard the tail end of a joke. Seats in the living room were pulled into pairs. Social workers, he thought; more bloody Deep and Meaningfuls. It's a party, for God's sake.

Rachel was in the bedroom. She sat in the big, ugly reading chair with a biography of Thomas Merton across her bare knee. He knew she hadn't been reading.

'You've ruined it.'

'I know.' He saw the mahogany sheen of her folded leg.

'What's the matter with you?'

'I don't know.' He couldn't bring himself to mention his father. *You should know!* he wanted to bellow. 'I really am sorry.'

Her mouth closed against him. When she did that he could see her age. He picked up a little orange gumboot from the floor.

'He insists on wearing these bloody things all summer,' he said with a weak laugh.

'Where *is* Sam?'

'I don't know. Out the back somewhere. Probably scoffing the horses' doovers. He'll stink of anchovies tonight. I'll have to sleep in the spare room. Come on. We better go outside and be hosts.'

But out under the party lights of the pergola, his new resolve waned. His smile split his face, his jokes petered out mid-sentence; he couldn't look their friends in the eye. Ann stood with two other women beside a table bristling with bottles. He caught her looking at him, looked away.

You're thirty years old, he told himself; be adult enough to go and smooth things over. He got himself a glass of Semillon. He took a few serious breaths. And he stayed where he was. He stood rigid beside Rachel as she spoke with their guests.

There was a hole in him. Something was lost. The tall man in loose grey trousers with that stooped, expectant stance. The big hands so often hairy with pollard. Only a memory now. He was dead. Actually, finally, dead. And now there was nothing for Jerra Nilsam to fall against. He thought about the ride home. His heart beating. It was riding down that street, as though he had been balancing a bicycle for the first time. There was no exhilaration in it, only a terrible sense of gravity.

The party wore on. Bottles emptied and the lawn was flattened with sporadic dancing until, in the middle of it all, someone gagged the stereo and brought out a guitar. A thin droopy young man began to play 'Stairway to Heaven'. Nilsam groaned. Dancers bitched quietly beneath the frangipani.

'It's 1985, for God's sake,' he muttered. '1973 is over.' Someone shushed him. Someone else tittered.

'Amateurs not good enough for you?' a woman hissed from across the courtyard.

Nilsam found a chair at the end of the garden. He'd wait it out. From there he overheard the same conversations about IVF, family therapy, AIDS. After a while, Sam came by, slit-eyed and cranky. He put the child over his knee and put him to sleep with 3/4 time pats on the back.

Nilsam weathered it out, protected from conversation by the sleeping child.

'Use the brakes, Jerra!' Old man running behind. Tinsel on the lawn. Christmas. Old man holding the back of the seat. Charging around the yard on the reddest bike in the world. And then the grip gone, no old man. Sudden grave feeling of independence. Turning, turning. 'You'll be right!' the old man calls. Then the roses, the thorns, looming. Whooaa!

He woke with a flinch. Craziness in his belly, as though he

was about to fall. He put his face to the little boy's neck and closed his eyes.

Neither Rachel nor Ann spoke to him when he helped them clean up. He collected bottles and broken glasses, picked up cigarette butts with dramatic disdain, swept, sighed. When they went inside he knew better than to join them. Philip was asleep in a deckchair, face disfigured by snoring. Nilsam unlocked the studio behind the courtyard, went in and shut the door.

The studio was foetid and dusty. Egg cartons on the walls gave it a spooky look. There was little room in which to move; the place was full of microphones on stands, cords, a piano, an organ, various guitars, mandolin, banjo, the eight-track recorder, a drum machine, mixing desk, metronome, sheets of paper, bits of carpet and blanket and rickety chairs. Here Nilsam wrote songs and sold them to singers who never quite sang them well enough or in the presence of people influential enough to make him rich. They were not love songs and not particularly sad. Rachel sang them to Sam at bedtime and bathtime, and having her sing them was enough for him to continue. But she never sang in front of him. He had to eavesdrop to hear her husky, wavery voice. The sound of it made his skin prickle the way it had the first day he saw her on Scarborough Beach. It had been autumn and he had come back to the city with his mind cooled enough to set a little and see the shape of things and bear it.

He turned the eight-track on. He listened for a few moments to his doodlings on a keyboard and then he switched it off. For a long time, he did nothing but sit in the haven the old man had built for him. It was his father's idea to build it before the cancer beat him down and his blood turned to water. He knew his son was no handyman. It was something between them, like the old days. The old man said it was his Ark. Rachel teased the old man and called it the Tower of Babel. He built it anyway and at the end of summer he died.

When Nilsam went out into the warm night, Philip was gone from the deckchair and the house was in darkness.

Sam and Rachel were asleep. He slid into bed beside them. He lay a while, listening to their sounds, and the old melancholy took him. He lifted the blind a little so he could see them in the light from the street. Rachel's hair was plaited and thick on the pillow. Sam was face-down between the pillows, looking – as always – as though he'd fallen asleep crawling, and in a moment he saw the birth again, the awful rending of flesh, the tiny blue slug tossed on to Rachel's belly, the crew snatching him away to work on that sunken little chest, that hiccupping little chest, and letting go the blind, he fell back on to his pillow.

Rachel and Sam slept on, and in time Jerra was left limp, and his mind was clear.

In that dim room with its smells of talcum and incense and anchovy breath, Jerra remembered how he and Rachel took him to the old man's bedside, the last time when the toddler smiled and quivered and the old man drank him up, his flesh, his scent, his life. 'Blood,' the old man said. It was his joke.

Nilsam was a father. He was a husband. He was a son.

Cars rattled past on the street outside. The Bulgarian's dog was barking again. Nilsam pulled Sam to him. He slipped an arm under him and cupped the little buttocks in their pyjamas.

Rachel turned with a sigh. He lifted the blind again. The faint light showed him her face. It was so familiar it might have been his own. He felt her breath on him. The house creaked. He knew where he was. The Bulgarian's dog barked. A Volkswagen pulled in next door. He even knew the time by that; it was four o'clock. A rooster crowed. Something receded in him.

At dawn he took Sam in his arms out to the toilet. The grass was cold. Sam pissed on the seat. The homely ammoniac smell made Nilsam grin. He hoisted the sleeping boy on to his shoulder and took him across the dewy lawn towards the house.

Sun moved across the rooftops. A phrase of music came to him, something fresh which made his heart tic. This afternoon he would go and see his mother. Today he would do many things. He took the boy inside, put him in bed beside Rachel and climbed in. Sleep came to him and he was not afraid.

THE WATER WAS DARK AND IT
WENT FOREVER DOWN

THE GIRL left her mother in the rented cottage with all the shades drawn and went down to the packed white sand of the beach. She passed the jetty with its whirling braid of gulls and followed the line of the bay. She was tall for her age, but years of training in the pool had taken lankiness from her. Her hair was cropped close. In the summer sun her big nose had gone scabby. She just wished her mother would put the bottles away, raise the blinds, and come outside into the world again, but the girl knew she had a better chance of making the Olympics than changing her mother.

Eight years ago, when the girl was six years old and her father had been gone a year, her mother had a terrible accident. Depressed and drunk, she passed out while smoking in bed and woke in flames. Her nylon nightie crackled and hissed. She beat herself out on the floor and threw a jug of water over the bed, but she did not call out to the girl across the hall. She sat shaking in the dark with a bottle of sherry until dawn when she phoned an ambulance. Because she waited, her scars were hideous. Years later, she told the girl she hadn't wanted to alarm her by shrieking and waking her in the middle of the night looking the way she did, like a charred side of beef. From that moment the girl was convinced that her mother was either stupid or sick.

Down the front of her bikini, the girl saw her tiny breasts and was grateful that her own body was unblemished. Even these days, the sight of her mother caused her teeth to clench. She kicked up a string of kelp and watched it settle back on the sand. This holiday was so boring. There was no one her age. Already she'd run out of books. It was no different from home.

Following the curve of the bay, she saw the small island offshore – low, rocky, spotted with vegetation – and she wondered how far out it was.

She knew her mother was sick and bitter and afraid. She just wished she could pull herself out of it, get a job, stay out of mental hospitals, save for some special surgery, find a man. God, to be *normal*!

All those stupid, recurring statements ran through her head. *'All a person needs is a bit of land,'* her mother would say, *'that's what makes the difference.' 'Men hate us. They hate our bodies.' 'God has been cruel to me.' 'Your father never loved you.'* These came up during TV programmes, at meals; the girl heard them shouted in the night, heard them screeched from their sixth–floor window as she slunk home from training. Over and over.

A hot breeze blew off the land, from where the colossal white backs of dunes humped at the edge of town, threatening the place with their shifting weight.

She's gonna send me crazy, she thought.

Every night after school, the girl trained in the swimming squad. It was three hours of blind, busting effort, away from home, and though she didn't love it the way the others did, she knew she couldn't be without it.

The girl stopped walking. It was stupid to walk, she knew. Walking made you think. What she needed was a swim; to be an engine.

By now the island was directly out from her. Crayboats passed it, their motors coming from weird directions in the wind.

An old man on a sailboard skimmed past with a ludicrous smile on his face. With a grunt, she ran to the water and speared into the channel and swam.

She had good style. Her breathing was metrical. She was tuned for it. She swam and thought the thoughts of a machine.

Out in the centre of the channel the water was dark and it went forever down. The island seemed no closer.

She moved all her parts. Everything did its task. She was not tired.

When the water suddenly became warmer, she knew she was there. Standing in the shallows, just out from a little sandy beach, she saw a cloud of birds and heard the blood chug in her ears.

'All a person needs is a bit of land,' she said aloud. She laughed and it wasn't all derision.

She stretched her arms. She noticed that she'd left her watch on. It had stopped. She guessed the swim had taken her fifteen minutes. The easterly was drying her already, leaving streaks of salt on her flesh.

The island was a bird sanctuary. There were signs and warnings. It wasn't a big island. Maybe ten hectares she guessed, or less. She climbed up from the beach and wandered across the island's humpbacked plateau. Seabirds filled the sky; they nested in holes in the ground and limestone nooks; they chased each other in territorial battles and shrieked from places unseen. On the packed sand, scrub and limestone monoliths offered little shelter. The tracks of birds peppered every soft surface. The whole place smelt birdy. On the seaward side surf creased across reefs, and small, sunken lagoons and potholes stood still and full. From the low cliff she could see fish down in the water with birds diving on them. Underfoot, wherever she went, broken eggshells mashed and blew. As she walked, a murmur grew and birds fled before her. One ran blindly from its hole and skidded off her shin. Thousands, thousands of black birds.

In their midst, in the centre of the island, the girl sat down to watch them soar and stitch about her. She wondered why they thrived so. She thought of Biol. class and tried to think. There seemed to be plenty of fish for them to eat. No predators that she could see – no sign of snakes. Just birds, and she didn't even know what kind. Hatching, growing, hunting, mating, dying. There was something relentlessly single-minded about the whole business.

After a time, she stood up and more birds rose with her, taking their atonal music with them. By her foot, she saw the carcass of a small bird. All over the island she found dead birds: whole, mutilated, broken. And shells and feathers. And shit. A constant layer of debris. She felt within the grasp of something important, something she might understand. From Biol. What did that skinny teacher with the tobacco breath call it? That was it – the web of life. She saw it all before her. The sick and the weak died and the young and the strong lived and thrived. It's the way things are, she thought. You need to just *go*, that was it; survive, win.

All you need is a bit of land . . . something solid under you. Ah, what rubbish, especially from her mother. Something solid, and there she was all day in the dark, drinking. A life of fluids. A whole ocean she must have drunk by now and she talked about *land*! Bird sanctuary for a lame duck. She was tired of fighting it all, always always swimming over the top of that sea of grog. Maybe that's why I started swimming, she thought, to stop her drowning me.

She went back down to the sandy beach and she took off her watch and bikini and lay in the sun. Her body was strong and hard. She was young. There was no more room, she decided, for feeling sorry for dead things and dying things and sick things; for her mother or even herself. Now there was only time to live, to survive. Live. Survive. They're the same thing, she told herself quickly. No difference.

She got up and saw that she had left her perfect shape in the sand, and then she cried out in triumph and ran naked down to the water and pierced it and began to swim.

Be an engine. Don't complain. Don't ask. Don't hesitate. Swim, don't think.

Pushing out, she knew that as soon as she was old enough she would leave her mother. There was no room. She had to look after herself, leave her mother to the web. There wasn't time enough any more for all this swimming through craziness and ugliness and dumbness, sherry, beer, Scotch, gin.

Be an engine.

But she faltered.

Don't think, breathe!

She moved her parts. Swimming machine.

Think.

No, you old bitch. I can swim.

She cut through the water and filled up cold with anger and went harder.

I can be a machine. Like a fish, you old bitch. I can swim away.

Harder.

Go.

Do.

Cut.

Harder.

That body thrashed and whitened the water, throttling out, vibrating, parts shearing away, roaring white hot, and all the way down she felt young and strong and perfect in the cold darkness.

NILSAM'S FRIEND

for Galloway and Chambers

LOOKING UP from the page Nilsam saw his friend come up the path, distorted in the gentle convexities of the leadlight window. He stood and the chair crashed into the wall. The window shrieked as he opened it.

'Well, butter my bread,' Nilsam said with his head stuck out.

His friend looked up with a grin. His hair was thick and his beard was long and lustrous in the creamy sunlight. He was thin and barefoot as usual, but hair and beard formed such a magnificent mane that it made him seem bigger, thicker.

'You look like a lion.'

Nilsam's friend stopped below the window. The air was congested with the sounds of birds and cicadas. A dog barked. It was spring in Perth. Nilsam's friend wore the tiger-striped calico pants his girlfriend had made, and a black T-shirt bearing the words SURFERS AGAINST NUCLEAR DESTRUCTION. He squinted in the sun.

'Got in last night.'

'You're early.'

'Ran out of money in Athens.'

Nilsam shook his head. 'Athens.'

Both of them broke into laughter.

Nilsam left the window and went through the house to the front door. It was cool in here. The dark boards croaked as he went. So the old romantic is back, he thought; the perpetual adolescent. He wondered for how long. Nilsam's friend could not decide whether or not to marry. He embarked on trips to 'get his head together' but a decision was never forthcoming. There were always stories; he brought back atmosphere by the suitcase, but never a solution to his dilemma. At least this time he looks well, Nilsam thought. Last time he looked like something out of Belsen.

'The boy asleep?' Nilsam's friend asked as they embraced at the door.

'Yeah.'

'I bet he's twice the size.'

'He's learnt to say shit.'

'I turned thirty in a monastery.'

'Good grief, let's get some food and go out into the sun.'

In the kitchen, Nilsam pulled the cork from a bottle of wine and he gave his friend a salami and a cheese with a little knife in it.

'Thirty.'

They sat out on the back lawn which was strewn with bright plastic toys. They ate and drank. Nilsam's friend looked hard and wiry. His eyes looked good and clear. He told Nilsam stories about the crazy Greek peasants living in the old church, about the lump on his girlfriend's breast they'd flown to London to have removed; about the airlessness of the English; about Greece again and the tavernas and the white light and the donkeys; about the surf in Spain and the ecumenical monastery in France where he'd arrived sick and been taken into the infirmary like a medieval pilgrim; about the icons; about things that happened in him that he couldn't explain properly, and Nilsam listened and felt overweight, sluggish, ignorant and still a little disdainful. He was working. He had a son to look after, and a wife to consider. He didn't have time for romantic jaunts. He didn't have the money or the hide. And, dammit, he didn't want to go.

'I wished you were there, sometimes, you and Rachel and the Terror.'

'We'd have slowed you down,' Nilsam said. He poured some more wine. It was thick and red against the liverish grass.

'Well, I missed you all like hell anyway. Greece, mate, you'd love it.'

'Greece? I've got most of it in this neighbourhood.'

'But the retsina, the tavernas, the light, the colour of the ocean.'

'People say the light, the sea, the . . . well, it's the same as here.'

'It doesn't matter. Yeah, it's a lot like here. But it's not here.'

Nilsam shrugged. It always came to this.

The back door opened. Nilsam's son, rumpled and squinty from sleep, toddled out into the sun and fell into his lap.

'He *has* grown.'

'He's crapped himself, too,' Nilsam said with a smile, and he put his lips to the child's hay-smelling hair.

'You're good with him.'

Nilsam shrugged. He felt dowdy. He was a man and he felt dowdy like women were supposed to feel dowdy.

'Did you see the rooster?' He pointed up the back.

'What's it, a leghorn–emu cross?'

'Biggest rooster in the world.'

Nilsam's friend laughed.

'Reminds me,' Nilsam said. 'A little girl bumped into me coming out of a record shop yesterday while I was riding past. She must have been eight or so and she'd dropped her Bach record. I asked her about it. She looked at me and said: "Bach was the greatest composer in the world. So was Handel." I had to ride a whole block before I could laugh without a conscience. Nearly fell off me bike.'

The child rolled over in his lap and reached for the knife on the grass.

'Ta? Ta?'

'No, not for boys.'

The child turned over and began to cry.

'I'm winding down,' Nilsam's friend said. 'Got in at four this morning.'

'Go home and get some sleep,' Nilsam said, grappling with the child.

'Yeah.'

They walked through the house to the front door and on the veranda they stood in the noonday shade and looked out across the suburb with its close-set houses and smudges of smoke from the spring burn-off.

'By the way,' Nilsam said, 'what's the verdict?'

'I turned thirty. It put me out of kilter. Couldn't decide.'

Nilsam smiled and his friend went down the steps.

In the afternoon he sat out there as the sun ate into the shade. He watched his son climb the steps with fierce concentration as he waited for his wife to get home from work, and he caught himself wondering what it was like to see the same creamy light, the same blue eye of the ocean, the same sky-colours somewhere else.

Minimum of Two

I FELT Greta in the dark and her buttocks were cool as honey-dew. She stirred. Her breasts came my way and puckered against my face. I hoped to God she would stay asleep. I ached with my own blood. Gently, I squared her hips to me, displaced a bent knee and settled in between her legs. Her fine hair fell across my mouth. She breathed her sweet melon smell. I felt the curve of jaw, line of neck, heard the satin whisper of a shifting thigh and all the caution went out of me as I pushed her back, writhed up into her, levering on my toes until I prised her open. She gave a little cry. Her knees locked me at the hips. I scrambled and shunted with my head blank. Greta, my wife, began to scream. Her nails lifted buds of flesh from my back. She head-butted me and I yawed off her, spilling across the bed into the cold. There was a small silence before a car started up across the street and Greta began to make broken noises that might have been retching or weeping, though I couldn't tell because I got the hell out.

Among the sawdust drifts in my workshop, I threw tools at the wall and kicked drums, lurching in a sweat from one end to the other until I could barely breathe any more and I fell in a corner against an old chest full of bolts and brackets. The fluorescent light made me feel puny. I was still naked. I smelt of Greta. I was ashamed. That hatred came back and I got frightened of myself.

I thought of that bastard Blakey cornering her in the dungeon-shadows of the car park, and of the features of her face collapsing as she backed against a fender, then a pillar, then a wall. The things he did to her, those details that everyone heard at the trial, the things he said, the things I listened to her say in a dead tone. I thought of her quiet on the piss-smelling concrete and her blood on his business suit; now in my mind I couldn't stop from seeing her pulling her clothes together as he showed her to her car and strapped her in and sent her on her way to be on her best behaviour. The look of her when she came into the house that night nearly three years ago made me want to die.

She was like a ghost for two weeks. I couldn't get a word out of her but I heard her crying in the bathroom at night. When I found the bruises on her I forced it out of her. I took her to the police. A week or so after that, she thawed a little and I knew she was coping. Her big laugh came back and the softness in her eyes. There was a rash on her chest sometimes that came and went but she seemed OK. After my first rage I put it all to the back of my mind. I told myself that what was important was getting Greta back into herself. I wanted to give her all the time she needed.

It was some time before she could be touched, but she softened up. We stayed home, felt intimate again. I was frightened to even suggest sex, but it was her idea in the end. We decided to have a baby. Big and round and rich, Greta never looked better. Seeing her pregnant made me happy and I knew it was all right with us again.

Blakey was Greta's senior in the Department. She took too long to act. The jury procrastinated as though maybe the whole thing was Greta's fault, but Blakey got five years with a minimum before parole of two. We sat like wood in the courtroom, Greta and me. The lawyer was smug. There were photographers. They begged us to smile.

After the trial, I stopped work for a few weeks. The house was quiet. Greta went back to what she was like the months after it first happened; it was like a relapse. She cried a lot, moved potted plants from place to place around the house, smoked three packs a day, had nightmares, wouldn't talk about it. A few weeks passed. I took her out for a game of tennis; she wore a tracksuit even though there was sun. We drove up into the hills. Had big dinners at home and got drunk and slept well. I'd worked hard on the house ever since the first night she came home like a ghost and now it was good to be in. Winter was coming. Greta stayed around the house. Because it was cosy, she said. I knew I was helping.

She got better. The twins were born and she cried for three days, but she pulled herself together. I worked hard and brought in a lot of money and improved the house still more. Everything was good. Greta was content with the boys.

But something went wrong somewhere. Six months after the twins were born, Greta changed. She seemed distracted. She was a scrupulous mother, she did everything right, she spared the twins nothing, but I'd come into the room and find her suckling them, one on each breast, with a look of awful sadness on her face. She looked as though she was waiting to die.

Not long after, she stopped eating meat. It didn't bother me. When I saw it made her ill to see me eat it, I quit too.

The kids grew. I climbed into work each morning, and for eight hours I thought of nothing but the smell and the feel and the weight of wood. I made us a lot of money.

For a long time Greta hid the rash from me. It was red and ugly and puckered. Her skin felt as though it had been embossed. Greta said it was a side-effect of the pill.

We didn't linger over sex. It was a gradual thing. Greta never joked about it any more. I started going without. It was weeks, then months. The boys took my mind off it. I used to laugh at their crazy infant dialect as we played under the big purple lilac in the spring.

I waited for her – she was my wife – I knew she needed time. But there was nothing. Even Greta's affection for me seemed to dry up. She never touched me, never said anything gentle; there was no intimacy in her. She hardly looked at me. Every now and then she would get drunk and melt a little,

enough to laugh and to hug me and even lead me to the bedroom, but it always ended with her in tears and me going mad
out in the workshop.

It was like starving to death.

Greta saw doctors about the rash. She saw a psychotherapist
about sex but he wanted her dreams and I could have told him
that Greta never remembered dreams.

Some nights when I fled to the workshop, her weeping
sounded wrong. I thought I heard laughter. It was a sick noise.
My whole life was warping like a plank in the sun. That's when
the hatred came into me.

The night I was desperate and pitiful enough to try to make
love with my wife while she was asleep, the night that made her
look at me as though I was diseased, that was the night I decided
to kill Fred Blakey.

When I went back inside that night, the house was quiet. I went
to the big grey filing cabinet in the study and took out all our
documents relating to the trial: letters from the lawyer, copies of
legal documents, some rape pamphlets, a few notes I'd made
during the proceedings. I sifted them on the desk. It made me
cold to see the letterheads, even the shape of my own hand-
writing from the time. In the file there was a slip of paper which
bore nothing but the words: a minimum of two. Blakey might
be out already, I thought. I checked back through the dates. No,
he'd still be inside, but nearly due for parole. The twins found
me asleep in the reading chair in the morning. They thought it
was great fun.

During the day I looked up some old telephone directories
and found where Blakey's house was and at dusk I went driving.
On my way through the city I passed the Public Service building
where Greta had worked. The sight of it did something to me. I
turned into the entrance of the multi-storey car park just down

the Terrace, stopped there for a while, and backed out. I couldn't make myself go in. From there I went across the bridge and found Blakey's house in the suburb by the river where all the doctors and the lawyers live and everything stinks of new money. Blakey's place was an open-front, glassy shoebox arrangement with the lights of the city on the river melting up towards it. Outside, I sat for some time. I don't know why I got out of the car. I was just doing things; my brain seemed a step behind every action.

I walked up the long, wide, curving driveway, found the double doors in a portico dense with bougainvillaea, and rang the bell. A small woman came to the door. She looked drunk.

'Is Mr Blakey home?'

'No.' She leaned carefully on the door.

'When will he be back?'

'Are you a friend?'

'We have someone in common, I suppose.'

'He won't be back. We're divorced.'

She shut the big jarrah doors in my face.

All the way home I thought about Blakey, tried to remember what he looked like. He was taller than me and about as broad. Thick hair the colour of dead grass. He had a strong-featured face that was going to fat and he sat like a man who was used to sitting. At the trial, and at a work party where Greta introduced him to me once, he looked to me as though he'd only be comfortable at a desk or behind the wheel of a car. He talked a lot and loud.

The day after I visited Blakey's wife I did something I promised Greta and myself I would never do; I rang my old school friend Tony Mitchell. I knew then that I was serious. I really would kill Fred Blakey.

Tony Mitchell was an education officer at Fremantle Gaol.

He'd made a lousy teacher in the state school system. I hadn't seen him since he began at Fremantle. He owed me a favour. In those early bare months after the trial, I sometimes wondered whether my old friend Tony Mitchell ever saw the man who raped my wife. I wanted to know what it was like for Blakey in prison; I needed to know he was scared and unpopular, but Greta didn't. The rape is over, I told myself; the man is in gaol. The past is the past. I determined never to use Tony Mitchell to satisfy my curiosity.

Tony Mitchell took a while to remember who I was. When he did recognize me on the phone he sounded vexed, as though he deserved an explanation.

'What do you say to a drink?' I asked.

'Well—'

'Lunchtime tomorrow?'

'Been a long time, Neil.' Tony Mitchell was the only person alive who called me by my first name. Even Greta and my mother in Sydney called me Madigan.

The bar was crowded in the pub where we met in Fremantle. From it you could see the prison buttress above the tin rooftops of houses. Tony Mitchell had a stool saved for me at the corner of the bar. He was thin and looked as though he didn't know what to expect. We shook hands, made the tentative connections again. I bought him a few beers. He seemed worried.

'I need a favour,' I said after twenty minutes. 'As an old friend.'

He went stony. 'And it would have to be illegal.' Tony Mitchell owed me some favours. He had married young. Foolishly, I'd made him and his wife a whole dining suite for nothing because they were short of money; it took me months to recover financially.

'I don't know,' I said. 'Unethical, maybe.'

Tony fooled with his glass. 'You in trouble?'

I shook my head. 'You don't know my wife, do you? She was raped—'

'Madigan! I can't—'

'So you know him?'

'Shit, Madigan.' He drank off his beer and looked ready to leave. 'Yes, now that I've blurted it out. I know Fred Blakey.'

The old curiosity got me. 'What's he like inside?'

'He's all right. Getting old quick. Doing a degree in literature and politics externally.'

'Popular?'

'The screws like him. The boys like him well enough. Rapists aren't pick of the crowd inside.'

'He gets parole soon, doesn't he?'

'Madigan, I can't talk to you about Blakey. Give me a break.'

'All I want is some information. For a favour. You remember favours.'

'What're you gonna do? You can't dish out your own justice. Blakey's been punished. It has to stop somewhere.'

And I was thinking: What about for Greta, when does it finish for her? And me, when does my bloody life go back to normal, when do I get back everything that once belonged to me, for Chrissake?

'I'm not dishing out any justice.'

'How is your wife?'

'Fine.' I shrugged. 'I just want some information. I sort of know the guy – he's not a stranger. I thought I might clear the air.'

I bought him another drink, kept him on his seat. He looked hard at me. He didn't believe me for a moment.

'I just want to know when he gets out and what his address'll be outside. Just so I can contact him.'

'I'm sure he's in the phone book.'

'Didn't you hear about the divorce?'

'I'm in the business of helping guys improve themselves—'

'And I'm not gonna stand in the way of that.'

'I've got principles, Madigan.'

'Must be improving yourself, while you're at it. Things changed since the state schools, have they?'

He put down his beer. 'I've gotta be back.'

'One phone call.'

'Don't hold your breath,' he said, already walking.

I finished his beer and ordered myself another.

He rang three weeks later. Greta was beside me when I took the call; I felt her looking at me.

'June 12. Morning.' He hung up. That was all, but it was enough. I got to wondering why he did it at all. We were school mates and team mates from football. There was a favour outstanding. It was about a rape. We were men. I would have done the same.

Five weeks passed. Greta and I didn't speak much. We had the boys for a buffer. Greta had never been a weak person. She was independent – wilful even – when I married her. People said she wasn't afraid of men, of anybody. They liked her forthrightness and her kindness. I loved her for the way she looked and the way she could tell you to go to hell. She took charge of a situation. I just liked wood, happy to work as my own boss, confident that Greta and me had our own domains and the shared privacy of the house and the place our bodies made when we made love. We chatted and gossiped. We did things. People liked the sight of us together.

But those five weeks before Fred Blakey got out, we lay straight as nails in bed and Greta dressed in the dark and scratched herself and whimpered in her sleep. Doors were always locked and windows closed. Greta was no longer strong. I worked distractedly, got so far behind schedule that it seemed hopeless. All day I thought about Fred Blakey and at dinner Greta looked at me as though I might pounce at any moment.

The days were short and never warm. At night Greta sat with the twins in front of the TV until they were asleep, then she went to bed herself and I sat up alone, picking splinters from my palms. My body began to feel as though something had been hacked out of it.

One night I went in to bed and in the dark I heard her talking. I stopped before she heard me and I discovered that she was praying. I got into bed and hugged her hard. She yelped.

'Fred Blakey will pay, Greta,' I murmured in her ear. 'I swear it.'

She writhed free and I let her lie nail-straight beneath the quilt.

On the evening of June 11 I did two things. First I rang Tony Mitchell and he told me to go to hell. Someone, a woman, was shouting in the background. I'd had some Scotches; it was a bad idea to ring him. I had nothing to say to him in any case.

The second thing I did was more hopeful, but it went bad all the same. I took Greta out to an Italian place we'd been regulars at soon after we married. I drove her, organized the babysitter, opened doors for her. She needed to know I cared and understood.

We sat by the window with its ferns and baskets and bottles, watching people walk past to the cinemas and cafés. Across the way, a club washed the street the colour of sunset. I bought wine. The food was good: things in butter and rich sauces, pasta without meat on the sort of china we used to slip into handbags when things were tougher. Greta wore a light suit, all crushed and sultry-looking. The collar of bone beneath her throat was sweet to see. Her dark hair was short and showed her ears and that neck and I felt grateful for her. When she moved, in those nervous jerks she'd acquired, her breasts shifted and her hands furled and unfurled and it didn't seem so bad that there was no talk between us.

As we finished our coffee, Greta picked at breadcrumbs on the tablecloth and spoke quietly without looking up.

'What did you mean about Fred Blakey?'

Now that I looked at the top of her shirt I could see where she'd tried to disguise the ugly rash with powder.

'What I said. Only that he'd pay.' I smiled. 'I didn't know you had any religion.'

She continued to gather crumbs, eyes down. 'You wouldn't do anything stupid, would you?'

'I've done stupid things before.'

'If you ever—'

'You were praying. I heard you. What do you pray about?'

'I want to go home, Madigan.'

When we were out on the street, a dog ran from an alley and Greta shrieked, flattened herself against me, then after a moment, as the dog, running circles around the traffic lights, began to stop traffic, she unpicked herself from me and we walked back to the car like acquaintances.

June 12 was a Monday. By seven fifteen that morning, I was parked outside the football ground that backs on to Fremantle Gaol. Rain fell in short turns. There was no wind though I could smell the harbour plain enough. All the limestone buildings downtown looked pretty in the dull light with the sky behind. The long, high walls of the prison were of limestone also, but they were grim and no light, no weather could ever pretty them up.

No one seemed to take special notice of me. There was a hospital and some houses and the football ground close by, and the prison entrance was sixty metres down the hill, so my being there didn't need to seem suspicious.

I'd thought about what Blakey might do. If he was anything like me, he'd head straight down the hill for the nearest pub, walk those narrow streets to smell the fruit and coffee and see the women and the docks. Beside me on the seat of the rented car were a big wide roll of masking tape for the number plates, a stocking for my head and claw hammer in case of something unforeseen. When Fred Blakey came out on to the street and headed downtown, I would have plenty of time to tape up and disguise myself before running him down.

Cars came and went just after eight; the shift changing.

I wasn't nervous; I was like a lump of wood.

At nine twenty Fred Blakey drove past in a white VW with a woman at the wheel. The car came out of the entrance-way, turned up towards me and went past, going up the hill. They didn't appear to have seen me. I didn't know it was him until he was past and up round the bend. For a few moments I sat still, hands on the wheel. Then I started the little sedan and threw it into a U-turn up the hill.

A woman! I'd expected a broken man, spurned by all, shuffling out on the road, walking into Fremantle to survey his chances, here he was, the bastard, with a woman collecting him at the gate. I drove hard. I had no plan.

Around the bend the VW wasn't to be seen. The lumpy road intersected with the north–south highway and on instinct I turned left to go north towards Perth. Buses and trucks stagnated the traffic. I found gaps, worked my way through, made good ground, and after a few minutes, I saw Blakey's car on a hill ahead. Eventually, I got within five cars of him and I kept my distance.

We wove round the river past shipyards and boatpens and yacht clubs until the better suburbs ran to the foreshore. I saw the two heads in the VW tilting towards one another in conversation, and all the time I tried to organize the business in my mind, to make some plan.

In time we reached the suburb where Blakey and his wife

lived, but instead of passing through, as I expected, Blakey's girlfriend turned into a sidestreet away from the river and up through the trees and rich verges into a quiet avenue. I hung back without the cover of other cars. The VW slipped into a gravel drive between pines and I coasted past, got the number and drove home.

All day I sat alone in the workshop. Greta hung out the washing with the boys at her knee. When she reached up and exposed the back of her legs I saw her with Fred Blakey and I could hardly breathe. She saw the hire car later in the day, just looked hard at me and I kept away.

At dinner I joked with the twins and drank some beer. Greta brought out a lifeless vegetable casserole. She was remote, When she passed I had the feeling you get as a schoolboy when the prettiest girl in the class slides past: helplessness and gloom.

'Where did you go this morning?'

I said nothing. I wanted so much to talk. Later I said, 'Things'll get better. They will.'

For a moment her eyes lifted. The lines beneath them made her older than she was. She looked tired and sick. I wanted her. She turned to the twins, gave them toneless baby talk and supervised their meal.

Late the same evening I parked in the street where I'd left Fred Blakey earlier in the day. In the dark, I walked past a few times until I had an idea of the place. It was a closed-in kind of house, thick with trees and shrubs, every kind of creeper, rockeries, retaining walls, small pools of lawn. Not a vast place, but very comfortable; it made mine look quaint.

I took the stocking and hammer with me when I finally went down between those pines towards the house. The grass was wet and quiet. Neighbouring houses were obscured by walls and vegetation, so I had no reasonable fear of being observed.

The first window I came to had a faint light in it. It seemed to be a living room: couches, a roaring stereo, standard lamp, and a sleeping dog. The stereo saved me; the dog seemed overwhelmed by Elton John. I couldn't match up Fred Blakey with Elton John. Mantovani, perhaps.

I picked through the garden to other windows, but they were dark and had the curtains drawn. From out there the manic piano of the record sounded weird and set my nerves awry. The final window, a big paned bay window, was carelessly draped with a faint pink light sifting out. I eased up from a crouch in the flowerbed and saw through gaps in the curtains that the room was a bedroom and occupied.

I saw two pairs of legs. The man's were hairy, varicose and white. The woman's were shorter, darker, younger. I tried another space in the drapes and saw a profile of the woman's face against the hairy white shoulder of a man. She didn't look twenty years old. Her hair was blonde and cut short. She had full lips and a small jaw. Her eyes were closed. I couldn't hear what she said when her lips moved. At another space in the curtains I saw the man's heaving back. I saw him stiffen, roll aside. The man was Fred Blakey. He looked old, with the road-map face of a drinker, and with his greying hair all scuffed up, he looked forlorn.

I stood in the garden with the claw hammer in my hand and one of Greta's stockings wrapped round my wrist. I saw that heaving white back on Greta, saw his smooth old hands pushing her head into the concrete, the spittle at the corners of his mouth, her breasts strangling in his fists, those places I knew he'd dribbled over, the stain of his big white body on me.

Greta would be in bed by now. Her body would be shut tight; she'd be lying there hard and straight in our bed where things used to be whole and sweet. Maybe she'd be scratching her rash, or praying like a scared kid, cold and straight. And in there, twelve hours out of gaol, was Fred Blakey heaving and lurching on a girl who seemed to enjoy it. He had hair on his shoulders. I turned the hammer over in my hands. I went out to my hired car and waited.

About midnight the lights went out in the house where Fred Blakey was. At one thirty the streetlights went out. The radio in the car put me to sleep. I dreamt I was walking down a passage that got narrower and narrower. I ran down it, faster, crazier. When I woke it was four thirty. I switched off the radio. The windows were opaque with condensation and the ceiling of the car was wet. I opened a window, cold air rushed in, my head cleared.

Suddenly I felt sad, as though something had slipped from my grasp. I sat like that, like a bereaved man, until six fifty when Fred Blakey and the girl jogged out on to the road with the small dog. They wore red tracksuits.

I hadn't planned this. I hadn't planned anything. My mind was bogged. I just acted.

When they were out of sight down the hill, I tried to start the car, but it wouldn't catch. I kept trying. I was calm; I didn't curse. I let off the handbrake, took the car out of gear and rolled. At the fourth hop, the motor started. I revved it hard and braked. I waited a full minute. I couldn't have told you my name.

By the time I caught them up, Fred Blakey and the girl and the dog were at the road by the river. It was the side away from the river. He was on the grass verge. She was on the road. The dog zigzagged between them. She turned and fell, mouth wide, as I rode up the kerb behind them, but Blakey never turned around. She went under. Something flew off to the side.

Blakey rose out of the ground and starwheeled up over the bonnet and I felt him thwacking across the roof and down the boot, and then I was around the bend, collecting sprinklers and the edges of parked cars, trying to get back on the road. There was mist on the river and skyscrapers looked like giants rearing from clouds.

I went in quiet at home. Greta woke as I crawled in beside her. She rose on an elbow and looked at me through sleep-narrow eyes. The look on her face. She hid her breasts. She got out of bed, pulling on a shaving coat and jerked up the blind. A small sound hicked in her throat. The morning light flattened me.

'It's all right, now,' I murmured.

'No, Madigan,' she said. 'It's not.'

And in that moment I knew that I had lost my life. I was a dead man.

DISTANT LANDS

THE GIRL they called Fat Maz worked in her father's news-agency. Her father had a club foot and he was an angry man because the army had never wanted him. All day he clomped up and down between the racks of magazines keeping an eye out for thieves and making sure people bought things instead of standing and reading for free. The girl's mother sat all day at the register and watched the cars pass. Once a day a big Greyhound rolled past going north to the city. Only the dull drumming of the old National reminded the girl that her mother was there. She was always relieved when her parents went home for lunch and left the shop to her.

Every day at the lunch hour, a tall dark man came in, paused for a moment just inside the door as if to adjust his eyes or to get his bearings before heading straight to the paperback novel called *Distant Lands*, opened it, and with his foot on the bottom shelf, read for fifteen minutes. The first time he came in his reading was furtive; he spent as much time looking up to see if he was being watched as he did reading. His eyes showed white and worried over the burst of exotic purple on the cover, and to show that she couldn't have cared less, the girl smiled at him and shrugged.

'Interesting?' she asked that first day as he walked out without spending a cent.

The man said nothing. He just passed the register with his eyes downcast. When he got out in the street, he adjusted his tie, buttoned his jacket against the smelly harbour breeze, and went.

After that, the man came again, but he did not look at the girl or give any sign of recognition. Her father would have thrown him out. Not only was he freeloading; she guessed he was a Pakistani too. His Nescafé hands were clean and well manicured. His suit was conservative and cut sharp. When she inspected *Distant Lands* she saw that he had marked his place with a long, black hair. The book looked as though it had never been opened. On the back cover, the blurb said: *You will want this book never to finish.*

As weeks passed, the girl wondered whether she should read *Distant Lands* for herself. The dark man seemed to draw such energy from it; she could see it in the way he buttoned his jacket against the wind each day. But the book was so long and she'd hardly read a book since leaving school, and, besides, she felt somehow as though it might be eavesdropping. For now, it was enough just to look forward to the lunch hour and that strange feeling of comradeship she felt when the dark man was in the shop. She was part of a conspiracy. For an hour, her rules were shop rules. Just watching him up the back with his polished shoe on the lower shelf and the gloss finish of his down-pointed brow shining in the fluorescent light gave her pleasure.

She was not a sporty girl. She did not read. She had no boyfriend. Sometimes she would bicycle out to the edge of town and look along the highway. She felt herself growing fatter every day. She hated the smell of the harbour and she often wondered whether she smelt of it after all these years.

Several times she almost asked the man how the book was coming along, and once she nearly left the register to confront him, ask him why he read it at all, but even as she opened her mouth or got up from her seat, she knew she might spoil lunch hours for them both. For even though he never even met her gaze after the first day, and even though they'd never really conversed and he'd never actually bought a single item from the newsagency, the girl knew they understood one another. She had never felt this tacit understanding with anyone before.

Once the dark man came in late. The girl's parents had come back from lunch. She felt her arse tighten. She saw the dark man walk down to the back, oblivious. She held her breath. But before he even touched *Distant Lands* the man seemed to sense the girl's mother craning over the National, and he left immediately. He was back next day, dead on time.

There was a more serious crisis. One day, a big red woman in a shiny cardigan brought *Distant Lands* to the register. At the time, the girl's mother was out on the pavement dragging in wet bundles of the *Daily News*.

'I'm sorry,' the girl said. 'That book's reserved.'

'What's this – a libr'y?' The big red woman deepened a tone.

'It's on order. Sorry.' It seemed desperately important to save it for tomorrow's lunch hour. It might take weeks to get another copy down from the city and the thought of lunch hour without a visit from the stranger sent a gallop of panic through her.

'Haven't you got more?' The big woman put a meaty beringed hand upon the register.

'I'm really sorry.'

The woman stood there for a moment as though deciding tactics, but in the end she slapped the book down on the glass counter and rolled out. At the sight of the great rump in retreat, the girl felt fear. That could be me, she thought. It wasn't the fatness so much as the . . . the . . . whatever it was that seemed so patently missing. The woman hadn't even really wanted the book, she began to suspect. Their little confrontation was just something to do.

She watched her mother drag in the newspapers. Her father passed, throwing his foot angrily ahead of him. Outside the Greyhound was pulling away empty.

As she helped close up that night, she felt the oddest seesawing inside her. By dinner it was gone and she watched TV until she slept where she sat.

Next morning she felt guilty. She had no friends, but her mother and father looked after her. They'd given her a job when she quit school, and jobs were impossible to get in this little town. Maybe things weren't as bad as all that.

That day, the dark man came in as usual. Watching him read, she noted that he was not handsome, though she did not object to his colour. His teeth had the look of polished rice. She felt a smile wedge her face as he turned a page. Was that little snapping movement in him excitement? Now she was happy; there was no doubt of it. This was happiness, not everything else.

The shop was empty. There was only the dark man reading *Distant Lands* and her peering openly at him over the register. Nothing else but a thousand garish glossy covers. He's happy, she thought, seeing him turn another page.

As she watched, the Nescafé coloured man turned what she'd swear looked like the last page. Her throat closed her heart off. She heard him sigh. She saw him shut the book and place it back on the shelf. She saw him coming to the register.

His small teeth showed in a smile.

'Thank you,' he said.

The girl opened her mouth.

'And this is for the bus,' he said, putting a note on her palm. 'Goodbye.'

The girl they called Fat Maz watched him go out into the main street, turn his collar against the harbour wind, and go on his way.

After a moment, she went down to the back of the shop. She was excited and confused. *Distant Lands* stood on the shelf. She picked up a long black hair. It was strong enough to wind around her finger like a tourniquet and turn the flesh blue. She stood with her back to the shelf and let out a grunt. The fifty-dollar note was starchy-new. She stuffed it down her jumper and into her bra. Leaning against the shelf for a moment, she looked towards the door. When she breathed, the money sounded electric between her breasts.

She met her parents at the door. She saw shadows in their brows. She fairly crackled.

LAPS

AFTER SEVEN years, Queenie Cookson began to swim seriously again. Each morning she drove to City Beach and swam up and down between the groynes. Out behind garlands of surfers and waist-deep swimmers, she scored the swells with her strokes. It hurt; she felt as though she was etching herself on the sea. As she tilted her head to breathe, she would often see on the beach her husband and daughter keeping pace. All this time, she thought, they've been growing, and I've gone to fat. It took her seven years to find will again, to shrug off defeat.

She had come from her home town a loser, an outcast; she left behind a grave and a crusade and a well of bitterness, and somehow she'd turned her mind to being a mother and relearning how to be married. These things were good shelters. But seven years of softness hadn't taken all will from her. Queenie Cookson did not like to be beaten. She did not like to cower. Her big, brown body and everything that lived in it was not trained to be that way. In the first month of summer she lost ten kilograms, and she knew she could be hard again.

Every stroke of her dogged freestyle was a blow, and with each swim she knew she was shifting more than her own weight. Somehow, out there that summer, Queenie changed. Early on, the morning swim was like doing penance, but in time it became a pleasure. She began to feel she belonged in the dawn-brown sea, as she had when she was a girl, when her grandfather was alive, when the world could only be good. The old man had taught Queenie to swim. He threw her out of the dinghy and rowed just ahead, calling, coaxing, hounding her. He was all she had. She'd left him buried on a hill she no longer owned.

These mornings, Cleve and Dot mooned along the beach indulging her. Sometimes Dot paddled out on her board and Cleve watched her hassling for waves with men twice her size. It made him laugh to see her cut a long bottom turn; she was dwarfed by the most puny wave. She put the men to shame zigging and zagging under the churning weight of water. Cleve stopped joggers and pointed her out. He could not let her go unnoticed.

Like her mother, Dot swam before she could talk. Her short honey hair was cut and shaped like a mushroom and her skin was the colour of sherry. She had the body of a miniature athlete. She was six years old. Though a strong swimmer, she was lazy like Cleve, and swimming laps bored her motionless. Most mornings, unless the swell was good, she just walked with Cleve, not saying much. Both of them would prefer to be at Scarborough; it was just down the hill from where they lived and the surf was better, but it was safer at City Beach for laps, and besides, the little men with big money were tearing up the beachfront to build hotels for the Americans and neither of them could stand the sight of the cranes and steel skeletons and hard-hats and the awful wound in the ground where the burger joints and pinball parlours had been.

'They're tearing up the fount of my youth,' Cleve would say and wave his arms like a Shakespearean actor.

Dot would shove her hands into her pockets and drop her head. 'They're making a rotten mess.'

So out of duty, and with sadness, they went with Queenie to City Beach.

One morning, near the end of summer, as Cleve handed her a towel, Queenie shook the water from herself and told him she was ready now.

'For what? What are you ready for, more laps?' He elbowed Dot.

'Ready to go back.'

'Where?' Dot screwed up her face and sucked on the strap of her bathers. 'Cor, swimming.'

'Back to Angelus, Cleve.' The soberness of her tone surprised even her. Weighty. Yes, she thought, there's weight to lose.

'A holiday?' Dot straightened.

Queenie smiled. 'A weekend, maybe. You might see a whale. They're coming back there, these days. It was where we used to live. It's my home town. We had a different life, then, Dot.' She noticed Cleve's old apprehensive habit of kicking the sand. 'I've been thinking about it all summer, Cleve, and I reckon it's time We can't avoid it any more. We're older. Places shouldn't frighten us any more. We got screwed by the place – OK. But a place can't screw you for ever. It'd help me, Cleve.'

She saw his face set. Dot looked from her to him. They all walked up the blenching beach to the car park. The sky and the easterly gave warning of another withering day. Summer: watermelon, flyscreen doors, sleeping on the back lawn in the haze of mosquito coils, the sweet smell of water on dying grass, undisciplined sunsets. It was what they lived for.

No one spoke on the way home in the rattling Land Rover. The Cooksons lived in a little weatherboard house, thick with passionfruit and grape vines, on the hill above Scarborough Beach. It *was* a new life they had here. The hurt of seven years before had healed them together in a way they had not expected. It was only lately Queenie had come to notice it. She had been numb for longer than she could recall.

Dot stomped from room to room, getting ready for school. Cleve fried eggs on the gas range. Queenie fingered the ever-dull *West Australian* on the table. She didn't pretend to be happy.

'You don't agree then,' she said.

Her hands before her were big and salt-wrinkled. The kitchen smelled of potted herbs and last night's fish batter. She looked at Cleve's peeling shoulders. He was thinking hard, she knew. His legs were too thin for him; it looked as though the bottom half of him went hungry. He didn't seem afraid of turning thirty-two next week.

Dot crashed in and sat down.

'Sunny side, Dad.'

'Why?'

Queenie prepared herself. Breakfast Banter.

The little girl replied: 'Cause I like the yellow dot.'

'A flaming *dot*. That's what we got.'

'A dot. So what?'

'Yeah, could have been worse. Imagine twins. Two dots. A colon. Three, an ellipsis.'

Dot pouted.

'Not those lips, dill. If you were twenty dots I could get a pair of scissors and cut along the line.'

She made a sound of a fart with her mouth.

'But all we got was one lousy Dot. A dot with a bot.'

'The whole world is a dot. From a long way.'

'So is an egg. Here, eat it. Actually, an egg is a world, too, for a while.' But Cleve had lost her. Dot had punctured the yolk and was tamping it with wads of buttered toast.

Queenie watched him back at the stove. He knew she was watching, but it didn't spoil the morning's ritual. Queenie saw him shuffle around the kitchen. He had changed a lot. She liked him so much more since Dot was born and they'd lived here. He was frumpish and good, these days; he'd stopped trying to be someone he never was, now he had no country mettle to prove. She imagined people would like him at the hospital where he lifted them and wheeled them through the labyrinth into the operating room or out the big glass doors to freedom.

She received her egg and a kiss on the brow.

'You don't agree, then?'

Cleve sat down and bit into a big, green capsicum. 'Yeah, let's go tomorrow.'

'For the weekend?' Dot wore a dag of yolk on her chin.
Cleve nodded. Queenie laughed and was afraid.

2

As soon as Dot was home from school, the Cooksons left for
Angelus.

Just after sunset, near the town of Williams, they hit a
kangaroo and Cleve had to get out and kill it with the wheel-
brace. It took five hours' driving to get to the small town on the
south coast. When the lights of the town rose from the dark like
a new galaxy, Cleve woke Dot and she watched dumbly.

Angelus was no longer a whaling town. These days it lived
by farm produce and traded hard on its English climate. Tourists
came to see its awesome cliffs and beaches, the wildflowers in
their season, the museums, the relics. Angelus had learnt to live
off its dying. No one mentioned the protest any more. It was a
town looking bright-faced into the future.

The motel Queenie checked them into had a spouting concrete whale in its floodlit forecourt. Their room stale, drab. It
stank of cigarette smoke and Pine-O-Clean. Dot fiddled with
the TV and the motel notepaper, flicked through the Gideon
Bible without enthusiasm and went to sleep. Cleve and Queenie
turned the light out for her and sat in the dark. Cleve pulled
some cans from the smelly little refrigerator and they drank beer
in silence.

Pubs closed. They listened to the sound of men weaving up
the street to their wives.

'Nothing's changed,' Queenie whispered.

'We have.'

'Are we any better, do you think?'

'We try harder,' said Cleve.

'I suppose we should see everything.'

'I guess it's the point of the exercise. Exorcise.'

'I just want to come back and see the place and be normal in it. And maybe see Poppa's grave. I want to . . . confirm things.'

'Like what?'

'Like us growing up. Like us being properly together. Like this town being the past.'

Fresh from their antiseptic motel breakfast, the Cooksons went out into the bright, windy morning, and without much sense of purpose or direction, began to walk. Fat clouds bundled up from the south. The air was mild; it was not the summer they had left. As they turned into the main street, the steel surface of the harbour came into view.

'Pretty,' Dot said.

Queenie put a hand on Dot's mushroom head.

'Yep. Pretty.' It was. It still was. Queenie saw it better than she ever had.

All morning they visited familiar places: park benches, a certain rose garden, some historic cottages, delicatessens. All morning Queenie hardened herself. Sooner or later someone would recognize her, she knew. She just had to tough it out. But no one did. And as the morning proceeded, anonymity began to peeve her. No one recognized her as Queenie Coupar the local girl who turned coat; she was just another tourist come to see wildflowers and replicas and plaster whales.

Cleve took them out to the deep-water jetty to show Dot the tiny shack where he huddled when he was a watchman, when his life was creaking and falling around him. It was a long walk to the end. Some boys fished. Down on a landing near the water, two old drunks lay in each other's arms and the morning sun set alight the dew on their backs.

'Was it cold?' Dot asked.

'Yes.' Queen answered for him. She recalled the fights, the hardness between them, the emptiness of the bed at night.

'Rats used to crawl everywhere,' said Cleve.

'Ugh.'

'A man jumped off here and drowned one night,' Queen said.

'Yes. One night.'

Dot went to the edge with a wrinkle on her brow.

'It's hard to understand I know,' Queenie said.

Dot nodded. Gulls stitched the sky behind. Queenie felt as though all this was a story she had read somewhere; it didn't seem part of her life.

By midday the harbour lost its sheen. The Cooksons ate lunch in a quiet pub with a view of the water. Queenie felt Cleve watching her as they all chattered and rattled cutlery. Below them was the town jetty where the tugs and official craft berthed. Once it had been the mooring for the whale chasers.

'This is a nice town,' Dot said. She stuffed a chip into her little oval mouth. 'I'd like to live here.'

Queenie felt herself flinch. 'Wait till you see the beaches. The beaches are the whitest, the cleanest . . .'

'Cleaner 'n' brider an' bigger 'n' wider,' Cleve said in an American drawl.

Dot giggled. Two men in business suits left off dismantling their T-bones and looked at Cleve with open suspicion.

'Oops,' Cleve whispered. 'The accent. They think we're greenies. Let's not talk French either, eh? Let's just be rubbernecks for the day.'

'It's all we ever were, Cleve.' Queenie pulled back her bread-coloured hair.

'No,' he said. 'We cared about things. No one can take that away.'

★

On the crest of a hill, Cleve pulled up before the tall timber house. It seemed to have been dug into the granite flank of the hill. It was old and solid and lovely. An English house. At the sight of it, Queenie felt the veins in her neck thicken.

'This is where we used to live,' she murmured to Dot who was sleepy and listless.

'Why didn't I ever live there?'

'You weren't born then,' Cleve said. 'It used to belong to Queenie's family. Like the farm.'

'Now it doesn't.'

'Oh!'

'Yeah. Oh.' Cleve looked at her. She smiled.

'Houses don't matter, though, do they, Dot?'

'Ya just live in um, that's all.'

'Glad you came, Spot,' Cleve said. 'You're good counsel.'

'I'm tired.'

Queenie pulled her springy little body across the seat and put her head in her lap.

'I learnt to swim in this town, Dot. When I did everything else lousy. I knew I could always get in the water and swim like a fish. Like you.'

'I surf, Mum.'

'Yeah. Well.'

Queenie looked away from the old house. Someone had opened a curtain. Cleve put the Land Rover into gear.

Despite the sombre afternoon light, the beaches along the peninsula glowed. They struck Queenie as almost gaudy in their whiteness.

Dot slept, but Queenie still addressed remarks to her, even though they were meant for Cleve.

'Yep. Learnt to make love here, too, Dot. And I learnt to stick to my guns no matter what. An' then I learnt about how

213

stupid it can be to stick to your guns after your ammo's run out.'

Cleve smiled. 'I wanted to be a hero too, you know.'

'Now you're just a dag. Thank God.'

'Cheer up. This is the good bit coming up.'

'You know we didn't stop the killing.'

'You helped stop it. That's enough. Jesus, you're so proud.'

Queenie smiled. 'Yeah. One thing I did inherit.'

Dot awoke at Paris Bay where the huge, rusting oil tanks still stood. As they coasted down the long hill overlooking the Sound, Queenie saw the tiny whalers' cabins, the fallen jetty, some paint-smeared sheds, and she was full of memories.

A caretaker met them at the gate and took two dollars from them. 'We're making the place into a museum, since the bastards closed us down,' he said. 'Been here before?'

'A long time ago,' said Cleve. He found himself grinning and he caught Queenie's eye.

And there it was. The long ramp of the flensing deck where once Queenie had lain in the blood and offal with the others, the cogs, the great windlasses, the chimneys from the boilers, the oily shorebreak. Beside the ruined jetty, the *Paris II* was aground and bloody with rust, the harpoon gun up-tilted on the bow.

As they walked on to the flensing deck. Cleve was grim-faced. Queenie was surprised to discover in herself a sadness for the place. She had campaigned so bitterly to destroy it. Now there were only gulls and wind. It was pathetic.

'Hey, check this out!' Cleve called to them from the base of a vast tank. It stood forty feet high and silver paint came off in great shaley leaves. Cleve turned a wheel and a circular hatch squawked open.

When they reached him, only his legs showed from the little hatch. His voice thundered inside the tank.

'Let me in, Dad.'

'No, Dotty, it's a bit smelly,' Queenie said.

'Used to be full of whale oil.'

'Bet it took a million litres. Let me in, Dad.'

The legs disappeared and after a moment Cleve's face poked out. 'Here.'

'Cleve.'

'It's all right. Come on, mate.' He pulled the child in and she let out a gasp.

'Cor.' Her footsteps echoed. The tank vibrated. 'Come in, Mum. It's mint.'

Queenie stood outside with her back to the flaking metal. Some weak sun came out and retreated. She heard Cleve and Dot charging about inside. Every now and then she caught a hint of the unforgettable stench of burning blubber. But the place was dead; she knew it now.

'All right,' she shouted into the hatch. 'Enough.'

As they walked back up the gravel drive, Dot grabbed her hand and Cleve's and the wind blew and she was like a sail between them.

Then there was only the farm to see. They didn't stop now; Queenie knew if they stopped they'd never drive out there and she'd never be satisfied. It rained. On the old road parrots sputtered green and the sky hung low and they hissed through sheets of fallen water. Rich milking pasture gave way to a more austere landscape where sheep stood still. Oh, she knew that land, that road.

On the farm gate hung a sign. NO TRESPASSERS. ROO SHOOTERS SHOT. KEEP OUT. In a century and a half no one had put a sign up before. No one had been denied entry to this place. Cleve and Queenie sat dumb in the idling vehicle. Beyond the gate, the rising land was overgrazed and guttered. In the distance, the hill showed signs of tree-felling.

'A hundred and fifty years,' Queenie murmured. 'And now this.'

'We'll talk to them, tell them who you are.'

They opened the gate and drove up the bone-shaking track to the old house where they were met by a thin, red man with amber freckles. Queenie felt it all: the smell of wet soil, hay, the slummocky sounds of cattle, the stone house built by her ancestors, the windmill where she'd climbed as a girl . . . she was dizzy with it. The man waited for neither request nor explanation.

'You saw the sign. Get the hell off.'

'My wife's Queenie Coupar.'

'I know who she is. Get off.'

'She just wants to see the old man's grave. It's on the hill.'

'Mr Pustling's orders are for no one to—'

'He doesn't own the grave, for Chrissake!' Queenie began.

'Then you'll need a helicopter to land on that six foot of ground, lady. Get off the place.'

'C'mon, Cleve.'

'We should have known better,' Cleve said when they were outside the gate again. Queenie got out to close it.

'I want to go home,' Dot said.

'Let me drive, Cleve.'

He looked at her a moment and got out. She got in behind the wheel.

'What about the gate?'

'Leave it open.'

Dot and Cleve exchanged looks. The farmhouse was obscured by trees and rising ground. There was no one near. Queenie swung the Land Rover around and back through the gate into the firebreak along the inside of the fence.

'We're going to the beach, anyway. Stuff 'em.'

'She used to be like this all the time, Dot.'

'She drives like a loony.'

The beach spread itself white between two granite head-lands. Queenie churned the Land Rover past places where she had played and loitered. She met Cleve on this beach; he'd been a trespasser once before. Dot was conceived here. And a few years later, this was where everything came aground. A pod of whales. The Coupar line. Their marriage.

'This is a special place, Dot,' she said, pulling up near the tidal smear of weed.

'No,' said Cleve, 'it's just a beach. Just a place.'

She looked at him a moment. 'Yes. You're right.'

It started to rain again. Queenie pulled off her T-shirt. She had the back and shoulders of a rower. Wholemeal hair settled back on her shoulders.

'I think she's gonna swim,' Cleve said, and dug Dot in the ribs.

Dot rolled her eyes. 'More laps.'

Queenie jogged down to the water, breasts beating, and dived into the shorebreak. She bellied into the path of a breaker, pierced its back and struck out to calmer water where she floated and waved. Up behind the vehicle on the deserted beach she saw the dunes. Further back was the hulking shadow of the hill where the old man was buried. In his own six feet. Well, that's all anyone needs, she thought. More than I need.

She launched into a crawl, smacking across the tops of swells as she had done behind the old man in the boat all those years back. She kept the hill in sight. She struck out, not invin-cible but strong. And she knew she could swim it all out of her; it was only a matter of time.

BAY OF ANGELS

I SAT WITH him by the river. The big, sad peppermints gave us shade and the breezy scent of their litter. Across the rumpled water, on the opposite bank, freeway traffic glittered in miniature and city towers took the white sun on their flanks. Full-bellied yachts were passing; they floated by like light and music. There were children near us, and gulls. It was beautiful to see. But I knew my friend saw nothing. There are times when all you can do is feel, when there's nothing but alarms ringing and you can't even see yourself in the mirror.

I sat by, in the world outside him.

'Ah, God, the water,' I said. 'My grandmother called this the Bay of Angels.'

My friend gave an all but imperceptible nod.

'I can't think why,' I said.

I sat with him. Neither of us was young any more. I couldn't see those nerves blue-sparking in him, but I knew it was happening. I took off my shirt and saw again that I was tanned and going to fat. What the hell, I thought guiltily; who cares.

I sat outside of my friend and waited for him to tell it all to me. That's why we were there. He said these afternoons helped him stay float; it was like jettisoning cargo. His mother looked after his wife and kids once a week, and in return she expected him to cope.

I learnt to walk on that soft strip of sand by the water. My mother took me down there as a baby. In all the photos we're brown as nuts and she looks like that old film star, Esther Williams.

I thought: It's safe here – next week I'll bring little Sam down.

I was waiting to hear it all.

My friend was trying to understand, but he just didn't know what it meant to seize up altogether. Though I heard him speak of it, he'd never been unable to continue the way a swimmer, cramped up and beaten, prepares to drown. Thinking about it made my mouth taste electric. I remembered that year, hiding out in the bush. I remembered the four walls of that hut and the suggestions of the sea and the lapping of family voices and the ultramarine light slowly deepening inside.

But today I was alive enough to be going to fat and to see the city as beautiful. I felt grateful and, somehow, guilty for not being able to explain myself.

'Want a dip?' I asked.

My friend took off his singlet. He was white and not going to fat. What the hell.

We waded out. The cool water was stained from its path through the hills but it was clean. We breast-stroked out toward the line of moored boats. I dived to the bottom and came up laughing.

'Middle of a city and it's clean water!'

My friend cut the water beside me.

From there it seems as though the city block was resting on water. Kings Park sat green above it. The sky was the colour of sleep. I rolled on my back and saw the old university, pretty and fatuous in its nest of foliage. At night the shores here would germinate with the light of lamps and the sound of people laughing and wading with nets and calling after children. There would be fires and the smell of cooking prawns, the hiss of beer-cans, faint music and the commotion of somebody stung by a cobbler. There would be cars revving. There would be the dark way of the water.

And I forgot I was swimming, supporting myself in water. My friend laboured beside me. Sobered, I said, 'We always come back to water. When things happen.'

I waited for my friend to tell me, but he stroked along eyes shuttered against the sun.

Swimming back through the boats, we came upon a yacht swathed in nets to keep children off. Hanging strangled in the net, a gull swung above the water like a cheap symbol in a film. I swam wide. I sensed my friend tiring; his stroke was ragged.

We scattered tiny smelt before us in the shallows as we waded in.

We sat on towels.

'C'mon,' I said. 'Is she worse?' He had kids. He believed in a God somewhere. His wife always told mine he was good in bed.

We sat there a long time, and as I waited for it all to come out I saw a host of white-sailed yachts sweeping down in the wind. Bay of Angels. The sails were like the wings of Angels. My heart fattened with joy.

My friend began to weep.

I sat there with my mouth open.

THE STRONG ONE

I

ONE MORNING at the beginning of summer, Rachel left them asleep and walked down through the peppermints to the caretaker's office to post her letter. The office had wide plate windows pasted with maps and announcements. She stopped to witness her reflection in the glass. She looked good. Her skin was clear, there was light in her hair, and when she put her hand against her belly it looked as firm as it felt. The ponderous weight of her breasts was gone. She had survived something to become Rachel again. No; she knew she was more.

The caretaker took her letter and slipped it under the old hinge he used as a paper weight and a filing system. He looked at the city address.

'The university, eh?'

'Applying for social work.'

For a moment his eyes settled on the front of her T-shirt where her nipples stood out dumb from the morning chill. He was a short, dark man. In his fifties, she guessed, with a strangely turned foot. It seemed that every caravan park they stayed in was run by lame men. Rachel wondered how it must be for him to gimp across the grass every morning knowing that from behind curtains in caravans all around, people were watching, discussing.

'Well, good luck to yer.' He smiled up into her face and she felt no malice. 'Hubby studying?'

Rachel shook her head.

★

When she got back, she heard little squeals of glee. She climbed the step of the sagging, rented van. It was small. There was no way to keep it tidy.

Jerra looked up. He was still in bed. Sam straddled his chest, shrieking. An arc of drool fell on Jerra's chest like a little silver lasso.

'He's teething again,' Jerra said.

Rachel filled the kettle and lit the gas. 'I applied. Sent it just now.'

Jerra sucked Sam's fingers. 'Uh-huh.'

Rachel licked her lips. 'Could we live on a student's allowance, you reckon? What is it, these days, less than the dole?'

'Dunno.'

She watched him blow on the child's wet fingers to make him giggle. He did it purposefully, without humour.

'God knows,' he said, 'we barely survive on the dole.'

'Maybe your mum and dad'd help us out.'

Jerra pushed Sam's glistening hand away. He looked at her. 'You know what I think about that.'

Rachel shrugged. He didn't know that she'd had a cheque from his parents every month since the winter. She'd come to love the Nilsams. They were good people, not like her own parents at all. She couldn't understand Jerra's attitude towards them. She knew there'd been problems when he was younger, but it was so long ago. Jerra seemed to bear weights from the past as though they were treasures he had to take with him. It made no sense. She'd had to jettison more than he had to stay afloat: the lousy luggage of family memory, the self-hatred other men had seized upon and cultivated – even bearing Sam and having him torn out by force. She knew how good Jerra had been for her. He'd helped her to free herself, only she wondered if he'd ever want it for himself. And lately she'd come to suspect he enjoyed bearing it all, as though the past, as well as being his source of pain, might also be his only source of comfort. One day she'd drive it all out of him. One day.

'Maybe I could play a few wine bars.'

She snorted. 'Music.' Even she was surprised at the level of contempt in her voice. Their eyes met. 'No, I s'pose you're right.'

Sam squirmed. They both watched him. Rachel felt them drinking up the sight of him.

'Jerra?'

'Yeah?'

'I really want this. The studying, I mean. You know I never had a chance before. You always said I'd go back and do something one day. I'm ready now. I've had enough of this kind of living. It was good to come here. There was nowhere else to go. But I'm better now. And I'm tired of toilet seats warmed by other people's bums, and I'm tired of standing in other people's shower water when the drains're blocked. I had ten years of that when I was a kid. It's time to go, Jerra.'

'The mill. What if . . . ?'

His voice trailed off as she sat down. There was no anger in her. She spoke out of a weird, sensible calm.

'I've followed you round a long time now, Jerra. The band, these other jobs. Now that Sam's weaned and I'm well again . . . well, I reckon it's time you followed me for a while.'

Jerra held Sam by the leg. She saw his thumb traverse firm, sweet skin. A lawn mower started up across the park.

Rachel tried to get eye contact again, but he was intent on Sam.

'I mean, at least you know what you're good at—'

'Even if it is a total bloody dead-end.'

'Well, at least you had a chance to find out. While you were cruising up and down the coast in a Kombi, I—'

'All right. You're right. Let's not expose my piddling middle-class self-pity.'

Suddenly, Sam seemed alarmed and reached for her. She smiled to reassure him. He put his hands slowly into his lap and looked at them in wonder. Rachel ran a hand across her belly again. She'd get out into the sun this summer and tan that skin till those marks were fine and silver as fishbones, yes, that's what she'd do.'

'What'll I do?' Jerra asked. 'If you study.'

'Look after Sam.'

His eyes narrowed and she saw him let go of Sam. It was only a moment.

'Me? I can't.'

'You what!'

'I . . . mean I'm not—'

'A woman?' She got his eyes at last. He looked trapped.

'No, that's not what I—'

'Hell, Jerra.'

He looked away.

She saw him look away.

'Isn't it good enough for you, looking after a baby? All that talk!'

He turned back. There was heat in his face. Rachel stood and laughed. And then for a moment she thought he might actually begin to cry.

'Well, what then?'

'Can't you see? I'm scared, that's all. That I won't be able to do it properly.'

She pounced on him and drove her teeth into his shoulder. He yelped and Sam fell back on to the bed.

'How do you think I felt? Eh?'

She lay across him and watched him lie there with his eyes darting. She felt she could burst with anger and tenderness at any moment. A neat moon of welts darkened on his skin.

2

As they walked out along the road to the beach on Christmas morning, Rachel wondered if it would ever happen, if there'd ever be a change for the better. The past two years seemed such a mess: the band folding, the pregnancy they couldn't decide to end, the lousy odd-jobs, and the illness and frailty of the last, long winter. Jerra was stiff and hard with surviving; sometimes she didn't know him at all. He seemed happy still to mark time, as though he wasn't ready yet for another battle. But Rachel was bursting, ready to act.

Sam burbled and spat. They took turns wheeling him. The road was flanked by the estuary on one side and the bush on the other. It wasn't hot enough for a swim, but even when it was cool these days they walked down to the rivermouth to sit and watch the sea move and sigh and disguise itself in the glitter of sunlight; it gave shape to the day. Waiting, Rachel thought as she pushed; all this bloody waiting. But it didn't feel so futile any more, now that there was something real to wait for.

The estuary was full. It was the colour of strong tea. Near the mouth, the limestone faces of the cliffs looked hollow and wracked by morning shadows. The scent of river mud stood in the air.

Jerra took off his shirt. He was getting his tan back. She'd seen photos of him nearly black from the sun. The roasted darkness of him made him appear bigger than he was, and, narrowed in the sun, his eyes bore the shuttered shape of obsession. But those were old photos from his teens. Mrs Nilsam had shown her. Rachel knew they'd worry her if she looked at them long enough.

'See that track?' He pointed to a faint break in the vegetation on the bush side. 'Forms a nice little cul-de-sac. Sean and I camped there once. God, what a time.'

'Jerra.'

That look had come on his face, the look he got when the past had hold of him. She knew he kept the deepest, the most important things to himself, but there was no end of surface stuff – names and places and anecdotes of boyish adventures – that began to drive her mad.

'The ranger never found us tucked away there. We used to sneak back up the road at night and pinch a hot shower from the caravan park—'

'Don't, Jerra.' Not today. It's Christmas. There's things ahead.

'What?' He looked at her, annoyed.

'That nostalgia stuff. Don't.'

'Why not, for God's sake?' His face hardened. He seemed ready to fight her on it this time.

'Because—'

'Because you weren't there. I'm excluding you when I remember. I'm sorry.' He slapped his arm and held up the crushed body of a march fly.

'No, because it makes you pathetic. You do it like an old man who can't handle the present.'

She gripped the handles of Sam's pusher and strode out. He opened his mouth but she spoke first. 'It makes me despise you.'

Labouring up the final hill in the windless hollow where cicadas belted out their unified note, she felt him lagging behind. He didn't seem to have any resistance left. You can follow, she thought; you can bloody well follow.

At the crest the salty breeze met Rachel full in the face, and at the sight of the sea, something rose in her.

'I'm gonna cut my hair off,' she said when Jerra came up alongside.

He looked at her, then down at the sea which he seemed to behold with relief. That feeling in her, yes, it was triumph. She had pushed down walls to live, to give life. She had been where there was no dependence, only a battle of solitary forces. And she had survived. After twenty years of confirming her own ineptitude, Rachel found she was strong. Never before had she felt such strength. Sweat cooled on her. She touched the welts on Jerra's shoulder. In her ocean of new feeling she knew she had to be the strong one.

'Yeah,' Jerra said, apprehending her again, 'me too.'

3

The whole car stank of sweat and cooked upholstery. Sam grizzled and squirmed in his seat. On the passenger's side, Jerra sat low with his head tilted back and the wind in his stubble. Rachel drove. They'd agreed on it. Everything they owned was stuffed into the old Holden; it was all of them driving back through the city, and neither heat nor traffic could stifle Rachel's spirit. This was her return. Every movement, every driving action was laden with purpose.

'Oh, Jesus.' Jerra sat straight in his seat as though something had bitten him.

The river was flat. They passed the old brewery. It wasn't far to Jerra's parents' place.

'Don't worry.' She reached over to touch the bristled surface of his head. 'It's only for a couple of weeks. We'll find a flat.'

'No. It's something else.'

Rachel drew in breath and held the wheel. 'Don't spoil this for me.'

'Hey, listen —'

'Something's happening for me, Jerra. I'm getting somewhere. Don't stuff it up.' She saw him stay stiff upright in the corner of her eye.

Sam cried and struggled. They rolled through Jerra's old neighbourhood, found the street in silence.

Pulling into the driveway, Rachel looked up at the big red

house behind the silky oaks and saw Mrs Nilsam at the window. She wasn't waving. She looked quickly at Jerra, and then she got out and galloped up to the shady porch where the old woman stood, swollen-eyed and shaky. Rachel hugged her fearfully and spoke into that big, tanned neck.

'What's happened? Is Mr Nilsam all right?'

'Rachel. Oh, your hair – it's lovely.'

Rachel stood back and looked into the old woman's handsome face and then followed her down to the car where Jerra was unstrapping Sam. She felt herself go tight inside.

Jerra passed the child to his mother who touched him hungrily.

'It's Sean, isn't it?'

'In a car. Yesterday.'

'Funny. Back up the road, I knew.' He looked at Rachel with a sick smile and shrugged. 'I knew.'

Rachel looked down at him and a chink of panic opened in her. She felt Mrs Nilsam take her hand and squeeze it. There was strength there.

From the house, a faint call.

'That's your father. He's crook.'

Jerra looked up.

'One day, Sam,' the old woman said, holding the child up in the light, 'you and your kind'll have to carry yourselves.'

Sam looked at her and bared his teeth.

HOLDING

for Derek

HART SAT back and listened to them speaking quietly in front. The station-wagon floated through the night streets towards the inner city, and Hart felt warm and fed and happier than he had been. Jan sat low in the passenger's seat. Clive drove. Clive was Hart's best friend. He was ten years older than Hart, and he still seemed like odd company to keep. Clive was like a friendly alien. He managed several companies, had a passion for technology, and he owned more credit cards than seemed necessary. He belonged to the Liberal Party, and to compound Hart's mystification, he was also a Protestant Christian. But for all that, Clive Genders was the most generous, compassionate man Hart had ever known, someone who wasn't afraid to admit ignorance or weakness. His laugh was warm and settling; he had a penchant for the scatological; he was always more than the sum of the things he stood for. To a man like Hart who worked with social workers and psychologists, Clive Genders was worth holding on to.

Hart watched them from the back seat. He'd been thinking about tonight's news footage from South Africa. A black mob. A woman in flames. It was soothing to watch the two little Genders boys beside him on the back seat sleep in an embrace. He pulled the blanket gently around them and heard Clive guffaw.

'Oh, tell 'em to shove it up their arse!'

'Oh, Clive.'

'I mean in a loving way, of course,' He laughed. 'Bloody bureaucrats.'

Tonight they'd drunk wine from 'the private collection', the Margaret River reds Clive kept in the grease-pit of the family garage. He was a man with good taste and no class.

'Don't be a twit, Clive.' Jan's dark face was greenish in the light of the old dash panel. Hart found her difficult; he never let on to Clive. She had a strangely downturned mouth which always made her seem disgruntled. Hart looked away, realizing he'd been observing her all evening. That mouth was so damned irritating, but, in a way, watchable.

'Send 'em a telegram: GET STUFFED, RUDE LETTER FOL-LOWING.'

Hart laughed.

'Don't encourage him,' Jan said, softening a little, 'he's done it before.'

They reached Hart's street and sailed in to the kerb. He slid across the seat to the door and squeezed Clive's shoulder. He didn't flinch like he used to. As he turned in his seat, Clive's meaty face and receding hairline were illuminated in the light of the streetlamp. The boys called his baldness 'Daddy's growing forehead'.

'See you Friday, eh?'

'Care of the Magic Plastic,' said Clive.

'The teddy bears' picnic,' Jan said with that rich mouth of hers down at the corners. Her teeth were perfect.

'Thanks for dinner, Jan.'

'See you, Hart.'

'See you, Bleeder.'

Hart got out into the cold. The engine ran in the still street.

'Picnicks, Friday.' Clive worked the clutch.

The car's tail lights shrank away. Hart stood alone in the street with his breath hanging before him. The sky was clear. Dew glittered on the grass verge. Hart decided to walk. On nights like this, after fights especially, Andrea and he had always walked. She used to say it was cleansing. In his mind's eye he

saw the shadow between Jan's lips. He needed a walk. The cold
night scoured him.

*A telephone ringing. He swam up, floated across to where it shook
spastically on the wall. Took up the receiver. He heard a calm, authori-
tative voice. 'I am obliged to tell you that your friend Janice Genders
has died as a result of a miscarriage. Goodbye.'*

Hart sat up, awake. A dream. He felt bad, sick. A dream.
He got up and drank some water. People didn't die from miscar-
riages any more, he thought. Besides, she's not even pregnant;
they don't want any more kids. If I trusted any of the bastards
I'd ask one of the psychs from work what it could mean. He'd
never dreamt like that before. It scared him.

Before long he slept again, but in the morning, and for
many mornings thereafter, he remembered that cold, adminis-
trative voice.

At work on Thursday, Hart admitted to the Unit a small boy
whose eyes were like cinders. The boy looked at everything as
though trying to will it away. Hart read his report and kept up a
friendly, confident smile. The boy's parents seemed fastidious
and bossy and suspicious; they seemed ashamed to be in such an
institution. They kissed the boy and left without much reluc-
tance. Walking down the corridor with that little boy, reading
the awful case history as he went, Hart felt grateful that Andrea
and he had never had children. Every day he saw these victims
of carelessness and neglect and abuse. He and Andrea, he
realized, in their clutching unhappiness, could have maimed
children as easily as they'd maimed each other. He supposed it
was something to be grateful for.

★

Clive strode into Picnicks burring the wad of credit cards in his fist. Hart was already at the table.

'Put 'em away, you don't fool me.'

'Just to remind you of the company you keep,' Clive said with a grin. 'How's the Bleeding Hart?'

'Fair.'

'Come on, old son. Fair? On Friday? What's wrong, is the *National Times* late on the stands, or something? It's Friday lunch. Picnicks!'

'And the Protestant deity's in his heaven.'

Clive's eyebrows went up the way they did when he was hurt. Hart squirmed. There was an unspoken agreement they had about humourless jibes. He felt muddled.

Just then Nick brought menus and friendly talk to their table by the window. Cars rolled past down Oxford Street. With his old gesture of boyish expectancy, Clive lay both hands flat on the inky-green linen. His new beard suited him, balanced his face, hid the strain of work. Nick told them the day's specials, joked with them as always, and Hart lightened a little at the sight of Clive's eagerness. The business of being here at Picnicks with him, ordering food and drink, distracted him from a creeping panic.

'It's still the best place, you know,' Hart said. He felt his face break in a grin. 'Look at it all, the china, the menu, the wine list. There's nothing like . . .'

Clive flounced his hands about. 'The ambience . . . the sweet ambience.' And they fell into laughter.

'Put those bloody credit cards away,' Hart said when they had quieted down. 'That one's a parking token, for God's sake, and this one, is this for opening other people's hotel doors?'

'Just a simple man with a simple man's capitalist foibles.'

Their bottle of Rosemount came. It lay awhile, sweating in its bucket of ice.

Clive's face straightened out. 'You look tired, mate. How's work?'

'Rough. The whole Unit's in chaos. We admitted this kid yesterday who prolapses his anus at will. No one knows what the hell to do. Medical staff gave up, that's why we've got him.'

'He does what?'

'He sits in a corner and pushes so hard his arse turns inside-out. After meeting his parents, pushing arse doesn't seem such a silly thing to do.'

Clive winced. 'Parenthood.'

'Oh, don't worry, you do all right, you and Jan.'

'Actually,' Clive said, eyes narrowing, 'Jamie has this habit of sticking his finger up his bum during his bedtime prayers. Gives him a rather contemplative look, really. Should I worry?'

'I'm a nurse, mate, not a theologian.'

They poured their wine and sat watching the traffic pass. It was peaceful here away from all that hopeless tangle.

'Speaking of theology, I rang a black clergyman today,' Clive said.

'Oh? Where's he from?' Hart watched a woman ride by with a laundry basket on her back.

'South Africa.'

'What?'

'Yeah.' Clive grinned. 'I rang Bishop Desmond Tutu. Toots to his friends.'

'Bullshit.'

'I did, I really did. We had a good old chat.'

'What, for your Tory mates?'

'Cynic! No, for myself. I asked him a few naïve questions. He was late for a dinner appointment. I taped it for you. Just to show you I've got a social conscience.'

'What'd he say?'

'Pray. And get ready to pick up the pieces.'

Their entrée arrived. Hart picked at his terrine; it was perfect but his appetite was leaving him. Clive ate and drank, and Hart felt him watching. Hart could feel himself sinking. Hold on to this, he told himself; this is good, this man, this food, this day; hold on.

'Another announcement,' Clive said.

'Let's hope it's good news.'

'Unexpected, but good. Jan's pregnant again.'

Hart felt the shock drop in him like a stone in a well. 'Oh.'

'Three months gone.'

'Are you sure?'

'A doctor told her. Technology told him. You know my weakness for technology.'

'Congratulations.' Hart saw the puzzlement on his friend's face. He ordered another bottle of Chardonnay. The meal was beautiful, dreamlike, graceful, but Hart felt disabled. He was unequal to it. Clive and he talked on, moving from children back to politics, on to their mutual hatred of football, then back to children, but Hart felt as though he was impersonating himself. He felt himself slipping. He drank more; ordered another bottle to cover his strange feelings of grief and anxiety.

When they parted just before three, Hart was drunk. He left Clive bemused in the car park and walked home along Oxford Street to sleep up for the evening shift. He thought about that voice in the dream. Yes, it was the voice of a public servant, a hospital administrator. Contempt soothed him for a moment. Bloody dreams. The thought came to him: What if she did die? What then?

During the next week Hart spent hopeless hours with the little boy they called The Pusher. Too much time, he knew. But it seemed desperately necessary to break into that ten-year-old before the case conference at the end of the week. Hart was agitated by the idea of this child at the mercy of the psychs and their useless academic curiosity. Hart wanted him out, better, gone. He knew he was panicking; it was as unprofessional as hell and he didn't care. Coming across The Pusher alone in a corner, pushing till his eyeballs surged, Hart whispered, 'What, you trying to move the fucking world?'

He gave himself till the end of the week before he'd sign himself off. He was losing it. He was lost.

When he woke in the afternoons, the house was big and empty. After all this time it was still hollow without Andrea, and now he wondered whether he mightn't have lost himself as well. He watched TV. There he was, every evening, that little black priest at the head of a snaking mob with the white soldiers looking on from their armoured cars. *There* was a man who'd found himself, he thought.

On Tuesday he saw a woman in the street whom he mistook for Jan Genders. He called out to her and when she turned around he saw it was a stranger, a woman with a small bright mouth and green eyes. He wasn't so much embarrassed as angry. He felt robbed. His fury did not abate. On TV that nervous little black man stood with his mouth open in the rising dust.

On Friday morning, Clive rang to cancel lunch at Picnicks.

'The old girl's a bit off colour. Think I'll go home and have lunch with her.'

Hart rang the Genders home.

'I heard you're a bit crook,' he said.

'Hart?'

'Yeah.'

'I'm having what you call a suspected miscarriage.'

'Oh, God.'

'You don't believe in Him, leave Him the hell out of it.'

'Do you?'

'When I can.'

'I had a dream.' Jesus, he was desperate. But for what?

'Martin Luther King.'

'What?' What? What? God, he was gonna burst into tears any minute.

'Forget it, boy. Clive isn't home.'

'I . . .'

'The doctor says I probably won't lose it.'

'Clive believes in doctors.'

'The doctor told me to stay in bed.'

'Oh. Sorry.'

She rang off. He stood there, hot, breathless. He went for a walk.

Across the road from Picnicks in a greasy little pinball joint, he ate a hamburger. He could see the flashing neon sign and the table in the window where he and Clive always sat. He was filled with self-contempt; he felt like a waif with his nose against the glass.

Home again, he rang off sick. He couldn't work. He couldn't force it any more. The case conference would be in progress now; the psychs would be devising a neat theory; The Pusher would be turning his arse out in a corner. Opening his fists by force of will, Hart said out loud: 'I am not coping.'

The weekend came and Hart stayed in the cold house. He took out the cassette Clive had given to him and played it over and over.

My friend there is terrible violence to come, but we must resist. There is no choice for us. There is no choice for me. Pray for us. If you can do nothing else, pray . . .

On Saturday afternoon Hart walked down to the local pub on the corner. Its walls were adorned with smoke-stained fishing trophies, a turtle shell and a jumbo crayfish, the tail of which had fallen off years ago. Andrea and he had decided here one afternoon to get married. They were back two years later arguing the terms of separation. Hart drank in tempo with that horrible slipping feeling. The foul cloud of smoke and talk and memories pressed in. She'll lose that baby, he thought; and I feel guilty already, like it's something to do with me. Me! He drank up. To hell with them.

Following his feet up the hill, he thought about that dream. What was it supposed to be, the voice of God, for Chrissake? Yeah, Clive's little Protestant deity. Yeah, I can see him as a bloody hospital administrator.

In the night he was woken by another dream. In it, Bishop Desmond Tutu led an endless procession like those he'd seen on TV. Funerals, mass funerals. There was dust and chants and black hands and pink upturned palms. As the crowd drew near he saw the coffins. There they were, atop the long, sealed boxes, the white bodies of people he knew. Andrea, Jan (so white), Clive, The Pusher. In his dream Hart leapt down from an armoured car, bashed through the cordon, and ran out on to the dusty road. The small, robed black man, spectacles glinting, paced with shoulders down. Hart ran towards him, but the bishop held a hand up to him, signalling him to keep away. Dust was everywhere like incense. That pink palm turned against him.

He was awake. His head throbbed.

Sunday evening the phone rang out in the cold house. It seemed about right to Hart. He answered.

'She lost it.'

'Oh, Clive.'

'She's all right. They say it was dead for a week anyway.'

'Was it . . . hard going for her?'

'Fucking awful. Worse than having a live one.'

'Were you there?'

'Of course I was. Oh, God.' Clive sighed; it was a dead sound.

'You all right?'

'She wants to come to Picnicks on Friday. All right with you? Wants to break a few traditions.'

Hart stiffened. 'Sure.'

'I know you find her a pain in the arse.'

'No, that's not true.' He looked out of the window and saw the lights of the city. He was lost. 'Christ, it's all so bloody futile, isn't it?'

'No, just a little complicated. Not futile.'

Hart sighed. 'The little Protestant deity, eh?'

'Ah, you see? We'll make a spiritual giant of you yet.'

Hart listened. He heard Clive pause as though swallowing something. He heard him sniff. And then, down the line, out of the hollow night, Hart heard him laugh. It was strong. It was rich. With the lights of the city presenting themselves dumbly to him, Hart felt his whole being straining, holding on to that sound.

MORE

I

HE PAUSES at the door and wonders about lipstick. The house is
in darkness. He breathes through his teeth, feeds the key in,
opens the door. In the bathroom he strips and he stuffs his
clothes deep into the laundry basket. He crushes them down.
The mirror shows him his white face. On the kitchen table, held
down by an apple, there is a note. *Gave up waiting.* He creeps to
the bedroom. Streetlight divides the bed. Two figures jack-knife
across it, one large, one small. He eases out. Down the hall he
folds into the little bed with the Mickey Mouse quilt. Mobiles
hang from the ceiling. He switches the light out, but he senses
the shiny bright things turning in the dark above and his heart
won't ease up. He puts the nightlight on again and looks up at
the mobiles: fish floating on some hidden draught. He gets out
of bed and goes to the little wardrobe. On it there is a photograph in a Perspex frame. It shows a blood-spattered, unshaven,
mad-eyed young man looking into a humid crib which holds a
baby. The baby is big and battered-seeming. The young man in
the picture looks hungry for it. He takes the paper from the
frame and holds it up to the nightlight. He watches for movement, but all that moves is his heart in his chest, butting blindly
against itself. And he sleeps. The bed smells of his son. He feels
himself sink into that sweet Johnson & Johnson smell, knowing,
even as he swims into sweetness with fish flying above, that
everything is not all right.

★

The weekend before Rachel's exams, they drove north to Guilderton for the weekend. The evening air was full of the smell of coming heat. In the warm night on the verandas they played their mongrel game of chess. Jerra liked a skirmish. He didn't care so much for victory; he just liked to mow a path now and then, to see pieces fall. Rachel told him he had the tactics of a blind bull. She was reading Hemingway. He nodded. He wanted to ask her how she was liking Hemingway, but he just made his moves and watched the streaks of smoke from the mosquito coils. Now and then, the flash of the lighthouse broke the night. He drank too much beer. He lost the game and followed her to bed.

'Hope no one turns up,' Rachel said in the darkness a moment before he was finally asleep. The curtains lit up a second before leaving them again in darkness.

'Who?' he asked, after a pause.

'Our friends. Anyone. I want some peace.'

'And quiet. Don't tell me, I know.'

'It's just the exams, and everything. I'm going mad.'

'Yeah.' Assignments, essays, exams, textbooks. God, he was sick of it. 'No one'll turn up.'

'I hope not.'

'Blame me if they do,' he said.

'Why?'

'I'm unlucky.'

In the night, Sam woke and he cried for two hours and ten minutes. He kicked and scratched and drooled as each of them tried to comfort him, and then they began shouting at each other and in the end Rachel wept.

'Why are you like this, Jerra?' she called, holding Sam away from him.

'Everything's gone to shit. Your misery is contagious.'

'Oh, you can't bear other people's sickness or unhappiness, can you? You can't tolerate it.'

Sam ceased wailing and fell abruptly to sleep.

'I know,' said Jerra, lowering his voice. 'I'm not patient enough.'

'Not mature enough.'

'Don't social work me, for Chrissake. OK, I know. That's how I got into this mess. I was too young. I was stupid.'

'Thank you.'

'Thank *you*.'

Jerra prepared himself for more sobbing, but she climbed into bed with Sam and left him there. He stood for a while outside the door. There was excitement in cruelty, and the idea of it burnt him.

At the bend in the river, before it deepened off against the bar sealing its mouth, there was clean, shallow water and shade in the lee of the limestone bluff. Sam sat astride Rachel's brown belly and splashed. A gull shadow passed over them.

'Burr-burr!' Sam yelled.

'Bird,' said Rachel.

'Bird,' said Jerra, wishing she would turn her head and meet his eyes with a smile.

He lay back in the water, shifting on the tide-ribbed bottom, until only his mouth and nose were above the surface, and with his eyes open he saw the sky through a shifting filter of river water. He stayed there. He remembered a night when the colicky sawing of baby screams pierced him finally and truly, when he tore Sam from his neck and held him out and shook him till his head might come away. It was in the moment before slamming the little body into the wall that he lay him on the bed and went outside into the scathing forest cold. The crying stopped suddenly, and he thought he'd killed him. Rachel was too sick to know. And Jerra stood alone out there with the Godlike silence towering at him. He knew then that he was capable of the darkest things.

Jerra lurched upright, sputtering.

'Allo,' Sam said.

'Hullo, mate.'

Rachel made no comment as he went off on his own in the afternoon when heat was fattening the air. He took a flick rod and a knife and bucket. The sun glowered and stung his skin. From a rock in a deep bend of the river, he fished for bream using worms and a small amount of lead. He stubbed a toe and lost a rig. Two little girls joined him, and they fished like experts. They giggled when he begged tackle off them. One of them caught a gobbleguts. Jerra then lost a second rig and was too embarrassed to ask again, so he left them to themselves. As he walked away, it occurred to him that they thought he was an old man. A funny old man. He was twenty-four years old.

Sam and Rachel lay asleep in the hot little beach house. He sat and waited, listened to his blood.

At dusk, cutting lemons for the salad, Jerra saw the knife-steel sink into his finger.

'Shit. I'm cut.' He began to dance. 'It's bad.' He stopped. There was blood on the linoleum. He went back to the sink. For a moment, in the madness of shock, it occurred to him that he might have cut the whole finger off, and he began to shift the gore-smeared dishes about, looking for his fingertip. But then Rachel grabbed his hand and lashed a teatowel to his finger. The kookaburra prints on the linen began to blush.

At the first-aid station beside the shop and garage, the little man told him the wound would need sutures.

'It's a biggun,' he said. 'Probably sev-eared the nerves.'

Jerra watched him wrap it in a constrictive bandage, and was disturbed by the grease on the man's hands. He'd never been ministered to by a mechanic.

'Have to get a doctor on to that. Gingin's the closest town. Do it in the morning, unless you're worried.'

Rachel looked at him. 'You worried?'

Jerra shrugged.

'Well, I'm not worried,' she told the man.

All night Jerra lay with his hand throbbing. Sunburn caused his skin to feel as though it was shrinking on him.

He saw oily limbs and the twist of momentum. His head in the cradle of her pelvis. Smelled the pungent shifts in her. He saw. He saw. He saw that she was not Rachel.

At dawn he woke and wondered how he could possibly move, get up, get out of bed and go on. He felt like the maze was closing on him.

Hot wind blew through the car on the way back from the doctor's. His finger was tight with numbness and through it he swore he could feel the sutures moving. His back stung. He winced at every bump in the road.

'I know about it, Jerra.'

It wrenched him around in his seat. 'About what?'

'Quiet, you'll wake Sam.'

'Know *what*?' he murmured.

She drove. He shored himself against her tears, but she just drove and nothing came.

★

They'd been back ten minutes when Rachel came running into the kitchen. Jerra braced himself.

'Sam's eaten Ratsak!'

He wilted with relief.

'Poison, Jerra!'

Sam smiled. His white hair stood at odds with itself. There was a rime of green around his mouth. Jerra seized him and took him to the sink. He prised open his mouth with a finger. Sam giggled. Jerra reached into the tiny throat. The giggle choked off into a cry of alarm. Jerra felt the teeth set into the flesh of his good hand.

'Start the car.'

'Who the hell'd leave rat poison around for kids to get into?' Jerra muttered in the surgery. He paced around the doctor who held Sam over a bowl. Vile black stuff was coming up. Sam bellowed and gagged.

'Dave and Debbie don't have kids,' Rachel said. 'They wouldn't have to think about it. It's not their fault.'

'Should have kept an eye—'

'Oh, leave off, Jerra.'

'Well, you'd think—'

'What?'

'It just shouldn't have happened.'

'Yeah, well lots of things happen that should never happen.'

The look he got from her sent him to the back of the room where light filtered down clean from a skylight. He stood there, thinking of something to say.

'Skylight'd save your money, Doc.'

The doctor looked at him, brow askew, and went back to the business of helping Sam vomit. 'There's no sign of anything,' he said. 'Probably just had it on his lips.'

'Christ.'

★

244

Rachel began packing as soon as they got back to the beach house.

'It's not working out,' she said.

Jerra could not fathom her control.

'No, it's a disaster, eh.'

She fell on the bed and hid her face from him.

Jerra went outside and watched crickets leap out of the lawn to escape Sam's trundling manoeuvres on the plastic trike.

On the highway heading back, he leans across to where she sits rigid at the wheel.

'Look—'

'Don't, you'll kill me.'

He opens his mouth again but she cuts him off.

'There's too much on my plate, Jerra. I can't know about it, I can't listen to you tell me how sorry you are or aren't. I have to pass these exams. There's no way I can live if I fail them. I have to not go mad. OK, melodrama, violins, I know.'

'OK.'

'It happens, Jerra.'

'It's over, it didn't even start.'

Sam sleeps between them, drooling and awry in his little seat.

A hard, tiny sound comes out of Rachel's throat. She pulls over and begins to take in long breaths.

'Look, I can't go home, just now,' she says.

'Wanna go back?'

'No.'

'Want me to drive?'

She shakes her head. 'I need to be with someone. Away.'

Jerra sits. The blue, dry land goes away from him in all directions. He sighs. 'Mum and Dad are down at the Cut. You mean them, don't you?'

She starts the car.

'It's a hell of drive from here,' he says.

She gets into top gear and good posture and he sits back with his eyes closed.

2

It was dark when they rolled into the peppermint clearing, and in front of the timber cabin a fire sent sprays of sparks into the night. The smells of rivermud and peppermint and boiling crabs met them as they got out, and Sam finally stopped crying.

'It's Jerra, Tom!'

The silhouette of Jerra's mother came from behind the steaming old copper and met them in the dark.

'Spare a bed?' he asked as she smote him with kisses.

His mother turned and bellowed back into the house. 'They're staying, Tom! Put some beer in the fridge! You've cut yourself. And oh!' She gathered Sam up and touched his tousled hair which seemed to glow in the dark. 'What brings you down here to your old Granma, Sam?'

'Disaster,' said Rachel.

'Unrelieved misfortune,' Jerra said, and to his surprise, they each managed a laugh. Backlit in the doorway, he saw the reduced outline of his father. He looked worse.

Piles of rivercrabs, red and steaming, covered the table spread with newspapers and battered china plates and bowls of brown vinegar. There was fresh white bread, mustard, beer and chilli sauce, and as they ate and broke and sucked, dunked, smeared, cursed, Jerra watched as though he were not quite present. On Rachel's knee, a revived Sam sucked the sweet, white flesh from crablegs. He reared and laughed his little screech at the sight of his grandfather with a claw on his nose like a clothespeg. The old man looked happy, even though the cancer had him for good now. Jerra watched his mother. Her tan made her leathery and easy to look at. She had broadened these past years and she seemed to have grown stronger. She took more of every kind of space. Right there in her balding armchair at table, she looked happily immovable and he was filled with affection for her. He watched them all around this florid mess of crabs, the room full of eating noise and baby talk. His family, his blood. Oh, God, it burned fierce in him tonight, the desire to serve to protect to be loyal unto death. No room for irony tonight, and the feeling grew in him, fattened and rose like bread in his chest until he threw down his fork and left the table.

Out in the smoky dark he found the outhouse and locked himself in and waited. Sooner or later, he told himself, in a while it won't seem so important. Perspective. Irony. Sense. But he waited in vain.

Late in the night, when the others were asleep inside, Jerra played his father a song on the guitar. The lamp hissed. Mosquitoes pressed the wire all around the veranda. There was a melancholic pleasure in picking out the simple melody. He felt the strings emboss his fingertips, the vibration against his chest. He picked clumsily, handicapped by the gauze on his finger.

'What'll you do when you get famous?' his father asked, pulling a blanket over his knees in the silence that remained.

'I'll never get famous, Dad. I just wanna get old.'

'Yeah, boy, so did I.'

Jerra bit.

'Would you leave Perth?' his father said without pause.

'Oh, I'd miss the sun.'

'There's sun all over the world, they tell me.'

Jerra laughed. Always the same game. When Jerra gets famous. He wondered whether it was a way for the old man to stave off disappointment.

'You weren't moping about me out there, were you?'

He looked into his father's dark, dry eyes and saw something new.

'I was chucking up. Must've eaten something.'

'I taught you never to lie.'

Jerra found a chord and sang.

'It's a sin to tell a lie . . .'

The old man looked away out into the dark and Jerra felt the chord die against his chest.

'No, not about you, Dad. I can't even believe *that* yet. No, it won't beat you. You won't die.' He rested his chin against the smooth wood of the sound box. 'No. I s'pose it sounds weird, but in there tonight I felt sort of . . . unworthy.'

'Was it us?'

'Me.' Jerra tried to laugh. 'Jesus, it's guilt!' Any moment now he was going to blurt it all out like a child. He ached to confess every kind of betrayal.

'Things you don't know about.'

'Rachel and Sam. You belong to them.'

'Sometimes I feel like pissing off like I used to. I haven't measured up, have I?'

'You've done orright, Jerra. You grew up through some rough business. You're not too proud yet to be guilty. And you've had your losses.'

'Yeah,' Jerra said, full of bitterness. 'I've seen a few buried.'

'You worry about the living. Like your mother says: don't be bitter, be better.'

'Want me to take you out in the boat tomorrow?'

'What – for a last ride?'

'Geez, Dad,' he winced, 'be better, for Godsake!'

'Play "Danny Boy".'

Jerra picked it out, best he could.

When his father got up to go in to bed a while later, he kissed Jerra's brow and touched the guitar.

'When a bloke finds out how long he's got left, he knows

there's more to it, son. Stupid thing is, there's always been more.'

Alone, Jerra listened to the mosquitoes. He sat on his father's reading chair. Frogs began to change pitch. A waterbird slapped away somewhere out on the estuary. He fidgeted with the small pile of books on the chair-arm. Beneath a volume of bush ballads he found *The Book of Common Prayer* and he lifted it in surprise.

Morning light lay on the water. The boat turned at anchor. In the bow, the old man sat mixing pollard. Jerra saw the lines in his face and knew he was in pain.

'Takes you back.'

His father scattered moist grains across the water. Jerra cast a line out and heard the sinker pop the surface.

'Remember the pelican caught out here in the net? Years ago.'

The old man shook his head. His face was hard-set.

'There were things I wanted to say that day, Dad.'

'Boy. I need to lie down.'

Jerra felt the chill on his father's face. 'I'll take you back.'

As he hauled anchor rope across the gunwale, the boat turned lamely in whatever direction resistance lay.

In the twilight before dark, Jerra and Rachel left Sam with his grandparents and went walking. The air was warm but the mosquitoes were not out yet and sounds of the bush were muted. They walked on a soft clay path between blackbutts. Bracken rose at the base of the trees. The ground felt damp and sunken. When the path was wide enough they walked abreast. In the narrow sections Jerra took the lead and held out a hand to fend off spiderwebs. For a long time neither spoke. Jerra felt the callouses on his fingertips. They tasted brassy in his mouth. He looked at the ugly sutures in his index finger.

'I s'pose your mum and dad walk down here a lot.'

'Used to. Mum still does, I s'pose.'

'I like her. I like them both.'

'Yeah, I know.'

'We could turn out like that if we tried.'

Like what, he thought. Old and dying? But he checked himself. Try. Be better not bitter.

'Yeah I guess there's worse ways to turn out.'

'How is it with your dad?'

'We talked.'

'Did you know he prays?'

'How did you know?'

'He told me. He was frightened to tell you. You must have jumped down his throat when you were younger.'

Jerra felt bracken sliding across his flanks. He smelt her near him. He reached and touched her and they stopped walking.

'Yeah. I did. I didn't understand.'

'What about now. Do you understand now?'

'Not really. Maybe you need to be dying to understand.'

'Your dad said we were always dying. He's pretty wise, in his way.'

'Gee, you two are as thick as thieves.' He felt her flesh cool beneath his palms. 'I'm not dying. I'm living.'

Half-way across the distance between them as he leant out to kiss her, the undergrowth exploded and shadows showered up in every direction.

He cried out in fear.

'Quail,' Rachel said.

In the silence he heard the blood beating at his throat.

DEATH BELONGS TO THE DEAD,
HIS FATHER TOLD HIM,
AND SADNESS TO THE SAD

I

WHEN JUNKIES came into his café to nod and mutter and make cloths of themselves on his tables, The Man knew he was looking upon death itself. But he served them because when he was a boy in Naples he had learnt to walk straight and not look over his shoulder. Death belongs to the dead, his father told him, and sadness to the sad. On this street, far from Naples, there was death, there was sadness, and he did not look over his shoulder. He served the dead, took their money, and walked straight.

But the street and the café were not without happiness. In the afternoons people sat in the bookshop down the road and gossiped as they flicked through books they could not afford, while their children made their faces hideous against the plate glass to shock passers-by. Old men on the stoops smoked and called to one another in strange tongues. Drunks woke beneath the Moreton Bay figs in the park to discover that death had not claimed them in the night. Taxi drivers double-parked to complain and shake their heads in contentment before the peak hour. And in the evenings, before the café was full, the old pub on the corner was jammed with young people and the roar of music from a band whose guitarist wandered out to play twenty-minute solos to strollers-by. Cars slowed up to listen. People stepped over the long cord that trailed him; they smiled and were confused. Detectives came every night to get him off the street, but they did not beat him up, and when they were gone he would hang out the window to shoot riffs into moving cars.

During the mornings, though, there was mostly sadness. The street was forlorn and the junkies came into the café, and there were people with hangovers or marriage problems or people who seemed worried about how they looked. It was in the mornings that the Dying Gentleman began to come in.

Each day the Dying Gentleman sat by the window and looked hungrily out at the passing traffic. He sat with his hat on the table and his brogues flat on the floor, and sometimes a thin beam of winter sun would give his head a tonsure. At first, The Man, who knew a hungry person when he saw one, offered him the breakfast menu, but the newcomer shook his head and asked for a cold glass of milk. His lips barely moved. The Man listened: it was the voice of death. He got the Dying Gentleman his milk and heard the voice of death thank him.

It soothes my stomach, the Dying Gentleman said. He put a white hand on his belly and moved it across. He had never been handsome, The Man guessed, but you could see he had once been young and vital. He was wasting. It looked like cancer. The Man took his money and did not look over his shoulder.

But in time, The Man found himself unable to resist the sight of the Dying Gentleman. From behind the coffee machine, he watched surreptitiously. Each morning, the Dying Gentleman came in looking a little more hollow, a shade whiter. The monkish spot the ascending sun made on the top of his head seemed more luminous every day.

How is the stomach today? he began to ask the Dying Gentleman as he brought his glass of milk. The Dying Gentleman shook his head and drank. He looked as though he was starving, but as though a meal would murder him.

2

One evening, a man came running into the café with blood issuing from great wounds in his face. His jacket was torn and a swamp of blood rose from his armpit.

Someone is after me! he screamed. The Man took him by the bloody collar and put him out on the street and pushed him away along the pavement. He watched him stagger down toward the roar of music and leave a trail of blood. The Man saw him collide with detectives who had arrived to shoo the electric guitarist off the street. When he turned to go back to his café, he saw a thin, dark man holding a cleaver. He had a drooping moustache and he stood near the door, the cleaver at his side. The Man took a breath, walked straight past him and went into the café without looking back.

3

As the days became longer, the morning sun lay heavy on the Dying Gentleman who sat by the window with his milk. The light made him ghostly and The Man did not like to look.

The stomach? he would ask. The Dying Gentleman shook his head and put the hand to the belly. His flesh was translucent. Sad world, The Man said, despite himself. His customer shrugged and looked for a moment as though he might disagree. The Man left him with his milk.

It was Sunday morning when the Dying Gentleman came in and ordered bacon and eggs and sausages and short black coffee. The hot sun cut the café in half.

Feeling better? The Man asked.

Yes, the Dying Gentleman said. He put his hat on the table and straightened the little blue feather in the band, and The Man felt a happy twitch in his chest as he called the order through.

When he brought the breakfast, he saw the determination in the Dying Gentleman's features. From behind the coffee machine, he saw him eat all of it – the bacon, the eggs, the sausages, and the short black coffee – before putting his knife and fork down to watch the traffic pass. Then he got up and went to the pay phone by the door. The Man poured coffees and watched him dial. He saw the Gentleman straighten and speak and then return the piece to its cradle. He saw him put his hand to the window. He saw the black hole his mouth made and he got out from behind the counter and caught the Gentleman before he fell, and the wind escaping his throat was like the gentle sound of passing traffic. The Man felt heat and there was a terrible stench. The Dying Gentleman's head was on his chest, his jacket was slipping up his arms.

Junkies nodded in the corner. The sun did not reach them. He looked down into the Gentleman's face and saw the black hole of his mouth. The darkness of it seemed to go for ever down.

The Man looked up and saw that people had stopped their talking and drinking, and as he held the body and felt it belong to him, he suddenly knew that Naples was on the other side of the world, that boyhood was further, and that death was a lifetime, a lunchtime, a breath away.

BLOOD AND WATER

Since it was the day of Preparation, in order to prevent the
bodies from remaining on the cross on the sabbath (for that
sabbath was a high day), the Jews asked Pilate that their legs
might be broken, and that they might be taken away. So the
soldiers came and broke the legs of the first, and of the other
who had been crucified with him; but when they came to Jesus
and saw that he was already dead, they did not break his legs.
But one of the soldiers pierced his side with a spear, and at
once there came out blood and water.

John xix, 31–34

RACHEL LAUGHED and there was water down her leg.

'It's coming,' she said.

Jerra leapt up and switched the TV off. For a moment they
stood there and regarded the trails on her thighs. A car acceler-
ated up the hill and passed with a hiss outside. Rain fell; the
gutters were thick with it. They heard it chug in the downpipes.

'This is gonna be the happiest night of my life,' he said. He
put on a record. Suddenly the house was full.

The midwife came, felt Rachel's abdomen, and commandeered
their bed. Fires purred in the stove and the fireplace. The street
was quiet. They played Haydn on the stereo and held hands
during Rachel's contractions. They heard the midwife's snores.
Her name was Annie. She was a tall, athletic woman who
always wore her hair tied back in a scarf. She believed in God
and healing and the goodness of people's bodies. Rachel and

Jerra thought she was a little weird, but they had come to love her these past months. She was gentle. She warmed her hands. Her smile was reassuring.

In the light of the fire, Rachel's flesh looked polished. Jerra rubbed her back and whispered in her ear. She breathed across her contractions.

'It's fine,' she said. 'I can do it. Nice here. Look at the fire.'

The rushes came on like advancing weather. Jerra saw her knotting up till her flesh became armour and she hissed and they counted and Annie came out to sit by the fire.

'Having a baby?'

Rachel laughed. In the lull, Jerra sponged the sweat from her. She rested her head on his chest and closed her eyes. Her long braid fell across his thigh. He saw Annie by the fire. She too had her eyes closed and she was moving her lips. Praying, he thought; she's bloody praying. He remembered the prayer his mother had sung him at bedtime when he was a child, before it all got too embarrassing.

Gentle Jesus, meek and mild
Look upon a little child
Pity his simplicity
Suffer him to come to Thee . . .

Maybe I'll even sing it to his little critter, he thought; just out of nostalgia – what the hell.

At two o'clock the contractions took Rachel with such force that pauses between became moments of irony rather than serious relief. Jerra rubbed oil on her lips. He massaged the small of her back. He felt the vibrations in her flesh. He tried, he stayed close, he felt it in his skin, but he couldn't know it for himself; he couldn't know what it was like.

Annie gloved up for an internal.

'Having babies'd be fine,' Rachel panted, 'if it wasn't for other people's hands up you.' She winced, writhed a little.

'You're not dilating,' Annie said. 'You're so angry in there I can't feel it right. We've got twins, people, or a breech. How you feel?'

'Better when you. Get. Your. Hand. Out. Ah. I got plenty left.'

'Better call the doc. We might have to go to hozzie.'

'I need a crap.'

'Get the commode, Jerra.'

He heard his footsteps on the plastic-draped floor. It was like walking on water.

Jerra drove and the women sat in the back. Though he knew the way, he needed to be told. Annie shouted directions over his shoulder and comforted Rachel at the same time. He saw their moving shadows in the mirror. The hospital loomed. He had forgotten a jumper. He wished he hadn't worn overalls. They'll think we're hippies, he thought.

'Don't cry,' murmured Annie to Rachel. 'You got plenty left.'

They waited outside the emergency entrance. It was a private hospital. They had saved for insurance in case this should happen.

In the lift they propped Rachel up during contractions. At the desk they asked her to fill out a form. Jerra tried to be calm.

'I can only be an observer now,' Annie said. 'But the doc'll be here soon. Let's hold tight.'

Nurses and orderlies crowded round, strapping things on, tucking, adjusting. Someone cheerful inserted an intravenous drip.

'Try it at home, eh?'

'Be tough,' Annie whispered.

Jerra saw Rachel on her back on the bed. She breathed slow and deep in a trough.

'Let's just get this little fella out and go home,' she murmured.

It was five in the morning. At six their doctor came. He was a small man, a conservative dresser. He seemed to like people to think he was a conservative man as well, though it was just a front. Rachel liked him. She said he was old-style, that he didn't play God. She called him Doc.

'Four centimetres,' he said, wiping his glasses. 'Like trying to drive a bus through a gas-pipe.'

Jerra felt hyperventilated. He wished the big clock across the room could be covered somehow. He saw blisters of sweat bursting on Rachel's face.

'We're getting two heartbeats here,' someone said. The room seemed full of people.

'Can't we get a scan?' Jerra asked. 'We don't really know what we've got here.'

Someone mumbled something. Rachel let out a tiny yelp of pain.

'Time for an epidural,' someone said.

'I got plenty left,' said Rachel.

'Can't we get an ultra-sound?' Jerra asked.

A masked face tutted. 'All that technology. Dear, dear.'

'That's why we're here,' Jerra said quietly through his teeth. 'It's not for the warm feeling it gives us.'

'What do *you* think, Rachel?' the doc asked.

'Can't you send them all out?'

'It's their hospital.'

'I didn't want drugs.'

'Neither did I. But you're tired. You've worked hard enough for two babies already.'

Her face went white-hard. Jerra breathed through the contraction with her. He kept his face close to hers. They had trained for this and it worked. She beat the pain.

'I'll think about it,' she said in the short lull.

'I've got to get back for morning surgery. They'll call me about the scan. Be yourself.'

It went on all morning. Rachel whooped and hissed and panted and turned to ice only to melt and begin again. Breathing with her, Jerra was almost delirious. His head was gorged with oxygen. The clock was cruel with him. Rachel got older and older.

At nine someone wheeled a trolley in and inserted an epidural into Rachel's spine. Jerra watched it happen as though he was absent from himself. 'We don't want drugs if it can be avoided,' he said to the white smock. 'We want to be reasonable—'

'This is a hospital,' the smock said.

At ten he paced the room alone. Annie was asleep down the hall on the floor of the fathers' room. Rachel had been wheeled out to the ultra-sound room and they'd stopped him going. I'm weak, he thought. I'm piss-weak. He paced like somebody on television and it didn't seem funny. He was almost jogging. He felt ill. He paced. He knew he'd die if he stopped. Outside, through the frosted glass, a day was happening; it was going on without him.

By the door of the delivery room he saw Rachel's candle-wick gown hanging from a peg, and below, her sheepskin boots. He picked up the boots and squeezed them; he held the gown to his face, and in that moment it seemed possible that they might not bring her back. He stood out in the corridor. A nurse smiled at him. He felt something logging up behind his eyes. He ran to the toilet down the hall. On the toilet it felt as though his blood was running out of him. He was afraid.

He woke with his ear against the white wall. Sleep. He had been asleep. A few minutes? A moment?

The flush of the cistern sounded like a mob in a stadium. Out in the hall, a thread of that old tune stuck to him. *Gentle Jesus, meek and mild . . .*

The delivery room was still empty. He paced in a wide arc from one corner to the other. His head ached. He began to jog. Fifteen hours. He wondered what he had been like fifteen hours ago.

Twenty minutes later a white crew wheeled Rachel in. They shepherded Jerra into a corner while they renewed her spinal block. Annie came in looking sick. He wanted to speak to her but he couldn't decide what to say. Instead he elbowed his way to the bed.

'Just one,' somebody said. 'Breech.'

'Will it fit?' he asked.

'Has to, now. Too late for a C-section.'

'You OK?' he whispered to Rachel.

She nodded. Her lips were dry. Her eyes had retreated. He found a flannel and squeezed some droplets on to her mouth. It was suddenly conceivable to him that she might die, that she was *able* to die. He lurched.

'Get him a chair.'

He heard Annie whisper in his ear from behind, 'They've brought in a gynie. Be brave.'

'Doctor O'Donelly will be down soon,' someone said, plugging in something.

'The Knife,' Annie muttered. 'Isn't there anyone else?'

'You don't work here any more, Annie.'

'I remember. But these people are paying for this. They're consumers. They have rights. Did the patient request or assent to the epidural? The IV? To be lying flat on her back?'

'I didn't consent to any fucking thing,' Rachel hissed. 'They're gonna do what they want.'

'Annie, I'm warning you,' a smock said.

'I want to squat,' Rachel breathed.

'You've got no legs.'

Jerra got down close to her. 'C'mon. We have to beat these fuckers. Let's breathe, c'mon, don't lose it, let's breathe.' He stayed close to her. He could not imagine what must be happening inside her; it was another universe beyond that hard-white flesh.

Shifts changed. Annie sat by Rachel, crooning and stroking, and he went to call his parents. They must know something's up, he thought. His mother wept. He wanted to throw up.

Breathing. Breathing. Walls bent. He was in a bellows. *Gentle Jesus, meek and mild, stop me going fucking wild* . . .

Eat, they told him.

Pant, they told him.

Die, they told him.

They told him.

The gumbooted gynaecologist strolled in at one after the pushing had begun.

'OK, let's get this job underway. She doing all right?'

'She's fine,' Rachel croaked. 'And. We been. Going. Eight. Een. Hours. Mis. Ter. Ummmmh.'

'Isn't she terrific?'

Jerra knew that all the hatred he had ever felt before was merely ill-will and mild dislike.

'Ten centimetres.'

Trolleys clattered. A ticking box appeared behind Rachel's head and someone connected it to the IV.

'I don't want syndemetrine.'

'You're tired, lovie.'

'And you're not me.'

Annie gave Jerra a defeated look. He whispered, 'Beat him, Rachel.' He saw she couldn't go much longer. When she pushed, her veins rode up through her flesh.

There was a crowning of sorts. The perineum strained. Rachel's anus dilated like a rose opening. At each contraction something showed like a tongue at the mouth of her vagina. It was flesh. Then he saw black. Merconium.

'That's shit,' he said. 'It's in distress.'

'Are you a midwife?' someone asked.

'Testicles,' he said. 'God, it's a boy before it's a baby.'

At each contraction the raw, swollen testicles came out a little further, only to be strangled in the lull by the closing gap.

'I love you,' he said in her ear.

Someone sniffed. A crowd of smocks and masks. O'Donelly moved in. Somewhere Jerra saw the white face of their own doctor. He saw the scissors opening her up. He saw them cut from her vagina to anus. There was blood. There were great silver clamps pendulous from Rachel's flesh. Almost from within hers there was another little pair of buttocks.

'Push, Mrs Nilsam!'

'Legs up round his ears,' Annie said in his ear.

'Heartbeat faint now, Doctor.'

'OK, let's get him out.'

Rachel reared as hands went up inside her. Jerra saw blood and shit on a forearm. Rachel let out a cry and unleashed a foot from its stirrup. She kicked. A smock took the heel in the chest. She tried again, but hands took the foot and pinned it.

Now there were legs within legs.

'Jerra? Jerra?'

'Beam 'em, Rachel. Beat their arses off. At least you can shit and bleed on 'em.'

'No heartbeat.'

They were wrenching now, and twisting out the little arms and applying forceps to the aftercoming head.

262

'Jerra?'

'Oh, fuck me.'

A little puce head slipped out, followed by a rush of blood and water. Jerra saw it splash on to the gynaecologist's white boots. Across Rachel's chest the little body lay tethered for a moment while smocks and masks pressed hard up against Rachel's wound. He saw a needle sink in. Someone cut the cord. Blood, grey smears of vernix. The child's eyes were open. Jerra felt them upon him. From the little gaping mouth, pink froth issued. They snatched him up.

'Should have been a bloody caesar,' someone muttered.

Rachel groaned to get her breath while they sewed her.

Jerra saw the child hollow-chested on the trolley where the smocks sucked him out. He heard the deadly sound of it and he saw the gloved hands on the shiny little valves. With its blacksmeared hair, their baby's head looked like the dark side of the moon.

That's a dead baby, thought Jerra. That's it. She can't see it. How will I say it?

. . . suffer him to come to Thee . . .

A chest flutter.

Oh, Jesus Christ, he thought. Gentle Jesus, don't play with me. Let him be dead but don't crucify me.

The chest filled.

Oh, don't fuck around with me!

A hand moved. Five fingers.

Oh dear God.

Other hands were gentle with it. There was grace in the plying of his limbs. A horrible ache rose from low in Jerra's spine. He knew it was love.

'Is he all right?' Rachel croaked. She licked her lips. 'Jerra?'

'They've got him.'

The paediatrician looked up. A little cough entered the room. Then another.

'He's crying,' Rachel said. 'I can't see him.'

They brought him over, wrapped in a blanket. In one nostril there was a clear plastic tube.

'On oxygen,' someone said.

Jerra hugged himself. 'Is he OK?'

'He'll need some help.'

Jerra felt those eyes on him. Blood and water bubbled out of the infant's mouth.

'Son of God,' Annie said.

'Grab that side of the trolley, Mr Nilsam. Let's get this boy down to ICU.'

As he ran out with the smocks, Jerra saw that the room was empty of white figures and only Rachel and Annie were left behind. They were holding each other.

Corridors, doors, potted palms. Past them, Jerra ran. People blurred by but he saw those black eyes on him and he wondered who he was a day ago.

The little boy held his hand and bleated up fluid as the paediatrician inserted a tube into the raw-cut navel. Jerra's eyes stung with tears.

'What's his chances? No bullshit. Please don't lie to me.'

The paediatrician looked up from his task. Only his eyes were visible, but he seemed to Jerra to be more than a technician. 'Not bad, I'd say. Then again, I don't know. His lungs're full of garbage, I'd guess. Kidneys and liver won't be too good. Have to wait. Hips might be busted. I haven't checked. He'll have a headache, that's for sure. All that time without oxygen. He's strong though.'

'Like his mother.'

The baby seemed to fill with colour before his eyes. He went a mottled yellow and pink. Jerra wanted to touch the little feet, but he contented himself with the firm grip the miniature hand had on him. So it's a reflex, he thought; what do I care.

'Will he have brain damage, you reckon?'

The man shrugged. 'I'm not God.'

He was sitting by the humidicrib when they wheeled Rachel in an hour later.

'I'm stoned,' she said.

'Pethedine,' said Annie. They'd been crying, he could tell.

'Can I hold him?'

'No,' a nurse said.

A person with a clipboard came in. 'Mrs Nilsam, you're in room six.'

'Is that a single room?' Jerra asked.

'No. I'm afraid—'

'You see, the thing is I'll need to stay with my—'

'I'm sorry, you—'

'Look, for one, we're entitled under all that blood insurance we paid, and two, because my wife's just had—'

'Mr Nilsam, I—'

'OK, I'll sleep in the corridor. I'm about to be hysterical.'

'I'll see what I can do.'

'He's alive,' Rachel said.

'Call him Samuel,' said Annie. 'I reckon you should.'

'Sam.'

'Sure,' said Jerra, shaking as though a fit had come upon him. 'He's alive, isn't he?'

They lay in the dark and tried to sleep. Jerra thought of the dead fireplaces at home. He thought of the empty little house. He turned on his folding cot and felt the huge load rise up in him and he began to weep. His body muscled up against the sobs. He tried to be quiet. Tears tracked into his hair and he tasted salt and it was as strong in his mouth as blood. Jerra Nilsam cried. He wept and did not stop and he thought his eyes would bleed, and when he found a pause in himself, he heard the big bed above him clanking. He got up and turned on a dim light. Rachel lay with a pillow between her teeth. Her eyes were breaking with tears.

'I feel so defiled,' she said.

He turned out the light and held her. She filled his arms.

In the middle of the night he crept out of the room and down the long corridor to the intensive care unit. The nurse looked at his matted hair and his bare feet. In the reflection in the glass window he saw there were bloodstains on his overalls. He went in to the lone Perspex box marked *Samuel Nilsam* and he sat down beside it. A heart monitor bleeped. It was a mournsome sound.

His son lay spreadeagled on his front with his head in an oxygen cube. His blood-caked body was bound by tubes and wires. Beneath him, his huge swollen testicles. He had black hair. He did look strong, sleeping there, sucking on a dummy; he looked strong enough to be alive.

When the charge nurse turned her back, Jerra opened the little portal at the side of the humidicrib and carefully reached in. He touched the bright pink buttocks. He ran a hand down the closest thigh and felt the textures of hair and dried blood. There was warmth there.

Footsteps.

He looked up. The nurse regarded him with indignation. Her mouth was tight. She put her hands on her hips.

Jerra Nilsam looked down and gripped an arm. His joined fingers were a bracelet on his son's wrist. He felt blood. Yes, that was blood there, and he looked up at the nurse in defiance.

'Go to hell,' he said. 'This one's mine.'